Pure

Terra Elan McVoy

Simon Pulse

New York   London   Toronto   Sydney

SIMON PULSE

An imprint of Simon & Schuster Children's Publishing Division

1230 Avenue of the Americas, New York, NY 10020

First Simon Pulse paperback edition April 2010

Copyright © 2009 by Terra Elan McVoy

Also available in a Simon Pulse hardcover edition.

For information about special discounts for bulk purchases, please contact
Simon & Schuster Special Sales at 1-866-506-1949 or business@simonandschuster.com.

The Simon & Schuster Speakers Bureau can bring authors to your live event. For more information
or to book an event contact the Simon & Schuster Speakers Bureau at
1-866-248-3049 or visit our website at www.simonspeakers.com.

Designed by Tom Daly

The text of this book was set in Adobe Garamond.

Manufactured in the United States of America

6 8 10 9 7 5

The Library of Congress has cataloged the hardcover edition as follows:

McVoy, Terra Elan.

Pure / Terra Elan McVoy.—1st Simon Pulse ed.

p. cm.

Summary: Fifteen-year-old Tabitha and her four best friends all wear
purity rings to symbolize their pledge to remain virgins until they
marry, but when one admits that she has broken the pledge each girl must
reexamine her faith, friendships, and what it means to be pure.

ISBN 978-1-4169-7872-5 (hc)

[1. Best friends—Fiction. 2. Friendship—Fiction. 3. Purity (Ethics)—Fiction.
4. Christian life—Fiction. 5. Dating (Social customs)—Fiction.]

I. Title.

PZ7.M478843Pur2009

[Fic]—dc22

2008033404

ISBN 978-1-4169-6748-4 (pbk)

ISBN 978-1-4391-6788-5 (eBook)

This book is dedicated to the Glam Girls book group

of Little Shop of Stories in Decatur, Georgia.

chapter 1

"It looks like an engagement ring," I tell the spike-haired girl at the counter. Behind me on the green velvet couch, Morgan is crying her face purple. "With a blue stone, like aquamarine?"

The girl flicks her puffy-lidded eyes at the other barista, a thin guy with a shaved head. Not like they both weren't just watching me as I scrambled under the table, lay flat on the nasty rug, and pressed my face practically against the floor trying to see Morgan's ring under the abyss of the incense-dusty couch. Not like they hadn't stood there, not offering to help, as I hoisted up the front end of the couch, revealing nothing but a bunch of wrappers and coffee lids. Not like they offer any reassurance when I write down Morgan's number and ask them to call if the ring shows up.

"It's engraved," I say to the guy, who looks at least slightly sympathetic. "'Our angel forever' along the inside? It shouldn't be hard to miss."

"People lose stuff here all the time," Spike Girl says, glancing over my shoulder at Morgan, who's still crying. She could be vomiting blood, her eyeballs boiling to a liquid, and still I think this girl wouldn't be fazed. I twist my own ring—a band of pale, multicolored stones set with an emerald-cut Swarovski crystal—on my finger. I pray simultaneously for grace, patience, luck, forgiveness, and for this barbed-wire barista to get over herself and help me help my best friend.

Enter Priah: midnight hair a swinging sheen of straightness, her tiny feet followed by tiny knees, hips, rib cage, shoulders, neck, all topped off with these gigantic violet eyes and a two-thousand-pound grin. Only now she sees Morgan hyperventilating, and her face collapses.

"Oh, sweetie," she squeal-groans, crouching at Morgan's knees. "What happened?"

I level my eyes back at the baristas. "Of *course* we'll find it," Priah's canary voice insists behind me. I know Priah is crossing herself (even though none of us are Catholic), I know this girl in front of me sees it, and I know what she thinks. I don't care. I turn my back on her. Though losing the ring wouldn't be *near* (God forgive me) as awful as losing the virginity it's symbolically protecting, to Morgan the two might as well be, well, One, and I gotta at least keep trying to help her find it.

The next morning I have two texts from Morgan, so I head to the hallway phone to call her back. I'm strictly forbidden to speak on my cell unless it's to my parents, and since Mom actually finds a perverse pleasure in looking line by line through the bill for unauthorized calls, there's no way around this, except for texting if I keep it under twenty per month and never during school.

"What are you doing up so early?" Morgan wants to know right away.

"About to go to work, duh. What about you? I thought I'd go straight to voicemail."

I'm legitimately surprised at her chipperness, really. After finally leaving Java Monkey yesterday with no ring and only a slim chance of getting it back if it *was* found, Morgan was beside herself.

"Oh, it's so exciting! I couldn't wait to tell you! Did you get my texts? Well, last night at dinner when I told Daddy all about my ring slipping off, he just got the sweetest sheepiest puppiest look on his face." Morgan's own face, I can tell from her voice, currently has that rapture look she gets whenever her dad comes into the conversation. "He said that it was a sign, really, because just this week he'd started to go looking for a replacement ring for me in celebration of my sweet sixteen next month, and that my losing that old ring just meant I needed a new one right then, so he'd do the ring now, and then for my birthday go ahead and get me the Audi he'd been considering, but not sure about. Isn't that *great*?"

"Of course it's great." I remember to add an exclamation point in there. It is great, really. But when you're on the ninety-millionth instance of divine intervention in your best friend's life, it's hard to muster the same excitement as the first time.

"So this morning we're going up to Buckhead to have a

daddy-daughter brunch and then we'll look at some new rings. Do you want to come?"

"What? To brunch? Can't. I gotta be at the Center in, like, twenty. Remember?"

"Oh. Right. Work. Well, call me when you're done, right?"

"Yeah. Probably around five? Mom can drop me off after, I think. We're still on, yeah?" We've been planning to get ready together for tonight's Jesus-Generation Co-Christian dance since we got the Evite last weekend. We're always excited about the JGCC events, but this one's particularly crucial.

"Duh. Why do you think I want you to come over right *now*? Ooh but soon-soon-soon *I'll* be able to pick you up whenever, and whisk you off *wherever* we want to go!"

"Presuming after tonight I want to be *seen* anywhere."

"Oh, come on. The worst that can happen is he's not there at all, right? It's not like he's going to publicly humiliate you or anything. Mainly because I'm not going to let you humiliate your*self*. And it's going to be fun," she finishes lightly. "Boys or no boys."

"Right," I mutter, convincing neither of us. She's referring to the fact that her own boyfriend, Cody, isn't coming (because the JGCC group includes churches that openly support homosexuals), and also my own nail-biting hope that Jake—the cute guy I met at the freezing-cold-but-who-cares JGCC hayride in February—will be there.

When I hang up I'm still a little jittery. Tonight's the first chance I've had to see Jake again, at least anywhere outside my mind. We'd gotten squooshed together in the back of one of the pickups during the Valentine's hayride; our conversation started when he stepped on my hand, turning somehow into episodes of *This American Life*, whatever happened to bubble tea, and having to read *I Am the Cheese*, which then turned into my crush. We didn't really get to say good-bye when everyone started piling out of the trucks and into their own carpool rides, so he never asked for my number, but nevertheless I've been increasingly butterflyville for the past six days.

After hanging up with Morgan, I dial Cara's cell. It goes straight to voicemail, which doesn't bode well for her attendance tonight, though she did say yesterday at school that she and Michael would try to be there. I leave a message saying we hope she's still coming. Calling Priah next for last-minute wardrobe requests is a good idea, but I know her family would frown on a breakfast interruption, especially over something so "superficial." I consider calling Naeomi and asking her again what she's going to wear, but Naeomi's not much of a morning person, and I already know when she meets us there she'll be wearing her favorite baby-blue capris with "something shimmery" up on top. Since there's no one else to call, really, it's down to breakfast I go.

When I tromp down the stairs later after my post-work shower, I'm still uncertain about the four tops and jeans plus backup jeans I've crammed in my sleepover bag along with the two appropriate, possibly matching pairs of shoes I have, plus makeup, flat iron, and pretty much every piece of jewelry I own. I've also called Morgan twice to say I'm thinking of not going.

Dad is waiting for me in the den, flipping through an issue of *The Week*, wearing his oh-so-hip cargo sweats and yellow rubber clogs. "You ready?" he says, arching his thick eyebrows halfway up his skull.

"Where's Mom?"

"Oh." He puts the magazine carefully back in the chair-side rack and frowns. "Well, she suffered an attack of partial-temporary amnesium ridiculosum this morning, and vanished about an hour ago."

In Dad-ese this means Mom's pulling one of her famous I'm Independent Even Though I'm a Mother moments and has left me in Dad's care so that she can shop or go have coffee or do some work at her campus office or whatever.

"Well, I just hope we don't have to put up Lost Mom flyers again," I say in an attempt to mask my disappointment. Dad can't help his dorkiness, and I know he wants to be my favorite. I do love him and all, but before going off to a dance to maybe see a boy she maybe wants to see again if he's maybe there and maybe remembers who she even is, a girl kinda wants her mom around.

In the car my throat is chalk and I think I'm sweating every drop of moisture in my body out through my palms, so I keep tapping them on my thighs in weak efforts to dry them off. He is probably not going to be there. Probably not. So this is stupid. But thinking that isn't doing much in the hyper-perspiration department.

"What band is playing again?" Dad asks when we turn onto Morgan's street.

"Not a band, Dad. A DJ. You know, like at a regular club? Gospel choirs are still reserved for worship only."

Dad chuckles. "Chaperones going to be there?"

"Yes, Dad."

"Cell phone charged?"

"Yes, Dad, but I promise to use it only if there's an emergency."

"And Mr. and Mrs. Kent know where you're going to be at all times."

"Yes, Dad. Gah!"

His eyes are twinkling and I'm only half as exasperated as I'm acting, but when the car stops I've got one hand on the door handle and the other undoing my seat belt.

"Okay, okay. I'll stop." He leans over to squeeze me around the shoulders and I quick-squeeze him back. "Have a good time and don't do anything I wouldn't do."

"Come on, Dad." I hold up my left hand and wiggle my ring at him—a routine he loves. "You already know I won't."

chapter 2

Mrs. Kent answers the door, and I turn to wave at Dad, who's idling there in front of the house just in case, for some reason, the Kents decided to take off for Mexico at the last minute *and* all their phones were dead so Morgan couldn't call to let me know. He salutes and pulls away, and Mrs. Kent reaches around my shoulders to give me a perfumey hug. "Taa-bitha. Come on in. Don't you look nice. Morgan's in her room. You need a fruit spritzer before you go up?" She gestures toward the kitchen with grace that is half Miss America, half flight attendant.

"Oh, no thank you, ma'am." I remember to smile in spite of my nervousness and head upstairs, hoping she doesn't think I'm wearing this to the dance.

In her room, Morgan's sprawled on the bed talking on her cell. She smiles and waves and makes space for me. "Uh-huh," she says, rolling her eyes for my sake. I look around at the piles of clothing possibilities discarded on her floor and the eyelet-covered armchair, then pick through the closest one to see what she won't wear that I might. "Uh-huh," Morgan says again, making a "wrap this up" signal with her freshly unpolished fingers.

"Priah wants to know did you bring your red tank top?" This to me.

"Oh. Uh"—I mentally check the contents of my bag—"um, no. Why?"

She talks back into the phone: "Tab says no. Yeah, she's here. But, sorry." She listens a little while longer, looking at me and making hand gestures I'm supposed to understand but don't quite. "Listen, Priah, just come over and we'll sort it out." Another pause. "Well, whenever your brother or whatever can bring you, just come. It's okay." Pause. "Yes, I promise we'll wait, okay? And yes, I'll tell her. But I've got to go."

"Gah!" she sighs to me when she's hung up. "Sorry about that. Priah doesn't know what to wear and we didn't find anything at Lenox this afternoon and she was hoping you'd bring that red tank top you have but we knew you were working and couldn't call you, so, what can you do?"

"Priah went shopping with you?"

"After brunch and after the jewelry store was a bust. Can you believe they'd never even *heard* of purity rings? Can you imagine? Daddy got so agitated that he asked for the manager. When he came out, Daddy said he was sorry to hear that such a well-reputed establishment wasn't familiar with a moral revolution that was sweeping the nation, and he'd been prepared to come and spend a significant amount of money there but now knew better, since they obviously didn't support vows of abstinence and chastity among teenage men and women. It was so impressive. And they, like, were totally stunned and had nothing to say and we walked out, both of us disappointed. So we went and got Frappuccinos, and then Priah called and her mom had to do something nearby so she dropped Pree off and Daddy let us shop the rest of the afternoon. She had to go home to eat with her family, but she's coming around seven."

Looking around at the Land of Unwanted Outfits, I can't help but marvel at Morgan's unquenchable need to go shopping for *more*, but I can't really complain since over half my wardrobe is a result of her shopping sprees: castoffs she's worn about four times and gotten tired of.

"Well, what're you going to do?" I ask.

Morgan shrugs and turns toward her vanity mirror, pulling her long blond hair up off her face, considering. "Loan her something of mine, I guess. We totally would have called, you know, but—"

"No, no. I get that. I mean about your ring."

She plops down on the dressing-table stool and frowns at her fingernails. "I don't know. Keep looking, I guess. Daddy won't let me just get one online because he wants to be able to talk to the salesman and ensure the quality and all that."

"Why don't you go back to where he got your first one?"

"Yeah. We might." She shrugs again. "I just, you know . . . wanted something special, you know? Something new."

Her blue eyes are swimming at me and I *do* know. It is important. We made these vows when we were only twelve that we wouldn't have sex until we got married. I hadn't even gotten my period. And now we're in high school and almost old enough to drive and it does feel like reclaiming that statement should be even more spectacular somehow.

"It just means you haven't found the right one yet."

She smiles, but it's only a sliver. "You're probably right. It's just . . . so weird not to have it on. It's like, I feel I could get violated at any time, like in some way it was *protecting* me, you know?"

I go to hug her. Sometimes it's annoying how Morgan is so special to (read: spoiled by) her parents, but when she's worried like this she just has this utter sweet softness that you really do want to do everything you can to protect.

"Well, you've got me," I say. "I'll look out for you in the meantime. Like, right now I'm standing up for those unpolished fingertips—let's get you painted and primed!"

"Ah, my hero," she gasps, fake swooning onto the plush cream carpet where we both dive for her pink cosmetics crate. We choose colors and sit, feet in each other's laps, pushing toe separators between each other's tootsies and getting ready to get serious.

By the time Priah's older brother drops her off, Morgan and I have done each other's nails (we both decided on French manicures instead of anything too loud), have tried on six outfits (all failures, except for the two punk costumes we knew were jokes anyway), and have eaten our new favorite—Thai brown rice bowls—in front of some old *Project Runway* episodes on DVD.

Priah, as always, is polite and smiling in front of Mr. and Mrs. Kent, but when we get into the down-pillowed haven of Morgan's room she collapses, moaning. "Oh my Gah, my *parents*! I had to swear—*swear*!—that there will be chaperones there, that I'd keep my cell phone on and would answer whenever they happened to call, no matter what, and besides that, I have *nothing* to wear because I can never buy anything I want because they always—always!— think anything *decent* is 'much too matoor for a guhl of my age and oopbringing.'" Here she does one of her perfect imitations of Mrs. Degali, and it would be funny if it weren't so true. Priah and her family used to live in this really close-knit Indian neighborhood up in Allegany, New York, before moving to Atlanta two years ago, and they all totally think Priah's going to be corrupted every moment.

"Well, I've already rescued one maiden today," I say, standing up and bowing deeply, "so let me see if I can help you." Priah claps and bats her eyes and I go for my overnight bag, since it's been determined I'm not wearing anything out of it except my favorite jeans and red Mary Janes.

"Oh but Tabitha, we should really concentrate on you tonight, right?" Priah shifts on Morgan's giant bed so that she can sit cross-legged. I totally blush.

"Well, he probably isn't even going to be there," I manage a semi-nonchalant voice. "So I'm not worried about it. I just want to have fun with you guys. It's silly to get worked up over somebody you met once, like, a month ago." *Even if you have been listening to his favorite radio show obsessively so you have cleverly informed comments prepared, just in case.*

"Give me a break! He's probably been dying since the Evite, knowing he'll get to see Cinderella again. You've got to be hot!

Look, I clipped this for you—did Morgan say?" Priah rummages in her bag and pulls out a picture she tore from one of the five hundred magazines she reads. "Here, I can totally do it. Your hair is the perfect length for this."

The picture shows a girl with what looks like five different tiny French braids along her scalp, with the ends tucked under and tied with a thin red ribbon. It's glamorously cool, but definitely not something I'd normally do. Most of the time I just pull a brush through my hair or do a ponytail. The fanciest I get is twisting the whole wavy mass up into a messy knot held up with chopsticks. If Priah can pull it off, though, I'll look completely fabulous. Different, but fabulous.

I hold up the picture for Morgan, who comes out of her closet wearing a paisley-print wrap dress. She tilts her head like a curious pigeon, squinting. "It's good you're wearing jeans," Morgan decides. "With killer hair and killer shoes, you'll really only need some kind of cute but not-too-crazy top. I mean, you want to look good but not like you're trying." She goes back into her closet and comes out with a couple of different tank tops—one in navy silk that catches my eye.

I visualize myself as looking funky in a fun, not freaky way, and do a quick prayer to make my hair behave. "Okay, Pree. Do your magic." I turn around so my back is against her knees. She squeals and grabs her smoothing spray and my brush.

"Ladies, you look lovely," Mr. Kent says when we go down to the ivory-and-mahogany living room. We twirl for him before posing in front of the fireplace for a photo. Morgan and I've had about six hundred similar shots taken since fourth grade when she moved from Texas right into the seat next to me.

Mrs. Kent comes in to admire us, smiling like she's showing us how to. When Mr. Kent shows our picture to her, she smiles even bigger; when we crowd over we see why. Morgan's in the middle, her hair softly waved around her shoulders and peachy-glow face. On her left Priah is sharp and stunning, with a sparkling white grin. I'm smiling over on Morgan's right, and thanks to Priah's successful machinations, I don't even look too out of place.

"All right." Mr. Kent claps his hands. "Let's get these girls off to their shindig, shall we?"

Since it's dark, Morgan's not allowed to drive, even though she's been practicing almost every day since she got her permit last April. We chatter in the back instead, Priah betting us both a Soycream pint that Cara's not coming. Though I'm hoping she's wrong I don't take the bet—Dad taught me only to gamble if you know you'll win. Mainly, listening to them, I'm just drifting between hoping Jake'll be there and praying he won't.

chapter 3

When we get to the Midtown YMCA the music's already slamming, and it's crowded. Twenty yards inside the main doors are throngs of people we both know and don't: kids from youth groups across the metro-Atlanta area, including a lot from Decatur, where we live, plus some who were bussed in from way outside the perimeter, just for this. You can feel everyone's glee to be here, which is what makes JGCC dances way better than ones at school, where everyone's too cool to do anything. The DJ is onstage with his mixing board: some prematurely balding college kid with perfectly broken-in Cons and rainbow suspenders; a guy who likely thinks DJ-ing for a bunch of Christian kids is some kind of ironic alterna-cool, though the joke's on him 'cause everybody's digging his groove so much, he's genuinely getting into it.

Right away, we see Wedge, one of the youth ministers at Morgan's church, standing close to the stage, nodding his head to the beat. There's this ten-yard radius of emptiness surrounding him, like everyone knows about his "Save Britney" website.

Regardless, Morgan bounces over to him, chattering like mad. The music's too loud to tell what she actually says, so Priah and I don't even try to pretend to follow the conversation. We scan the crowd instead: a mass of shirts and faces, people dancing, an arm going up—a head flung back. Out there on the back edge is Cameron, the Methodist poster child for gayness, surrounded by his savior angels: girls from his church and our school who are determined to love Cameron despite his refusal to See the Light (i.e., Convert to the Straight Side). More faces, more folks I don't know—I'm looking for Naeomi's face somewhere out there—and then, *omigah*, there he is.

"Come on," Priah says, just as the DJ starts a remix of some old Madonna, "I love this song." Pree's knack for timely diversions is so keen it's almost spooky, but I don't dwell on it as she pulls me into the crowd and we start to dance. I concentrate on the music, on Priah's big smile, instead of wondering whether Jake saw me, if he saw me see him, if he didn't want to see me, blah blah blah. Instead, I'm just dancing. Or trying to. This really *is* a good song, even if it is kind of old, and Priah's fun to dance with, because she's so good, though not the kind of good that makes you feel bad dancing next to her. I smile back, only occasionally looking over her head, telling myself I'm looking for Cara, and am not, in fact, trying to spot Jake again.

Morgan butts into us then, yammering excitedly, but we just swing our hips and jerk our knees and fling our arms, too happy to listen. She gets it and moves with us too, and soon we are all sweaty and grooving. Some girl from the Unitarian church near my house—the first one my parents took me to in their Tour of Houses of Worship back when I was seven and they thought I should at least be exposed to *some* religion, the one I think they'd attend if they still cared about church—bangs into us and we all smile and wave and do a little dip-you-dip together as a foursome, and the DJ takes us to another hip-hop level, and the whole gym seems to be smiling and . . . just . . . *dancing*.

About twenty minutes later Naeomi has arrived. We open our circle to include some kids from we-don't-know-where, who have this kind of tribal-edge vibe to them (shaved parts of heads, black cargo shorts, chains, "native" tatts on their forearms), and who occasionally bust into this awesome break dancing thing with each other. This DJ has a penchant for the old school, but it's okay because the music is good and my friends are here and everyone is into it. Even Naeomi seems in a good mood. When I scream to her "Where's Cara?" in the middle of the next song, she simply shrugs and smiles and lets this tall Rasta dude grab her hands and pull her into a cute swing-shuffle. I figure if Cara's best friend can take it, I'd better chin up over her absence too.

After another good forty-five minutes, it gets hot—really hot—and Morgan says, "I need to sit." Without protest we all grab hands and follow her to the back of the gym. We sit on the bleachers together about halfway up. Next to me Priah sweeps her hair off her neck. I give my own braids a little pat to make sure they're still holding, and am glad to find they are. Naeomi fans herself and then Priah, and Morgan leans back on her elbows, watching the crowd before us. Her face is even and cool, but when she catches me staring, she twists her mouth into this goofy grimace, stretching her lips in different directions, her eyes rolling back. We crack up.

The DJ starts a slow set then. The chaperones all take a few steps forward as couples immediately form and lean in together. I'm glad we're already sitting, so we don't look like we got driven off the dance floor just because we don't have slow-dance partners, like most of the masses now swarming to the bleachers around us. I've done a pretty good job so far of not really thinking about Disappearing Jake, but now I can't help it. I wonder where in the crowd he might be, if he's out there already somewhere, leaning on some other girl.

Ugh. Awful thought. So I watch Cameron twirl a chubby girl in purple tights and a scraggy tulle skirt around instead. A few other people start twirling too. We are all watching, not wanting to be. I look at Morgan and wonder if she wishes Cody were here, or is glad that he's not. She's been either quiet or exasperated whenever he's come up lately, which means, based on her track record, that a breakup is imminent, though I still haven't figured out if it'll come from him or her.

My eyes move to Priah. Of all of us, she's the one who wants a boyfriend most, and this makes her a prime candidate for getting wistful and sobby during the slow dances. There was this boy she had a "relationship" with back in Allegany, and even though they only kissed that one time, they kept up pretty well during our freshman year. After school started again in September, though, he stopped writing her back (Morgan and I figure he found someone actually in his own town, but whatever), and Priah got pretty melodramatic, especially since that was when Cara and Michael started getting serious for real. Priah's better now, but tonight I want to make sure she is still holding on to our shining happy dancing moments, instead of sinking into sad sighing. I want to catch her eye, to thank her for my fantastic hair, but as I'm trying I have to look away real fast because about ten feet beyond her is *him*. Jake. Jake Harper. Jake from Old United and Seymour High. Jake from Valentine's weekend. That Jake. Him.

Morgan sees him at the same time and pokes me. "I know, I know," I say, staring forward, trying to be cool, but my throat is doing a funny and I can't feel my hands. Or my butt on the hard bleacher seat, really. Still, I know *exactly* where he's sitting: to my right and down a bleacher.

He gets up. My head automatically turns toward his movement. I see him come over but it's like I'm not seeing it. He stands there, says, "Hey," and then—right in front of my friends—he's asking me if I want to dance. Morgan squeezes my elbow but all I can focus on is the inch or two of white hem poking out from under his gray ringer T-shirt and the gleam of his belt buckle. There is a loop, I think—one of those carpenter loops—on his jeans. I cannot fathom his shoes, his hair.

I'm standing up and I guess my friends are watching and I step around Priah and follow him down the bleachers. He stops and turns and offers his hand to help me the rest of the way down, like some kind of gentleman. And then we go into the forest of swaying couples—*is this* happen*ing?*—and suddenly we're a tree too. Somewhere near my neck is his breath. My hands make two shields over his shoulder blades. I'm moving with him. We bump feet.

I can't tell you what the song is. You're supposed to remember but I can't tell you the song. All I know is my funny throat and the way my hands are burning.

"I sloshed pergumber afidence," he says near my ear.

I pull back to see his face. Oh, hazel eyes. Hazel. "What?"

"I washed your number on accident," he says again, smiling. "So I'm really glad you were here."

I imagine tiny bits of my phone number, my handwriting, floating around in the sudsy water with his clothes.

"But I didn't give you my number," I blurt. It sounds like I'm offended. "I mean—you didn't—" Believe me, I lamented this for days.

"No, your cheerleader friend did. I asked her after. I didn't want to—"

Morgan gave you my number and this whole time she said NOTHING to me???? But I decide I can be mad at her later. "Well, I hope it didn't leave a stain."

This makes him blush for some reason and I move my chin over his shoulder so he can't see that I see it. Now it's not just my hands that are on fire; in the center of my back, where his hands are, and my chest, where it's against him, is lava.

We press a little closer together, but in a few sways we're both kind of just standing still, awkward, because the music has changed into this not-slow, not-fast hyper-ballad that's too slow for bopping and too fast for proximity. Everyone around us has stopped moving too, not sure whether to leave the floor or not, and at the same time Jake and I lean back and say, "This song is kinda hard to dance to."

We laugh, relieved, and he jerks his head toward the gym door. I turn to give my friends an "I'll be back" signal, but only Naeomi's sleek dark head is turned toward me. She gives a wink and a thumbs-up. I follow Jake through the other not-quite-dancing-but-afraid-to-quit-because-there-aren't-that-many-slow-songs couples to outside, where the air is cool and fresh even with a chaperone standing out there smoking a cigarette and trying to hide it. We walk a few yards down the sloping sidewalk and sit on the guardrail side by side. The smoker could see us if he wanted to, but he'd have to look.

"Feels good out here," I say, to say something.

"Yeah, I hate when it gets hot too soon. The coolness is more normal."

We look at each other and sort of quirksmile. Talking about the *weather*.

"I'm sure you're glad to cool off," he says. "Looks like you were having a pretty good time with your friends."

Please God, let me not have looked like an epileptic giraffe.

"Oh, well, we love dancing. My friends are all on the dance team, though, so I usually look pretty dumb next to them."

"What I saw you held your own."

I blush. Let's not focus on the idea of him staring. Or comparing.

"So, you guys doing anything cool in your youth group?" I ask.

"Oh, I don't know. I mean, I guess so."

I wait for him to clarify.

"I mean, I don't go there," he rushes on. "Not really. My cousin, Owen? He does. And since we fish Sundays a lot I end up going to church with him sometimes. And youth group stuff. When I don't have lacrosse."

"Oh, I see."

I am trying to remember which one Owen was. I am trying to think if lacrosse is the one with the sticks or the one like football where everyone gets in a big pile to hike the ball. I am trying to decide if it matters that he doesn't go to church.

"What?" he asks, leaning forward to look me full in the face.

"Is lacrosse the one with the sticks or the big pile of dudes?"

He laughs. "Sticks. And lots and lots of body pads. And running up and down the field. A lot."

"Gotcha. Soccer polo. Without the horses."

"Soccer polo. Exactly. But you don't have to watch your step."

We laugh but are having a hard time making eye contact. I see him see my ring and my thumb automatically goes to cover it up.

"Hey, I really like your shoes," he says, leaning farther forward on the bar.

"Thanks. I have these green-and-brown ones too—" But his face, his mouth in particular, has come back up and is now suddenly very, very close to mine. I can see the tips of his bangs caught in his dark eyelashes. I can see his lids lowering and *Oh wait I'm not ready oh help me be cool please Jesus here it comes—*

My entire shoulders, neck, collarbone heat up as his mouth touches mine. My toes, I think, are honestly curling. This is *nothing* like Adam Dietzler and the ninth-grade beach retreat. The tingles are exploding all over the back of my skull, and when his bottom teeth click my top teeth I honestly think I'm going to faint. When he stops I keep my eyes closed just so I don't fall over.

I feel him move away, though the warm of him is still there. "I didn't"—he clears his throat—"want to mess things up like last time." I am dying. "Do you think—I can see you again? You know, not at one of these group things?"

My eyes snap open. "Oh."

"What? You have a boyfriend?" He is very clearly not looking at me now.

I can't help laughing. "No." My head shakes. So do my hands. "I mean. I would love to. See you. You know?" My thumb is twisting my ring around my ring finger over and over and over. Jake is nodding. Mostly I just want him to kiss me again.

"Cool." He nods. "In the meantime I am definitely not washing your phone number again."

I think angels could fly out of my rib cage, my back unzip and spill out daffodils.

"Better get you back to your friends." He helps me off the railing. I cannot believe this is happening to me. Before we go back to the gym, he programs my number into his cell. "I'm gonna head," he says, nodding toward the parking lot.

Wait. What? You're leaving? And you have a car of your own to leave in?

"My friends scrammed pretty early and I've got lacrosse in the morning anyway."

"Bye." I wave. He tucks his hands into his pockets and lopes a few yards away before remembering and turning back, waving dumbly too. I smile. He smiles. He goes. And then it's just me standing in the dark with my hands buzzing, feeling the shape of his shoulder blades pressed there under them.

chapter 4

I'm still a helium balloon floating through the gym until Morgan's hand is suddenly a vise grip on my elbow and she's hissing, "Where have you *been*?" in my ear. I think she's mad at first, but she hugs me and she's smiling, and she pulls me to where Naeomi and Priah keep dancing. I melt into the crowd and try to clear my head while the lights sweep shadows over everyone's faces.

They're all sneaking looks at me, but fortunately the dancing is too good and we only have half an hour left anyway. Once, when Morgan looks over, I do try to mouth "He. Kissed. Me." But she turns away in a spin and I'm not sure she sees.

And then we can't talk about it in the car afterward either, because Mr. Kent's right there. I'm squooshed between Naeomi and Priah, who's squeezing my hand and grinning, while Morgan tries to goad Naeomi into saying something about Cara's not being there. I close my eyes and take a deep breath. I wish Cara had been there too, and I'm half waiting for Naeomi's sharp judgment next to me. But thinking of Cara makes me think of what I have to tell her now, and then Jake's face swims up and everything else just goes warm all over.

Once we get into our pajamas and are settled around Morgan's room, though, Priah's all over me: "Oh. My. Gah. Tabs! He is so *cute*! I didn't know he was so cute! You are so lucky!" she shrieks. Pree wasn't allowed to go to the Valentine hayride, but as soon as she heard about him, she was trying to find him on Facebook. Of course, like all of us and everyone else in the universe, he has a profile (though he doesn't log in much), but the info he posted was generically basic, and his pic is a still from an old YouTube cartoon.

"You were sure talking awhile," Morgan says, handing me the can of Pringles.

"I don't think they were doing much talking," Naeomi butts in, an inky eyebrow arched high.

Priah leans in to grab my hands. "Aaaahh, I'm so *happy* for you!" she squeals. "He is so *cute*!" And though Priah's overenthusiasm about pretty much anything that happens to me or Morgan is sometimes borderline annoying, right now it's actually kind of nice. "So, did you kiss?" she wants to know.

Morgan's focused on rubbing cuticle oil in her nails, so she doesn't see the outrageously telling blush I feel crawling over my face. There is more bubbling from Priah, and Naeomi goes "Uh-oh" in her half joking, half preaching tone.

"What church does he go to again?" Morgan cuts in.

I clear my throat. "Well, he doesn't really. Except with his cousin sometimes. Owen? They hang out a lot and he occasionally goes with him. You know." She's looking at me like she already knows all this, which makes it harder to answer. "Like Priah goes with you. Like I used to."

She shrugs and moves down to the floor.

"Well, so . . . ," Naeomi asks, smiling wickedly enough for me to see the little gap between her two front teeth.

I can't help it: "Oh. My. Gosh. You guys. I had *no* idea that kissing was like this. I swear. Total volcano or something!"

"Aaaaah!" Priah half screams again, grabbing me around the neck. "Tabs! This is so great. You deserve this, like, more than anybody I *know*." I can't help but squeeze her back, though I notice Morgan's just staring at her toenails. She's so disinterested, I almost challenge her with a shove and a "What?" but I don't want to make too big a deal of anything in front of Naeomi and Priah. Admittedly I was looking forward to a whole play-by-play super-scrutiny with my best friend, going over all the highs and lows of my first real kiss—like we do with all of *her* kisses, at least until the boys want more and she dumps them—but instead I feel more like we're in PE, and Morgan hasn't picked me to be on her team.

"So are you going to go out?" Naeomi wants to know.

"I don't know. He asked me. But I don't know what my parents are going to say." Naeomi nods in approval. "He drives"—screech from Priah again—"so that makes it kind of . . . different." I feel myself getting flustered, wanting to stay happy but not being able to. "I don't know," I finish. "I guess we'll see."

Morgan keeps up the toe-studying routine, as though I'm

Priah going on about her mother, like I'm an annoying idiot. *Say something*, I think. *Can't you be happy for me?*

Instead I just mumble about how he might not even call. Naeomi nods again and for the first time I wonder what her talks with Cara were really like in the early days of Michael, how she knows so much about boys anyway, seeing as she's so Ring Dedicated she's never even gone to the movies with anyone but us.

"He will totally call you," Priah says, squeezing her knees closer to her chest. Maybe it's just because Morgan's being weird, but I feel another What Do You Know About It twinge.

It makes me miss Cara. More than I just normally would, the four of us having so much fun without her. I know Michael thinks the ring is really important, and I know they keep everything safe and tame—strictly clothes-on and nothing below the waist since things got a little heavy and scary at New Year's—but she'd understand more than anyone else the burning sensation I still feel in my hands and along the back of my neck. She'd at least give me a big knowing grin, some understanding nods, unlike my own best friend, who's acting more like I've contracted a disease.

Morgan dismisses all of it with one exhausted sigh. "Church tomorrow. Let's at least get horizontal if we're going to keep talking." With the conversation cut short, we busy ourselves with the air mattress, the passing and extra-fluffing of Morgan's two hundred pillows, the unfurling of fuzzy peach blankets, the good nights.

After the lights are out and Morgan and I are lying side-by-side-silent in the giant sweep of her bed, I try to pray: Pray a big thank-you for Jake even being there let alone kissing me; pray for Morgan to be back to normal in the morning and then get the ring she wants; pray for forgiveness; pray for myself to not be a total spazz; and as always pray for my family and peace in the world.

The good thing about praying is that you really can say whatever you want to God, and you know you'll get heard. The bad thing is He doesn't exactly give any feedback, especially not on Jake's kiss or Morgan's indifference.

chapter 5

As soon as I walk into youth group the next afternoon, Evie runs up and hugs me. "How was the *dance?*" she wants to know. Evie is really sweet, and it's fun to see her at church, but privately I'm glad she doesn't go to my school. Even in our all-of-us-are-equal-in-God's-eyes youth group, Evie can be a little, well, *much*, and if she'd been able to come to the dance instead of babysitting her stepbrother and sister, I know she would've been hanging on my elbow the entire time.

It was great, I want to say. *And I got kissed by this really, really, really cute boy who I really, really, really think I like.* Except Evie has never herself been kissed, and she doesn't have a purity ring as an excuse, either.

"The DJ was good," I tell her instead, scanning the church rec room for Cara. She's there, sitting on one of the tables, swinging her feet and talking to Brandon, another sophomore like us. I've been dying to talk to her all day, but church and lunch with the

Kents didn't leave a lot of time before getting here, and her cell phone's been on constant OFF anyhow.

Cara smiles wide when she sees me. I telegraph her with my eyes under Evie's chatter: *I have to talk to you.* Her smile makes me think maybe she has to talk to me back.

Before we get a chance, though, our youth group leader Marilyn comes in with a big accordion file balanced on top of two boxes from The Copy Pot. Our other leader, Greg, lopes behind her, carrying three boxes of Rhonda's Luncheonette doughnuts and a grocery bag with what must be milk.

"The letters printed out great," Marilyn says. "So all we need to do tonight is sign, address, and stamp. We'll be ready to roll tomorrow."

She puts the boxes and the file on one of the rec room tables and we all help unpack the pens, envelopes, stamps, labels, and letters—all the stuff for the final stage of what's been a whole month of YG concentration. It started with Madeline's confirmation class presentation on Faithful America, a group she joined on the web. Every year, people getting confirmed make these service presentations to the congregation, and the youth group picks one of the organizations to support. Since Madeline was the only senior confirming this year, she was a total shoo-in, but we really liked the multifaith mission of Faithful America too. We decided to write a letter to every church member and recent visitor, telling them about Faithful America's work, why we endorse them, and the different things (donations, e-mail lists, local action, etc.) that individuals can do to help. Then we spent two weeks arguing over the body of the letter, before we whittled it down from six pages to three. After tonight, the letters will go out into the world and we'll see what happens.

It's this exact kind of project that made me excited about joining the Senior Highs here, instead of going to youth group all the time with Morgan, which I'd been doing. The summer before ninth grade, Marilyn came into our Sunday school class (Morgan was in St. Simons with her parents, so I just happened to be at my own church), and talked to us eighth graders about the Senior High group. She told us that two seniors of the group actually sit on the church's Session and get to help make important decisions, and about their projects like this letter campaign, and the themed discussions they have every month about youth-picked topics, like racism, global poverty, and alternative prayer. Marilyn made it sound like the Senior Highs here were really engaged, instead of basically a big social group like at Morgan's church. Listening to her I felt my scalp prickle and my ears turn up—my heart go: *I want to do that too.*

I was so excited afterward that I called Morgan as soon as I got home to get her to start coming with me. We actually kind of had a little mini-fight about it, because at first she thought I was accusing her church of being too superficial, which I totally wasn't. I still do stuff at her church plenty, but soon after that, we met Priah and the two of them started going to Blessed Trinity together, and then we met Cara, and I invited her to come to youth group with me, and now it's all fine.

To maximize our time together tonight, Cara and I sit on the signing side, so we can write notes to each other in between things.

So what happened? Right away she scribbles.

I sign a few letters with my full name, Tabitha Gretchen Carmine McAbe, before responding: How do you know something happened?

All over your face. Was he there?

Her eyebrows rise up half the distance of her forehead when I can't stop grinning.

Was it nice?

Again an ultrarevealing smile from me.

He as cute as you remembered?

Cuter. Though half the time my eyes were closed. ☺

This makes her reach down to bang her fist on my knee and nearly shake my pen out of my hand. For a little while we just bask in the yay and spend some time signing and passing, signing and passing. Cara's signature is scrunched up and tiny, always near the bottom right corner of the paper.

Any day-after worries? she finally scratches. I look at her boyish handwriting and feel a wash of affection; this is what I needed last night. Cara just *gets* how people's brains really work. Worries? she wants to know. You mean like how my best friend still didn't mention much about it at all, even this morning and all during lunch today, making me wonder if the whole thing really happened? Or how I'm not sure my parents will let me go in a car alone with a boy? Or that I have no idea what, if anything, to say to Jake about my ring? You mean like that?

He hasn't called yet. I finally write. Does that count?

Next to me Aaron is signing all his letters with just a big X in the middle of the paper, so there's a big pileup. It's a few minutes before I see what Cara's written:

No BECAUSE HE TOTALLY WILL.

We look at each other and smile.

Since youth group's only an hour and a half, and there are a lot of letters, we have to sort of cram to get everything finished. There isn't a whole lot more note-writing, or much time for the closing circle prayer even, but we do it anyway since it's the most therapeutic part of youth group, not to mention a tradition.

Across from me Marilyn starts us off, but everyone's kind of rushing to get out, so it's my turn before I'm really ready.

"Uh—I'm thankful for . . . um . . . encountering new people and experiences this week"—here Cara squeezes my hand—"and, ah—" I don't like to pray for specifics in circle prayer, but I do want to say something for Morgan's sake so I wrap up with "I pray for lost things to be found again." Another hand squeeze from Cara, whose own prayer comes out in a rush too: "Thank you Lord for the things you've taught me this week and please give me the strength to continue to do your will in light of them." She doesn't like to pray for specifics publicly either.

After prayers go the rest of the way around ("Please let me pass my chemistry test," "Thanks for Mom and Dad going to Asheville without me," "Be with the families and soldiers who are still fighting, and those back home now too"), Marilyn wraps up with thanks again, asking that we may go forth and do God's will in the ways best suited to our own talents. At the end we all say "Amen" and then hug one another and disperse out into the cool blue evening to wait for our rides. Cara and I squat on the curb together, picking up little twigs and breaking them into small pieces.

"So, what about you then?" I nudge her with my tennis shoe.

She shrugs, looks out down the street. "Yeah, I'm sorry I didn't make it."

"Well, it was a lot of fun, but we understood." I'm tempted to hint about Naeomi's disappointment, about how I could've used another ally in the face of Morgan's chilliness, but then her brother's truck pulls up and Cara offers me a hand.

"You need a ride tonight?"

"You mind?"

"Never. Come on."

We climb into the back, waving to Todd who, like always, has his ballcap on backward and is grossly spitting brown tobacco slime into a plastic Bulldogs cup. We hunker down as he drives off and the wind comes around both sides of the cab. There's a scratchy wool blanket in the back but we know it's disgusting with the Rawlson dogs and who knows how else Todd or one of Cara's other brothers have been using it. Instead we scrunch together, low, squeezing our knees to our chests.

"I love when the world looks like this," Cara says, looking up at the sky, "letting you know there are grander things out there at work than the normal day to day."

I take a deep breath too, and try to relax next to her, soaking in the dusking color and the branches of the trees and the geometric angles of the telephone wires overhead. I try to focus on the giant reassuring calm instead of everything else. I guess I get a little hypnotized by the black-on-indigo, the soothing wind, because too soon the truck stops at the light before my street and I snap out of it.

"You still haven't said what you and Michael did this weekend." I shove her with my foot. "Things still being special?"

She's so quiet, I look to make sure she's heard. Maybe her silence means something bad happened, but then I see she's staring down into her lap with this really pretty smile on her face.

"He's . . . amazing." She holds her hands out like she's trying to grip the whole sky. "You know how you're feeling, right now, about Jake? How it's all this rush and excitement and kind of like 'Holy cow, I can't believe how incredible he is'?"

I nod. I'm not sure I'm a hundred percent where she means, but I nod.

"Well, that's the thing. I've been with Michael a long time, but I keep . . ." She shakes her head in this unbelieving, happy way. "I keep discovering him."

Her smiling is infectious, and as we pull into my driveway, we're hugging. She jumps out quick, though, climbing into the cab where it's warmer. Honestly, I'm kind of glad she's in a hurry; Jake's not calling first thing Sunday morning makes sense, but certainly by now he's at least left a message?

"Call me later if you want," Cara says, rolling down the window.

"Okay, I might."

"Don't worry." She beams again. "It's all going to be wonderful."

Wonderful, I tell myself as I thank Todd for the ride, wave to Cara, and head up my porch stairs to unlock the door. *Wonderful, wonderful, wonderful.* Thing is, I'm not sure yet if I'll end up feeling the same kind of wonder that makes Cara smile like that, or the kind that leaves you scratching your head, confused.

chapter 6

Walking into the house, I'm washed with the same sense of freedom and total loneliness I always feel when my parents are gone. I drop my bag on the stairs, go to the hall table to pick up the receiver. No rapid beeping that indicates a voicemail. No message from my parents, either.

So he still hasn't called.

I wish this didn't make everything suddenly suck. I try to focus, instead, on the tiny weird sense of relief I also feel. He'd been too good to be true, anyway. Not everyone can have true love like Cara has. At least now I know the deal, and can just go on with school and friends and get back to normal. Naeomi would be proud of me.

Yeah. Who am I kidding? Suckville.

I go into the kitchen. On the counter is a frozen pizza and the ingredients for a spinach, mandarin-orange, and walnut salad, my favorite. A note in Mom's handwriting:

Pure

Dear Tabitha Carmine,

As you know, your father and I are at the Youngstons', nine doors down. Should the house catch on fire, please alert the authorities, as we may be in the Youngstons' basement examining their dehumidifier, and thereby unable to see the flames or smoke. Protect yourself of course darling, but do grab as many of your baby albums as possible. There is pizza and salad: what your father claims to be your current favorite. Our cell phones are on as usual. We will be home around 11. Morgan called for you twice. Also, there is another message. A Jake Harper called at 4:43. He left his number, which your father has thoughtfully left on the original Postie on your pillow. We asked no further questions.

Please do not forget your scholarly obligations.

As ever,

Your loving mother

I read the note again, making sure there isn't anything extra Jake said that I missed in my speed-read. Like, how nice it was that second time we kissed. Or that he was sorry but the whole thing had just been some kind of dare his cousin put him up to and he felt awful about it and had to come clean. Nope. Absolutely nothing. Just Mom being Mom. It would be a comfort if it weren't so maddening. But at least, *Oh thank you Jesus thank you (I think)*, he called.

I go back to the hallway phone. But I am totally not ready to call Jake yet, not on an empty stomach. Instead I dial Morgan, who picks up in half a ring.

"Hey, I know you can't talk long," I say, just as she's saying, "I can't really talk 'cause we're about to eat," and we both laugh.

"He called."

"You call him back?"

"I'm nervous."

"Why?"

"Well, because—"

"I mean, it's not like he's got some major hold on you."

"Well—"

"I mean, for all you know he could be Dork of the Universe over at Seymour. King of Pathetic Park. Mayor of the Land of Solitary Lunch."

I laugh, even though this isn't quite how I thought this would go. "Good point." *But he's so laid back and funny and cute. And his mouth is*—"So, is that why you gave him my number at the hayride?"

She is quiet for a second. "Oh, that. Well, I just wanted to see, you know? And we know what happened there, so."

"He said he washed it on accident."

"Well," is all she says. This isn't really making things easier or better.

"Listen, I have to run. I have stuff to tell you, though, okay? So, tomorrow?"

"Should I call him back right now or not?"

She sighs. "I don't think you should. Not yet. I mean, I guess yay that he called—you know he likes you, at least. But you've got a full life, right? More than boys? Hello? So what's the rush, right? You can make him wait."

"Okay," I say. *But—he called!* "I'll see you tomorrow."

"Okay then."

"Bye."

It's so awful when you need something from someone else, even though you're not sure what it is, and then you don't get it. Of course Morgan's right—what's the real rush? I mean, maybe that's what guys really want, anyway: to have to work for your attention, for you to be too busy with your amazing life to return calls promptly. But that doesn't seem in line with what Priah reads in all her magazines: that you should flatter guys and be extra-nice and make sure they know you're interested. And even if I *do* find out he's Dork of the Universe, right now I really like him. I mean, I can be a big dork too, a lot of the time. So, I should call him back, right? Maybe, like me, he's been waiting all day too. Maybe he's worried about being too pushy or looking uncool even though he's going crazy every minute. The idea is actually kind of nice.

I stare at the pizza box while the oven preheats, trying to get the chant *you are retarded* out of my head.

Three slices of pizza, a big bowl of salad, and two Punnett squares later, I'm staring at my curtains, my pen tapping against my biology notebook. I realize part of why I'm stalling. It's the ring. I mean, should I just *tell* him about it, like Morgan does when a boy even has a crush on her? He looked directly at it. He was holding my hand. Is he curious? Of course, he was also at a JGCC dance. He probably knows what it means already. And he could've looked me up on Facebook too, where I've got all those links and stuff. . . *So then why didn't he Friend me? Ach. Forget it.*

But even at church, there are a lot of people who don't know about purity rings. It's not like just because you're Christian you have this automatic abstinence impulse. My own church didn't go to the Ring Thing celebration when it was here. Instead I went with Morgan.

That was when I was going to Morgan's youth group way more than my own. I'd spend the night with her on Saturdays (sometimes Fridays too) and then we'd go to her church in the morning, go home for lunch and homework, and then go back to her church later for youth group. They did fun things at Trinity: roller-skating, movie outings, Six Flags, even trips to the mall, plus visits to people at the church-sponsored retirement home, which is how I got the idea of working at the Center. There was always praying, of course, but it was excited praying. And a lot of JGen activities.

The Ring Thing celebration was one of them. It was at the Civic Center, and we had to get permission from our parents to go because of potentially explicit material. Mom and Dad barely glanced at the form before signing it. Once I turned ten and could handle church on my own, they weren't involved much, outside of talking to me sometimes about how I felt about the sermon, Sunday school, and youth group discussions. That was more out of interest in my intellectual development, though. I think they expected I'd eventually grow out of the whole church thing, or get bored, or whatever, and I think maybe I would have if Morgan wasn't also so enthusiastic and I hadn't had Blessed Trinity to go to with her. Mom and Dad worried a little about the influence such Jesus Freakiness had on me (and do still sometimes); they were probably lax about the Ring Thing celebration because they thought it might help me see the light.

And it did. Just not in the get-me-out-of-here-these-people-are-psycho manner they definitely would have felt. While there *was* a kind of weird frenzied feeling about the celebration, it was mainly completely inspiring to be in this huge auditorium full of kids and adults who were just totally intent on doing God's will, and were happy about expressing it.

The preacher, Reverend John Howell of Memphis, Tennessee, was also this totally hot young guy. He came running out to this crazy techno-Bollywood remix of "Like a Virgin," with pictures of brides splashed across these three huge screens. He came right up to the edge of the stage, pumping his fist and saying "Praise the Lord" a lot, reaching down and shaking hands with people in the front row. Everybody was totally screaming their heads off, smiling and clapping and shouting "Amen!" It was nothing like my quiet, soothingly solemn church; I kind of liked actually being free to shout out "All right!" instead of sitting still and silent all the time. I liked seeing so *many* people my age, so many college students even, and not just being a minority among parents and old people.

After things calmed down a little bit, Reverend Howell started telling us about his life as a teenager, how he'd felt this pressure to "get" a girl—that sexual experience was a worldly thing to hoard, like gold, and show off. He said this always made him uncomfortable, but that he didn't know any other way. He told us how he started almost hating the girls he'd be with, how easily they gave up their bodies to him once he figured out how to put the moves on just right. He was ashamed, but had no one to talk to.

Then he was visiting his grandmother's house like he did every Sunday dinner, a practice that at the time he hated, mainly because it always made him feel even more ashamed. After dinner they'd read the Bible together, and Reverend Howell told us about how usually he'd listen as best he could and try to be respectful, but never felt anything resonating. This, he said, was because he was hiding himself from God, like Adam and Eve after eating the fruit, afraid to show their nakedness to Him. But this night his grandmother read the story of Jesus in the temple, how he threw out the merchants and turned over the tables, accusing them of making the temple into a robber's den.

"And that image stuck with me," Reverend Howell breathed into his headset. His voice was low and quiet, and the entire auditorium was deadly silent, breathing with him. "It wasn't a sermon about adultery, or fornication, or wrongdoings against women that did it—oh, no." He started pacing across the stage. "It was the image of the temple being turned into a place of stealing, a place of cheating, a place of *sin*"—and here he stopped pacing and looked straight at the audience—"that gave me pause. For I knew that the Lord saw my body as a temple. Oh, I had heard it many times. But it wasn't until I heard that story, the story of Jesus throwing out the money changers, that I understood what I had to do."

The next part of the celebration involved a lot of video clips of commercials and music videos and parts of movies emphasizing how we're surrounded by temptation, told that the body is a commodity instead of a sacred and holy place. How even in our schools we're being programmed to believe that sex is okay, that it's okay to corrupt our bodies, because they're teaching us sex education in science classes. Everyone was nodding and pumping their fists and saying, "Yes, yes," even Morgan and especially her youth group leader, Wedge.

The celebration escalated from there. Reverend Howell was bouncing around onstage, telling us it was good to love our bodies, to use them in healthy ways to express our love for the Lord, that dancing and even physical expressions of love like hugging could be good and positive and full of Heaven, but to know the limits, to treat ourselves and our bodies as something special, not to be shared with everyone. He told us that sex should be saved for the ultimate love, the ultimate person. That we should keep ourselves special and pure like Jesus for our own marriage.

Then he started calling people to come down and testify, to reclaim their love for Jesus and their commitment to Him. By this time Morgan was crushing my hand and smiling so hard it made her cry. I was excited and moved too, mainly feeling overwhelmed by *so many* people being so open and happy about their relationship and commitment to God. We went down to sign the Pledge for Purity—a huge banner that Reverend Howell was taking all across the country, full of signatures of people who wanted to promise their bodies and lives to Jesus. The overhead screens were full of different kinds of rings you could get as a daily reminder of your pledge, as a personal statement and symbol: a sign we were saved for the ultimate.

A week later Morgan showed up at school with a ring. It was beautiful and I was instantly jealous. I wanted an outward expression to show the world that I, too, felt as though my body, my love, was something special. Morgan spent the whole twenty minutes before the first bell describing how her parents had taken her to Rathbun's for dinner, how her mom had bought a new suit for the occasion and had taken Morgan shopping too. She told about the doting waiters, the candles, the virgin daiquiri her father had ordered for her, and how, between the clearing of the dinner plates and the bringing of the dessert menu, "Daddy actually came over and got down on one knee." He offered the small black velvet box to Morgan and said that in his eyes, her mother's, and Jesus's, she is a special child to be protected, cherished, and defended until the end of time. She described how she and her mother had cried and hugged, and how "even Daddy had to dab his eyes with his napkin when he returned to his seat."

At the time I did a good job of smiling and hugging and exclaiming and all that, but deep down I was sad, knowing my parents would never, ever do the same thing for me. But I didn't have to sulk long: in true best-friend form, Morgan arranged for me to have my own ring, too, binding us to each other as well as Jesus.

Now Morgan is going to have another new ring: bigger and

better, more sparkly and full of more Jesus power than her first one. I wonder if she'll make Cody get a new one himself or if she'll simply break up with him and get a bigger, better, more sparkly and more Jesus-infused boyfriend to go with it.

All the while scorning me my first real kiss.

I push my notebook off my bed and roll over to stare at my midnight-blue ceiling with the glow-in-the-dark stars and planets Dad and I arranged in made-up constellations. It isn't fair for me to think that about Morgan. I'm just mad about how she acted about Jake, mad that Priah was more excited for me than my own best friend.

Which leaves me, yuckily, having to figure out what to do on my own, for now. Cara would tell me to call him back, but I don't know what to say. Why *wouldn't* I want to tell him about my ring right off the bat? Am I ashamed of my relationship with Christ? Shouldn't I be excited to share my commitment? Wouldn't I want the best boyfriend ever—*not* that he's my boyfriend—to know about the most important promise of my life? But then again, why should I have to start talking about sex with a boy I don't even have the nerve to call?

The sound of Mom and Dad laughing on the porch, unlocking the door, snaps me out of it. I pick up my notebook from the floor and pretend to concentrate on biology while I listen to Mom come up the stairs and down the hall, and then there's a soft knock on my door frame even though the door's open.

I turn to her and stretch as though I haven't just been lounging on my bed for the last fifteen minutes, thinking about nothing. "You have a good time?"

She rolls her eyes but her mouth is pleased. "Oh, your dad always makes me laugh. And you know him and Roger." Her short honeyed hair is rumpled in a pretty way, and her face is pink and sweet.

She goes to my dressing table for my brush. I sit up and make room for her on the bed, my back to her. She pulls my hair into a loose pony, starts brushing the ends. My eyes practically roll back in my head from the hypnotic pleasure.

"Mom?" I try after a minute of brushing heaven. "When did you and Dad first . . . you know, kiss?" This is not very sly of me—we both know a boy called the house today.

"Oh, God," she snorts, splitting my hair into two sections so she can start brushing farther up. My whole body is tense with waiting to see what she'll say.

"Well, it isn't very romantic, if that's what you want to know." She tells me about being at a football game during grad school with friends, how they were all bawdy and laughing, and how Dad walked her to her car. She says she hadn't really thought about Dad in That Way, but that whole night she felt herself just watching his laughing face, the cords in his neck, the way his jacket hung around his shoulders. "I kept thinking at the car . . ." The brush has stopped; her voice is quiet. "*Oh, Eliot, just kiss me, please.*"

I turn to look at her. It's admittedly kind of weird to hear Mom talk about Dad this way, but her face is so happy, remembering. I wish Dad could see her right now too. I know exactly how she feels, and I think I could tell her, but then she gives me a small Mom smile and I blush.

"And then he did," she finishes. Her eyebrows give a little quirk then and she does that chicken-head jerk thing. "Why do you ask?"

I'm twisting my ring around again. "Oh, I was just wondering."

"Okay." She gives my bangs a quick stroke and winks at me. "Well, finish your homework. It's late. I've got three hours of lectures I haven't prepared for myself, anyway." She leans in and kisses my nose, and I kiss her chin at the same time.

I decide, *Screw biology*, and get ready for bed. But not five minutes after my lights are out, Dad knocks. "Night, Twink," he murmurs, coming over to stroke my back.

"I kissed a boy last night, Dad," I say, half into my pillow. "And I really like him. That's who called tonight. And I'm nervous to call him back."

To my relief his hand doesn't stop stroking. It's as if I didn't say a thing.

"Well," he says into the dark after a moment, "if he's worth two pounds of salt, he'll wait until you're ready."

His hand lifts away and it's like he takes this giant stone from the middle of my shoulders with it.

"Thanks, Dad."

"Any time, kiddo."

"Love you."

"Oh, you know I love you more."

And with that he's gone and I'm alone, and soon I am asleep.

chapter 7

Of course in the morning Mom sleeps late, which means I sleep late, which sucks because then I just feel perpetually scrambled and behind myself all day, not to mention missing hanging out with everyone before school, with so much to talk about.

But I can't worry about that because it's off to first period straight out of the car. I've missed homeroom and don't even have time to go by my locker. Instead I hustle to the chorus room, barely getting in before the bell. You'd think having a singing class at eight A.M. (when the schedule rotates that way) isn't the greatest thing in the world, but once our voices get warmed up and we get going, a good session in chorus can have your engines humming—literally—for the rest of the day.

This is true for me, but it's especially true of Cara, who always rocks in chorus, even when it rotates to after lunch. She's why I continued this year. You hear people talk about girls having voices of angels? Well, Cara really *does* have a voice like that. Honest, she somehow sounds like what they must broadcast through Heaven on a constant loop. She's amazing to watch, too, because she simply opens her mouth, and out comes this stream of beauty that feels like it's coming from her lips, chest, and forehead all at once. Maybe even the palms of her hands too. And she barely looks like she's doing anything. It just . . . comes out.

So of course she always gets the solos. And District Festival is coming up, and Mrs. Dew has us singing this really beautiful, really complicated piece with a descant. Because Cara is so good, and the rest of our soprano section is still so breathy, Cara gets to sing it by herself. We've only practiced it a few times but it sounds amazing already. In fact, I kind of can't wait to get to it today to take my mind off everything.

When we stand for warm-ups—the commotion of getting up, stretching—I catch her eye and mouth, *Good morning?* She smiles and shrugs, which could mean *Yes, great,* or it could mean she's exhausted from being up all night because one—or more—of her four older brothers got arrested again for vandalism.

During her solo she sounds beautiful and strong, giving everybody chill bumps, and making Mrs. Dew break out into this giant smile and tell us how proud she is to be our director. Like I said, a good session in chorus can really start your day off right— even if it started out wrong.

After chorus is the gigantic comedown of math, which Cara and I also have together over in the 600 wing. Down the long hallway connecting the music rooms to the rest of the school, Cara tells me the basic nothing everybody talked about at Morgan's locker before homeroom. We get to the teeming crossroads where the 600 hall meets up with the pass-through by the library to the liberal arts wing, and where it's always like Times Square on New Year's Eve. When we break through, Cara catches up and asks me how did my talk go with Jake.

"Ugh. I totally chickened out. He's going to hate my guts or at least think I hate his. I'm such a dork. Of course, Dad said, like Morgan pretty much did, that if he's a decent guy he'll understand and wait, which I guess is true, but—"

"But what, silly? You know they're totally right."

"Well, it's not that."

We stop by the set of lockers outside of class and wait for Lanetta and Sprockett—whose real name is Woody Brockett—to go in. Sprockett ducks his head and waves. Cara just waits calmly, like a mom or a therapist.

"I don't know," I say. "It's weird. I keep thinking it was all like really superfast, right? I mean, we barely even talked on Saturday. How does he know he likes me so much? How do I know I really like *him*? And maybe he's just messing with me. Maybe he saw this innocent little sweet girl and thought, 'I bet I can break her.'"

"Oh, come on, Tab."

"No, I'm serious. I mean, neither of us said anything about, you know, *the ring*, so does he know or not? And if he does, what? And if he doesn't, then what do *I* say?"

"Okay, um, whatever comes to you, duh."

"Well, why didn't he ask me about it?"

"Okay, first of all, maybe he thought it was nothing. Michael thought I was just wearing a ring of my mom's at first, remember?

And then, when I finally told him, he thought it would help keep us *both* pure, even if it made him even more scared of my brothers? So maybe Jake noticed it and figured you'd tell him about it when you wanted to. Like, perhaps, a gentleman? Or, worst of all"—she stops and makes a horrified face—"he is actually a *nice guy* and knows what it is and actually, duh"—she knocks on my forehead with her knuckles—"thinks it's cool?"

I think about this. The truth is I won't really know Jake's position until I talk to him. "Okay, maybe."

"Good." She pulls open the classroom door right as the bell rings and we slip in.

Just like I knew it would, talking to Cara makes me feel better. I start to consider what I might say to Jake, but Mr. Outif has different plans: pop quiz on the proofs we covered last week. By the end of it my brain is a total scramble, making my good-bye to Cara pretty hasty. We dash our separate ways but not before she shoves a note into my hand. I carry it unread to my locker, where there's also a note from Morgan:

BFF: Where are you are you ok? You weren't there before school so I hope you get this. I don't have my ring yet and am pretty bummed. But! I am really happy for you about Jake, honest. Did you call him or not I am dying to know. I know I have been guarded but when he didn't call you after the hayride and then was all Mr. Fast Action at the dance I got my suspicions that he was a rat. Just looking out for my girl, you know? But *if you think he is cool he must be so I will give him an honest chance! And he is c-u-t-e as Priah says. Just be careful and remember who really loves you. Hugz! M*

On the way to English I unfold Cara's note and try to decipher her tiny writing while I dodge soccer players, Cressida and her posse, and some giggling freshmen. It takes me twice to figure out what it says, and even then I don't know what to think:

THE WORLD DOESN'T REVOLVE AROUND PURITY RINGS, YOU KNOW.

chapter 8

Today of all days I would love it to be like last year, with all of us hanging out together at Java Monkey after school, but I have to go to *work* instead. I like my job at the Center, I really do, but sometimes having even just a part-time job really gets in the way of the rest of my life.

Hanging out with Lacey all the time is great, though. I basically want to *be* Lacey when I grow up, because she is smart and cool but also pert and sweet (like Amy Adams dressed up as Sienna Miller), but she is also dedicating her life to helping old people. Mainly she coordinates events and activities during the month, like tai chi or beach bingo or country-western singalongs, but her most serious project is the weddings, where once every other month we stage a full-blown (fake) one for the Alzheimer's patients. We have a "preacher" (he's just an actor, but he holds a Bible) and cake and a band and everything. She even has a grant that pays for stuff. Lacey is always the bride, and Sterling, the head of programming, is always the groom just because he's willing and handsome.

I, however, get to play all kinds of roles: last time the caterer, the time before that the videographer.

We do this all as part of Lacey's research, which is about promoting positive responses in Alzheimer's patients, especially those advanced enough to not remember much in either short- or long-term memory, but not sick enough to be completely incapacitated. According to her, the weddings raise the patients' endorphin levels, which improves their overall well-being even days later, whether they remember it or not. Even though there's no cure for what's wrong with them, this helps their quality of life. And I have to admit, even though the weddings take a lot of work, it is nice seeing these really frail and confused patients all dressed up and shuffling together like they're dancing, telling stories about their own weddings or—as Coyle Ann, the Center receptionist, points out—just making up whatever comes to them and telling it to whomever will listen. Anyway, it's fun and cool, and Lacey is pretty much my idol.

So I can't help but burst into a huge grin when I see she's hanging out by the reception desk in the main lobby, waiting for me to tell her everything about Saturday night. Even Coyle Ann is smiling, which is unusual, especially on Monday.

"Soooo . . . ," Coyle Ann says, peering at me over her bifocals when I reach her desk. "Still got that ring on, missy?"

I give Lacey a shove. "Did you tell *everyone*?"

"Come on, kiddo. You know all we do all day is sit around gossiping about you."

Coyle Ann "hmmphs," tapping her stack of applications and trying to frown.

"Wellllll?" Lacey does Groucho Marx eyebrows. "Ah? Ha? Yah?"

"You two are terrible," I moan, loving the attention. "But okay, yes. He was there. And he is sooooo cute. And we danced and then we went outside to talk—"

"Mmmm-hmmmmm . . ." Lacey winks at Coyle Ann.

"And yes, okay, we kissed."

"Eeeee!" Lacey bounces on her toes and gives me a hug. Then she drapes herself across the ledge of Coyle Ann's huge desk and plucks a lily from the giant arrangement that changes every other day. "Ah, Coyle Ann, remember the dizzy sweetness of your first *l'amour*?"

Coyle Ann snorts. "You two cuckoos better get hustling. Rogers'll be out here reminding you of med drop—"

"Ladies, med drop in five," Mrs. Rogers, our floor supervisor, says, whisking through the swinging French doors that connect the main lobby to the eating hall. She barely looks at us, flipping pages on her white enamel clipboard and heading to the conservatory. Lacey and I giggle and Coyle Ann gives us another fake stern look, so we snap to military straightness and skip off to the pharmacy.

"What have we got today?" I ask after we've delivered everyone's meds and settled into her office, where I'm supposed to help her with administrative stuff.

"Oh, right, sure. Fake like you're not *dying* to tell me every detail. Go ahead with your cool high school self." She sniffs and straightens an already-straight pile of folders.

"*Way* better than my first, that's for sure."

"Oh, the first kiss is always terrible." She reaches for the box of Wheat Thins in her desk drawer. "Everybody is just copying stuff from the movies or whatever. Mine was utterly gross. Tim Fries." She shudders. "He smelled like them too. Blech."

"Well, let's just say I think I'm a convert now."

"That's my girl. So'd he ask you out?"

"Well—"

"What?"

I tell her about Jake calling yesterday, about Morgan saying I should wait, and then my overall chickening out.

She leans in closer to me. "And our problem is what, exactly?"

"What do you mean, problem?"

"You haven't called him back because, why?"

"Well, because I'm not sure if—"

"Yeah. Right. Okay." Her fingers quack together in *blah blah blah* puppet motion.

"Okay okay okay." I stuff a Wheat Thin into my mouth. "I'll call him tonight. Are you happy?"

"Not till you come in here and tell me I get to finally be a bridesmaid and not just the bride." She laughs.

chapter 9

Dad's in the kitchen chopping vegetables when Mom and I get home at the end of our day. The wok is out and there's brown rice starting to boil on the stove.

"Uh-oh," Mom says, putting her satchel down on the kitchen table and going to kiss Dad's cheek. "Looks like Iron Chef again at the McAbe household. Look out, Tabs. Flying ginger."

"No, no, no, my beautiful doubtful Thomases," Dad assures. "There will be no flying ginger this evening. Just a simple vegetable stir-fry with a tasty hot peanut sauce."

"Anything I can do to help?" I snatch a piece of carrot from the cutting board, figure I should try to grease the wheels a little, in case Jake really does ask me out.

"Your bathroom's looking mighty football locker room-ish these days," Dad says, pointing at me with his giant chopping knife.

"*Besides* my bathroom."

"Cara called while you were at work. And Morgan. You've got about seventeen more minutes, I figure, before dinner and then the evil punishment of your homework. I will leave it to you to decide how to spend it, either wisely or wastefully."

"Ha," Mom says, heading upstairs to change out of her heels.

I look at the kitchen clock: six twenty. Dinnertime, unfortunately, in most households across America. While I'm not crazy about calling Jake at this weird time, I've got an English essay due next week that I've at least got to find some quotes for tonight, plus history and probably brushing up on proofs, as today's math quiz proved I ought. Maybe his family's eaten already, I think. Or maybe they'll be in the process of eating and all I'll have to do is leave a message. That wouldn't be so bad. Then I will have called but I don't actually have to *talk* to him. Just the idea of it makes my palms start sweating already.

"Okay," I say, more for myself than my dad. "I need some privacy then."

"Roger doger," Dad says without looking up.

I grab the phone and my backpack and carry both upstairs, shut my door, take a deep breath, and reach for the Postie on my desk. I punch in the numbers, listen to the ring, try not to puke. *Please be there please be there please be there*, I chant. *Please don't answer please don't answer please don't answer*, hot on its heels.

"Jake," he says, like some kind of detective novel.

"Uh, no, actually. It's Tabitha. I only know one Jake. And I'm pretty sure I'm calling him." I hold my breath. *Please laugh. Please laugh. Please don't think I'm a dork.*

"Tabitha," he says after a second. "Hey!" I imagine him smiling but can't quite hear it.

"Hey back." *Ugh. Stupid stupid stupid lame.* "My dad told me that you called."

"Yeah. Yeah, I did. How are you?"

I'm totally nervous and I think I screwed my geometry grade because I couldn't stop thinking about you; how are you? "I'm good."

"Good day yesterday?"

"Uh. Yeah. You know, a lot of homework to do. Youth group. Stuff like that. Today was a pop quiz in math so I guess I didn't do quite *enough* homework, but I think I did all right."

"That's good."

Anything clever I might've said to him has flown from my mind. "You?"

"Say again?"

"Did you have a good day yesterday? Lacrosse practice, you said?"

"Oh." I picture him scratching his head. Maybe he is sitting on one of those vintage-looking barstools with the vinyl seats and chrome legs. Maybe he is in his room. I have no idea what that room might look like. Do they *make* lacrosse posters? "Uh, practice was fine. You know, a lot of running around. Lot of jock stuff. No horses."

You could probably power half of Marietta with my frenetic energy.

"Rest of the day was kind of lame, though," he goes on. "Hanging around. Played guitar a little. School stuff. You know."

"I didn't know you played guitar."

"Ah, well, I don't really *play*. Just mess around. You know. It's something to do."

Um—what do guitar-playing lacrosse players play? "Do you write songs?"

"A little. Tunes mostly, but lyrics sometimes. They're usually pretty country."

I clear a sudden frog from my throat. "You like country?"

"Don't you?"

Crap. We are never going to be a couple. He likes country and I like Death Cab for Cutie and that's an abyss we'll never be able to cross. "Um, well, I guess I've never really listened to it much. Not a lot of square dances here in Decatur."

He laughs. "Out in Tucker we have a ton. I'll have to take you sometime."

"Sounds good." *He'll have to take me sometime!*

"But first I thought the movies? You already booked for Friday?"

"Uh, gosh. I'll have to check with my secretary, but I don't think so." *Gaaaaaa-aaaaaaaaaaaaahhhhhhhhhhhhhhhhh.*

"Unless they call an emergency board meeting, right?"

Wow, he's sharp. "Right. Unless there's the emergency board meeting. Or the Japanese cancel their contract. Then I'm totally booked until August."

"Ah. Got it." He doesn't skip a beat. "Well, I'll just have to call my Japanese correspondent and see what he can do."

This is fun. "Well, it's dependent on North Korea. But seems to me they're just bluffing."

"Hmmm. I've seen the M-ROSE report. Pretty unstable if you ask me."

Does that really stand for something, or did he just make it up?
"Oh well, that."

"But I'll keep an optimistic attitude," he goes on. "Maybe dinner before?"

Dinner and a movie dinner and a movie dinner and a movie dinner and a movie. "Uh, sure," I tell him. "I mean—sounds good."

"Good then."

"Okay so—Friday?"

"Friday it is."

I finally breathe a little. We are both grinning, I think.

"What else is going on for you this week?" he wants to know.

I call up a picture of my weekly calendar: "Well, yearbook after school tomorrow, and I work on Thursday. Pretty normal week."

"You work?"

"Tabster! Dinner!" Dad calls from the bottom of the stairs. My heart rate suddenly goes to 490, as though I've been caught doing something I know better about.

"Yeah. After school sometimes. Part-time. At the Melody Hills Assisted Living Center?" *Please don't think my parents can't afford my college tuition and so I have to work instead of drive around in convertibles and hang out listening to music like I'm sure most of your friends do.*

"Wow. Cool. You'll have to tell me about that."

"I will. I will. But Jake, I'm sorry I have to go—"

"I know. I heard your dad calling you. What's for dinner?"

"Ah. My dad's doing stir-fry. With peanut sauce."

"Sounds delish. But I'll call you tomorrow, okay? Just, you

know. To make sure the Japanese haven't invaded or anything."

Don't hang up don't hang up don't hang up! "Okay. Well, have a good dinner yourself."

"Thanks. I think it's astronaut ice cream tonight. My little brother."

You have a little brother! That is so cute I can't stand it. "Well . . . um . . . don't get carried away, I guess." *Gaaaah Tab you are so dumb please hang up right now and go to dinner please just shut up and go eat.*

"I won't."

"Okay, well—I'd better go?" *Breathe. Breathe. Breathe.*

"Yeah, you'd better. Have a good day tomorrow."

"You too, Jake."

And we hang up.

I plunge my head into my pillows, plunk one over my head, bite down, and scream as loud as I can, banging my feet on the mattress. When I jerk myself back up into a sitting position, the room swims for a minute. In the mirror over my dresser, my face is slightly red and smiling. I push my messy-wavy hair back in reasonable order and try on a few "Oh, that conversation was absolutely nothing" faces before I take a deep breath and go downstairs to my folks.

chapter 10

When Morgan and I see each other the next morning, I don't know who's more excited. I sent her two texts last night after calling Jake, but then Mom was on the phone with Aunt Heather from like eight to midnight, so when Morg texted me back at eight thirty that we had to TALK, and Dad was hogging the computer like usual, there'd been nothing to do but find some supporting quotes for my English paper.

As soon as I get to Morgan's locker, though, she rushes over and practically chokes me to death with hugging, squealing something Klingon-sounding.

"Check it out," she pants, holding a crumpled piece of pink paper two inches from my face. "Yesterday, Daddy picked me up from school and we went way-heck out to Smyrna and talked to this guy who has this totally old, cool jewelry place that does custom jewelry and we told him about my ring and I drew this picture and then, see, he made some small changes and Daddy talked to him a long time and lookit Tabitha I am getting this brand-new gorgeous ring!!"

I feel my face trying to make the same happy expression she's making while I'm also struggling to see what's on the paper in front of me. Morgan's squeezing my forearm so hard I think I'm going to lose all feeling in my hand.

"Hang on, hang on." I hold the paper out and look. In my periphery, Priah's bouncing on those toes of hers.

"Jesus bling," Naeomi says, sounding either impressed or revolted.

Once my eyes can focus and I can really see what Morgan's showing me, I give Naeomi a total mental *Amen*, because this ring is, seriously, a cathedral. The band is covered in filigreed hearts all swirling toward the centerpiece, which is, from the looks of it, a huge heart-shaped diamond surrounded by smaller diamonds. If the little penciled-in sparkles Morgan has drawn are right, she'll be blinding everyone with the Way, the Truth, and the Light.

"This is . . . amazing. Are you really getting it?"

"Totally!" Morgan claps. "This dude is so old-school. We did the drawing and he took my measurements and then in a couple days we have to go back so I can see this wax model he makes and then he'll get to work making the actual thing. Daddy got to pick out the diamond *right there*. I swear, Tab. Oooooo! Baby!" Suddenly Morgan bolts forward to meet Cody, who's shuffling toward us. She crushes him around the neck in a hug and kisses his cheek so hard it leaves a red mark. "Look! Look! This is what I was telling you about!"

Cody wraps his arm around Morgan's wiggling-puppy torso and leads her back to the rest of us. "Cool," he says, smiling in that shy way that makes other people think he's thinking something deep, but really just means he doesn't know what to say.

Morgan finally bounds from under his arm and comes back to me, her eyes and face shining. "Tab, we have to go there. You will totally love it. Not like those ugly boring rings everyone has on the Ring Thing site or anything. Completely original. You can totally pick whatever you want."

"I like what I've got, though," I say, twirling my band around my finger with my thumb. "You did perfect when you picked out mine."

"I know, but still. I—"

But then Cara sidles up in her loose jeans and boots, saying a small hey, asking did Naeomi finish her speech for English. Priah breaks in and starts nattering about how unfair it is that she has to write a six-page story for her own English class. Cody nods and complains about *The Scarlet Letter*. Morgan shows Cara the drawing of her ring and they both ooh and aaah. Naeomi asks if anybody saw *Project Runway* last week in prep for tonight, and when no one has, she recaps. Sprockett stops by to make sure Cara and I did okay on math homework, something he's taken to doing in the last couple of weeks. While he's busy doing some complicated handshake with Cody, Naeomi and Cara and I all exchange looks, watching Sprockett try not to stare at Priah while he talks to us. Morgan again squeezes my arm, grinning. It's the normal pre-day rush, and everyone's abuzz. The whole time, *I'm going out with Jake on Friday* is in my mouth, but somehow I can't make it come out. Not until somebody asks. When someone asks, it'll make it okay. It'll be real.

But no one does, not even Cara, and then there's the bell and it's time to spread out to our days. I'm slightly bummed, being alone in my excitement, but maybe keeping Jake to myself right now isn't so bad. I doubt, for example, that he's told anyone.

Though secretly I hope he's told his cousin, at least.

During homeroom announcements I write four notes: one to Morgan, one to Naeomi, one to Priah, and one to Cara, all of them in the same giant handwriting, all of them saying WE ARE GOING OUT ON FRIDAY!!! Because screw this clamming-up thing.

In chorus before warm-ups, I hand back Cara's note. When I look back during "vim vah voh vee" she winks and gives me a thumbs-up. On the way to math she reminds me about her first date with Michael: how the whole time she kept expecting one of her brothers to show up, and how she was so nervous when he kissed her she almost chipped his tooth.

Geometry is the same boring, and then Morgan's daily note to me between that and French is mainly centered around how much she hopes her new ring will be finished in time for Easter. There's nothing about me and Jake, but that's no surprise since she hadn't gotten my note about him yet.

She's waiting for me outside of biology though—our only class together this year—and she squeezes me around the neck. "So, your parents are cool?"

"To my face at least," I say, and she snorts. "You know how they want to be cool but aren't always. But pretty much it was okay. I think they were concerned at first, you know, being worried about the whole driving thing—"

"Well, you can't blame them, I mean—"

"I know, but then I brought up you, and eventually *me* driving, and said about a million times how nice he is, and they said, yes, so long as they could meet him first . . . and . . . so, we're going out."

A jigsaw puzzle of probably thirty-two different things scrambles through both our minds right then. For me, it's remembering the Valentine's Dance in sixth grade when Anthony Brooker asked Morgan if she would "go steady" and how she said no because he hadn't sent her a Heart-O-Gram earlier that day, and Dalton Riggs had instead. The time Peter Lake had a crush on us both at the same time. The whole eighth grade lock-in at her church, with Ben Twee—how he almost threw up with nervousness after kissing her, and after that for me the whole Adam Dietzler incident. Finally, if I read her right and I'm honest with myself, too, we've both got The Night Morgan Gave Me My Ring swirled in there, as well.

"Okay, well . . . ," she says, cocking her head toward our biology door, where Mrs. Laboutin is waiting to fill us with the glories of genetic recombination. "I just want the best for you."

A note climbs across the room to me later: pale green paper with swirly purple writing: U cn borrow my closet, of courz!

When, exactly, Morgan and I will be able to get together for me to raid her closet is going to be tricky. Though we hung out after school a lot in ninth grade, this year not so much, since all of us seem to be pretty consumed with various and sundry after-school activities most days of the week.

Today Priah, Morgan, and Naeomi are all busy with dance team until five thirty in the gym, their practice schedule upped from two days a week to three, now that Maverick Mayhem, the school's major spring talent extravaganza, is fast on the horizon. For Cara, it's filling in for Walt at their family's stables while he's getting the adult ed equivalent of his high school diploma. This means she has to do a lot of training and chores she used to only watch. Though Walt'll be finished this semester, Cara's so good at it she might just take it all over so he can get a real job. My Tuesday is yearbook, though admittedly now most of our major hair-pulling, maniacal deadlines are over and we're only waiting to get a few end-of-the-year sections filled in before final proofs are due mid-April.

When you're a senior, if you've done time on the staff already and get permission from the yearbook instructor, Mr. McClellan, you can take yearbook as a class, so seniors do the bulk of the layouts and the writing. The rest of us get to help with photos and captions and other things after school, which is a lot of fun, especially since it's not in your face every day. Yearbook seniors do take themselves pretty seriously, though, so there is still sort of a constant cloud of tension in the room all the time, especially if any underclassmen get any ideas about how something might be different. Mainly I keep to myself and my little pile of text corrections from the Clubs Editor, Yuhn. I know if I just do what

I'm supposed to do and am friendly about it I'll probably get Yuhn's backing for staff next year, so I just focus once I get there, and time always goes by really quickly.

Between home-arrival and dinner-with-parents I do get a chance to talk to Morgan for our end-of-day recap. I manage to squeeze in a few Boy-How-To FAQs before we have to hang up.

"Oh, well, just be yourself, Tab." She sighs. I'm squatting in the hallway against the wall between my bedroom and the bathroom—as far away as I can get from the open stairwell (and my parents' ears) without going into my room and being obvious about not wanting them to hear. "Relax. Stop worrying. The last thing you want to do is seem too serious, right?"

"Right." I nod, trying to imagine *not* being serious about Jake.

"And, you know. Just have fun. It's nothing *permanent*, right?" Her mantra. To Morgan, high school boys are just scenic-view stops on the road toward Mr. Forever: They're something to talk about, someone to go to dances with and get dressed up for, but in the grand scheme of things—I mean the *big* grand scheme—they're not a big deal until they're the Big Deal. Since that can't happen to us until we're at least twenty or something, right now what's the fuss? It makes so much sense it's hard to remember, especially in the face of Jake. But before we hang up I thank her about a dozen times and promise to tell her what happens tomorrow.

If, in fact, Jake calls tonight at all.

In the morning I seriously want to murder my mother, the only debate being by how many degrees and in what atrocious fashion. Except, genuinely wanting to murder my own mother is a relatively new experience for me and I'm not quite sure how one goes about expressing the desire without giving in to hatred and therefore failing to practice forgiveness and love. Jesus asked us to turn the other cheek, and to respect our parents, but His mother never "forgot" to tell Him until breakfast the next day that—while she was on the line with an unreasonably hysterical student—she had clicked over because the boy He was for the first time really really into was calling, but then didn't pass on the message. Not that Jesus was into guys, but you know what I mean. Pretend the Virgin Mary had actually *kissed Him on the forehead before bed* and still not said a thing about the important phone call.

Maybe then you'll get why it is a long, silent ride to school.

"I'll see you at tw—" she tries.

"Fine." I slam the door, not even rolling up the window.

"Tabitha—"

I don't want to start the day like this, but I also don't want her to have completely disregarded my feelings last night. SUVs are herding around our old station wagon; she's bent over the wheel, looking halfway indignant and halfway broken.

"Mom, I just . . ." My throat gathers itself around a crying and I have to look away. "It wouldn't be so terrible if you and Dad would just let me use my phone like a normal teenager. But I respect your rules. I comply." I shake my head at the embarrassing shame of this. I haven't even really had a *chance* to break curfew. I let Mom or Dad drive me everywhere, and Morgan and I don't even *want* to sneak out. "And in return? You just forget that I might have a life, a person calling me. Not just a boy, but even just my best friend. And you know?" I hate the way my chin is jiving around itself. I see cars, kids streaming past me. "It just totally sucks."

Mom says something I can't hear. She motions for me to lean in the window. Her face is tired, regretful. I feel horrible for not being able to forgive her.

"Listen," she says. "We'll talk about this after school. You may be right. I—" Her face goes all over me. "Okay," she says. "Okay look, I love you, Tabitha, and I hope your day gets better. We'll talk more later tonight. I'm sorry. Okay?"

I manage to nod. I can't look at her but at least, for both of us, I nod.

When I get to Morgan's locker after dropping by my own, it's only Priah and Morgan sitting together on the floor, poring over Priah's most recent Delia's catalog.

"Howdy, girls," I say, trying—willing myself—to be normal. "What's up?"

Priah shuts the catalog and they stand up.

Morgan hugs me. "You okay?" She knows the signs of a Tabitha freak-out.

"Just my mom being a jerk. No big deal." I let out a breath, pray for perkiness. "Whatcha looking at?"

"Oh," Priah practically apologizes, "just stupid stuff."

"Priah's trying to find something to wear for Easter. She wants to do her vows for real. Not just wearing the ring."

"Oh." I remember to be thrilled about this. "Priah, that's great! Are—are your parents cool?"

"Oh, well, I figure I shouldn't bug them with it, really." She twists the catalog into her book bag—identical to mine and Morgan's, except hers is in lavender plaid. "They still don't really get the ring, so—"

"They're used to her coming to church with me at least, so we're going to do it then." Morgan's face is a single beam of sunshine over Priah, then me. "You should too. Renew with me."

"But I like my ring."

"It's not about the ring, silly. It's about the promise. I mean, it was ages ago when we did it. We were tiny. So now that we're grown we should do it again. Publicly, together, you know? Especially if you're going to be locking lips on a regular basis. Might be a good reminder." She's smiling in that winking way, and the involuntary blush sweeps over me.

"So, where is everybody?" I'm changing the subject, and Morgan notices it and she'll totally call me on it later, not in front of Priah, but maybe by then I'll figure out a way to tell her that it's not renewal that makes me hesitate, but rather the spectacle of Easter: Easter at Morgan's church in particular, where the eight-hundred-seat sanctuary becomes completely necessary and everyone who is anyone is paying attention not just to what you say, but what you wear and who you sit with too.

"Who knows?" Priah groans. "Probably Cara had to do some horse thing and Naeomi's either studying or in a Future Presidents of America meeting." To this, Morgan giggles a little and she and Priah swap a glance I can't miss.

"Well, I just—" But then there's the bell, and us scattering after shoulder-hugging good-byes.

In homeroom all I can think about is Mom not telling me Jake called. It's not *such* a big deal, but suddenly all I'm aware of is my parents and their crazy, archaic rules for me—even e-mail and chatting have to be done on the family computer in the highly trafficked den—when the two of them get all the communication privacy they want. Not only is it unfair, but it makes me feel like a giant baby, to boot.

Cara's not in chorus to help me see the funny side of it, either, nor does she make it to math. I wonder if she's even coming to school today, and whether this has anything to do with Naeomi's absence this morning too. Instead Sprockett and I pair up to struggle over proofs together, and I just add it to the long list of How Today Sucks.

Morgan's not feeling it, though. When geometry is *finally* over and I drag myself to my locker, her note is full of swirlies and smiles. She is excited for both of us—a new phase for Tab and Morgs as she gets her new ring and I get a new boyfriend (maybe). What a great time to reaffirm your promise, she says.

I spend all of French filling up a note for her with the talking points I have come up with for Friday night. Also at the bottom I draw some Outfits Tabitha Will Not Be Wearing, including some of our favorite dress-up getups from grade school. It's so fun I don't even tell her about the fight with Mom this morning, which now seems far away and less important.

That is, it isn't important until we get to biology, and Morgan's all over me, wanting to know what my problem is, when I'd kind of forgotten I had one.

"Mom and I just fought this morning. You know, same old. Telephone and the fascist regime under which I live that prevents me from using it."

"Oh." Morgan's eyes are flashing.

"What?"

"So that's it? That's why you can't bring yourself to get excited?"

"Excited?"

"About my ring. My renewal, dummy. Or were you too preoccupied with your date to remember that?"

"What?"

"I mean, since that's all you can talk about."

"Morg, I was trying to make you—"

"Well, it's not funny."

Um. Oh. Okay. "Look, I'm excited. You know I'm excited. I think it's great. I'm so happy you found a new ring you really like and that you get to renew. There's just also a lot—"

"Well, I have a lot on my mind too, you know. You used to understand that."

Okay, obviously I have screwed up somehow without knowing. I reach out, grab her wrist, give her a little shake. "Hey. *Hey*. There's nothing for us to be tense about here. I was just off this morning, and I'm sorry. I can't wait to see your new ring when it's done and talk more about the service. Plus, I need to know how rehearsal is going. You've been pretty distracted yourself. I am behind on all my dance team gossip."

"Gaaaaaah." She grabs for my arm again. "You will *not* believe what Sidney did yesterday during practice—" And like that we're fixed, pretty much, which makes sitting through a lecture on DNA proteins a whole lot more tolerable than it would be otherwise.

The day ends on a fairly good note, so I'm sort of ready to deal with Mom when she picks me up. Really, it's only a couple of miles between school and home, and usually when it's nice out and I don't have to go to the Center, I'll walk, since now that Mom has tenure she has a lot more meetings. But today I figure Mom can inconvenience herself a little.

"You want to go anywhere?" she says, meaning Java Monkey or the Creamery for milk shakes, something we do after school when we don't have errands.

"Let's just go home and make curry corn or something."

She nods, her neck tight, and I get the feeling she's about to lay into me, that she's been thinking all day about how she was really right and I was wrong, and now I'm about to get another Inflexible Talking To. I feel the heat of protest already starting in my neck and jaw, feel the "It's not fair" already perched on my tongue.

"I don't know how to start," she says, pulling out of the pickup circle and moving into the slow post-school traffic.

"Mom—"

She detects the whine and holds up a forbidding hand. "Let me finish, Tab. You don't always know everything." I lean back, relenting, knowing protests don't matter, anyway. I watch her instead. She swallows a few times, squints into traffic.

"Look, I'm sorry about Jake. You're right, I'm not taking that seriously enough and honestly it's because I don't know what to do. Half of me is excited for you—horribly excited, Tab; you don't even know. You're so deserving and as your mother I want you to feel all the things you can feel. And yet on the other hand, also as your mother, I'm terrified. I don't know this kid, and on Friday he's coming to whisk you away in a car and who knows what will happen? I mean, I don't know how he drives—I don't know what he's been taught. All I want to do is protect you, even though, God help me, I have no idea how to do that. Not really."

This is definitely a surprise. Mom's unflappable sometimes to a fault. If she gets upset, it's over her students, the other faculty, or something Dad did, not me. But now it looks like for maybe the first time I've completely ruined her day because we had a fight. It's sort of nice, but it's also sort of irritating.

"Something bad could happen with Morgan driving, Mom. Or even with you."

"Yes, but with me it's different and I know Morgan. I've

known her since she was eight. I know her parents. I held her hair when she threw up spending the night."

We're home. There's the rummage of bags, locking the car, unlocking the house, letting ourselves in, getting water. We sit down across the kitchen table from each other.

"Mom, I don't know what to tell you except that . . ." But I don't know what to tell her, exactly, especially because I'm annoyed I have to tell her anything. "Just—you'll meet Jake and you'll see. He's really nice. I don't think he speeds."

"But what?"

"What what?"

"You're—clamshell a little."

I sigh, lean back in my chair. "Look, don't you think I'm nervous too? It so does *not* help for everyone to be all, you know, paranoid about Jake. I mean, I *know* I don't know him very well. We can all stop emphasizing that fact. But I want to get to, I think. Don't you think I'm scared too? I mean, what if he finds out he doesn't really like me?"

I can feel her looking at me. When I glance up she's got her Fond Face on—the one that is usually followed by a big hug and a kiss on the top of my head.

"Well, neither of you is going to know unless you can talk to each other, right? And I do realize this whole phone restrictions thing—even if it protects you—might ultimately drive us apart. Which honestly, I can't bear to picture."

Her face makes me feel suddenly very horrible for every bad

thought I've ever had about her, which, again, is a little annoying because I can feel we're about to do some important negotiating, and it gives her an unfair advantage if I'm saturated with pity. Still, I can't stand seeing her upset.

"Well, you can drive me wherever you want for now. Can't get my license until August, and Morgan has three more weeks to go."

To my relief, she smiles. "How'd you get to be so wonderful?"

"I'm adopted, remember?" This is our joke. When she smiles again, I go for it. "So—what does this mean, do you think? For me and the phone?"

"I don't know. I'll have to talk to Dad to see what he's been thinking. But until we figure it out, I promise to be more considerate."

"How about I just use mine whenever, until we reach a compromise?"

She smirks. "Don't kick a lady when she's down, kid. It isn't classy.

The house phone rings, startling us both and then making us laugh. Mom gets up and simply hands it to me.

"Hello?"

"Yes, is this Ms. McCabe's secretary?" he says.

I'm so overcome with smiling I think I am going to choke.

chapter 11

Good talk with Jake. Good, light chat with Morgan about nothing but dance team and gossip and me maybe getting phone restrictions lifted (she nearly deafens me with excited screaming). Good dinner with Mom and Dad. Good job getting my homework done early so I can chill out just watching TV before bed. All in all, a good end to a not-so-good day. I love when this happens, because it reminds me that nothing awful lasts for very long, which is hard to remember when you're in the thick of it.

Except at ten P.M. the phone rings. Since my friends know not to call this late, I don't even budge, especially since I'm concentrating on checking my chin for any blackheads, or signs that my skin is even thinking about starting to have maybe the slightest sign of a zit on Friday. When Dad sticks his head in the door, holding the phone out to me, I nearly jump out of my so-far so-good skin.

I give him Who Is It? Face and he just shrugs, but points at the clock.

"Hello?" I say.

There's a sort of muffled sound on the other line and then what seems like a chicken clucking under a blanket.

"Hello?" Again.

"Tabitha?"

"Cara?"

She's crying. "What happened?" I rush. "Where are you? Are you okay?"

She still doesn't talk, just this small "Eh, eh, eh," over and over, and struggling for breath.

"Cara, you're scaring me."

"I'm—I'm sorry," she finally says. "I just—I just—"

"It's okay. Take a deep breath." All I can think is something's happened to Michael or one of her brothers. Or Naeomi. "Where are you?"

"I-i-in the barn loft," she shudders out. "I had to come out here. I just—I don't have anywhere or anybody and I can't—Tabitha, I can't—"

I get up and go out into the hall. Dad's standing in their bedroom doorway, brushing his teeth but listening. I point to the phone and try to make a sign for crying with my free hand. He shakes his head. Cara's gasping on the other line, sort of jabbering about how she has no one to talk to anymore. I'm trying to soothe her and tell her everything's okay while I go into my parents' bedroom, where Mom is in bed reading papers. I reach for her pen and Posties, write Cara is in trouble as best I can while keeping the phone up by my ear with my shoulder. Mom frowns at the note but then nods, and I thank Jesus for our talk today.

"Cara, listen. Whatever it is, it's okay. You've got me. You've got Michael. You've got Naeomi. We're all here for you."

"She'll never talk to me again," Cara wails. "She'll never forgive me."

"That's not true."

"That's what she *said*." And again more gasping, more muffled sounds. Up in the loft there are several quilts and old blankets, and she must be under some.

"Of course she'll forgive you. She's your best friend." I go back to my room and shut the door, still worried but at least glad to know nobody's dead.

"Not anymore. And no, she won't. This. This is unforgivable."

"Nothing's unforgivable, Cara. You know that. Remember?"

"It's not like that."

My mind is swimming, trying to imagine Cara doing anything heinous. "Why don't you just tell me what happened. I'm sure we can work it—"

"The reason I wasn't at the dance on Saturday was that I was with Michael."

"We knew that. It's okay—"

"No, Tab." She starts crying again. "Do you hear me? I was *with* him."

I can't help it. Immediately I visualize it: Cara and her long brown hair and her tan cheek and her kissing Michael. Her hand on his thin chest. His hand moving. A shoulder. A flash of skin. And then it's not his hand and it's not Cara but it is Jake and it is me.

"Are—are you okay?"

Now her voice is hard: "What do you mean, am I okay? Of course I'm not okay."

"But I mean he didn't—?"

"No, no," she groans. "No, nothing like that. It was wonderful. Beautiful-perfect. Which is why I didn't really think—" She stops a minute. I'm worried she'll start crying all over again, and she does, a little, but then she gets herself together and tells me how they'd been talking about it for a long time. How they both really wanted to, not just out of crazy lust, but For Real. She tells me, her voice steadying, that they talked about it a lot, and she prayed. And waited some, and talked some more. "Ultimately," she sighs, calm and strong, "it just came down to the fact that we really love each other. And I know I'm going to marry him. So . . . since we're still too young to do anything official about what we know is a lifelong commitment, we decided to give each other the ultimate gift as a way to show each other, you know, how much we mean. And Tab, it was so—*that*."

I can't say anything because I'm pretty much just sitting on my bed thinking, *Cara had sex*, still trying very hard not to picture it and also feeling aghast, thinking how I was sitting next to her on Sunday—my arm around her, even—and the whole time she was completely changed forever, but I had no idea. Had no idea for *days*. It stuns me that something so completely major could happen—*The world doesn't revolve around purity rings, you know*—and nobody could even see.

"That's why I decided. Because it was so completely special."

I don't know what to say to this, so I divert. "And so you told Naeomi?"

She sighs. At least she isn't crying. "She's my best friend. At first I thought I wouldn't tell anybody, you know? After it happened it was so private and wonderful and I didn't want to . . ." She breaks off. I think of her sitting there at the dinner table, surrounded by her family, surrounded by us at school, not getting to share this major thing. "But then I could tell she knew something was up, and besides I just wanted to *tell* her. I thought maybe she'd even be happy for me, would know that it was different. But instead she got stony and cold, and when I pushed her, she said, 'I can't talk to you right now; I need to think.' Which at first I got, because sure, it's a surprise—it means certain things, and she needed time. But when she called back, I thought it'd be to say she understood."

"And did she?" *Because I don't think I do yet.*

"More like she needed to think about how many ways she could tell me I'd disappointed her. I can't believe *you're* not mad at me, actually."

"Well—" I take a second. "I'm definitely surprised. And I don't really know what to say. Annnd it is a little weird that you are suddenly, you know, my friend who has Broken Her Promise. . . ." I realize it's hard enough trying to grasp something, let alone the words to articulate what it is you're not quite grasping.

"And I'm not sure what you and Michael decided was right. . . ." *Oh God, I am going to have a lot of praying to do, aren't I?* "But I don't think any of what I'm feeling is anything like *mad*. I mean, that doesn't really help you much, does it? And if your brothers find out, you'll have plenty of *mad* to deal with."

It isn't really a sensitive thing to say, but we both giggle a little, which relieves the semi-awkwardness and helps me go on.

"Maybe Naeomi just needs to get used to it. Maybe if you give her some time—"

"Oh, no. This is it, I think. I think I really—"

"Hey," I say, trying to detour around the Path of Renewed Crying. "She'll come around. Maybe if I talk to her—" On my desk, my cell phone beeps that I have a text, but I ignore it.

"No, Tabitha, no. Please don't say anything to her. Don't say anything to anybody. I just—I just want to handle this myself."

"But it's a pretty big deal. What if you need help or something?"

"Well, of course we were *careful*."

"I know, but still. What if—"

"Tabitha, please? I mean it. This is mine. I just . . . I just called you tonight mainly because Naeomi wouldn't take any of my calls today, and I just couldn't take it, thinking about her never talking to me again, and Michael doesn't get why *I'm* not mad at *her*. I just needed to talk. I'll be okay, really."

And she does sound better. A lot better, really. Which means now I'm once again the one in upheaval with no one to tell. I tell her I won't open my mouth about it, even though things are going to be really weird at school now.

For one thing—it hits me—from now on Cara will have feelings that I can't comprehend, at least not until I get married. A million questions stir up in me, things I want to ask her, want her to explain. What did it feel like, of course, and did it really hurt? Will they do it again now, all the time, or was it just a one-time thing? Is it weird to see a boy naked? And more than that. Like, what is it like to love someone that much, to feel something so strongly and with so much conviction, that you'd be willing to break your promise even to God?

"Look," she says, "I'm really sorry for loading this onto you."

"No, I'm glad you did. I mean, you needed *some*body." Though admittedly I feel a little spike of anger at Naeomi for not being that somebody.

"Well, I think I'll hang out tomorrow around the chorus room before school."

"Okay. I'll try to come by then."

"Thanks, Tab. Thanks a lot."

When we hang up, about three minutes pass before my hand and face stop tingling from the shocked place where the phone was resting against my skin. The first thing I want to do is call Morgan. Not to tell her, but just to hear her voice, to know that things are okay with us, because even though she was a little weird about Jake at first, at least I could tell her about him. At least she didn't turn her back on me.

But since I'm still pretty stunned, there's a chance I might spill the beans. Instead I go tell my parents what I can. That nobody's died. (Though, of course, the part of Cara that was a virgin has, and maybe, I think, so has the part that was Naeomi's best friend.) That Cara had a fight with Naeomi, and was just kind of freaking out and feeling alone.

"I'm not sure this is what I meant earlier," is all Mom says, meaning I've pushed it. This is so beyond not the point that I don't even bother answering. Instead I kiss them both and go brush my teeth.

But once in bed I can only lie there thinking: about Cara thinking, and Michael thinking, and both of them doing all that talking about everything they're thinking—talking and thinking about this mega-humongous thing that maybe you can't tell anyone else, not even your parents or best friend. And I wonder if that's part of why Naeomi's so mad, that maybe she feels left out, is pissed off that she wasn't allowed to be involved. Or maybe it's that she doesn't really want to be.

I admit, sometimes I haven't always needed to know every detail of every bit of drama on the dance team, or every annoying thing one of Morgan's teachers did or didn't do, or what some boyfriend said or didn't say, or how fantastic once again her parents were about letting her do or get whatever, but when I talk to Morgan it isn't the information that matters, really. It's that she wants to tell me about it. When it comes down to it, it isn't really what you share but that you're sharing at all.

And Cara and Michael shared the ultimate. Now nobody—forever—can take that away, even if—not that I think they won't—something awful happens and they *don't* get married. And whether or not that's right, it definitely is important, isn't it? Which makes me realize that Saturday, with Jake, that kiss was something *we* irrevocably shared, even if it wasn't the most binding experience ever, like Michael and Cara.

And two days from now, we'll be out on our date and maybe we'll be kissing again. At least, I hope so. But what comes after kissing? I mean, if I'm serious about my ring—which I am—maybe I shouldn't be kissing at all. Because once upon a time, Cara and Michael were only having their first kiss, too.

I can't work it out, and now I don't have anybody to work it out with. Except maybe Cara, whom I do manage to go see before school the next day. She's sitting on the floor near the chorus room, doing geometry. She doesn't have any makeup on, her shirt must be one of Skip's, and she's definitely tired, but she's there.

"You okay?" I sit down next to her.

"You're tired, too."

"It's okay." I don't know what else to say, so I just press my shoulder against hers.

"You don't have to hang out here. I've actually got to finish this."

"I know. I just wanted to check on you."

She pats my knee. "Really, thanks."

"No biggie."

"No—you need to act like everything's normal, I know. And I'm really sorry, Tab. I shouldn't have put you in the middle."

I certainly don't want to be in the middle, to be already feeling this weird. But the saddest, saddest story to me in the Bible, sadder than even Jesus's march up the mountain with the cross and all the torment He went through during Lent and the Passion, is the story of the Garden of Gethsemane. It's right before Judas is about to give Him away to the Romans, and Jesus is all tired and exhausted and sad, and knows what's about to happen, knows He has to go through this awful thing and still people won't believe Him—that even His two best friends will betray and deny Him—and He's there in the garden and just wants some peace and some praying after dinner before everything comes down on His head. So He asks the disciples to just stay up and keep Him company. And they do, for a little while, but it's been a nice dinner and it's late and everyone's sleepy and they can't stay awake. Well, Jesus comes back in after crying and praying awhile, and He sees them all asleep and gets a little miffed. But they wake up and say they won't fall asleep again, that they love Him and they're sorry. When Jesus goes away again, though, of course they do. And He comes back again, and reprimands them, and it's just heartbreaking. I mean, there He was, about to die for them—for all of us—in this horrid way, and they couldn't even stay awake.

The least I can do is come say hey to Cara before school.

It only gives me a few minutes in front of Morgan's locker, though, since the chorus room is way over in the back of the school. At least Naeomi's there, which is a good sign, even though I can't really make very good eye contact with her.

"What's up with you this week, Tardypants?" Morgan wants to know. "I texted you last night to see if you wanted a ride this morning."

Gah, I totally forgot about that. I try to roll my eyes dramatically. "Stupid Mom." Hopefully that will be enough. "Can you hurry up and get your license, please?"

She's eyeing me a little at first, but the mention of her license launches her into a little brag/rant about how terrifying it is driving even short distances on I-75 or 85, all those lanes you have to cross and pay attention to, cars whipping on every side; how her dad is always telling her to close the gap between her and the next car because someone else is just going to cut in, and how she has to remind him that the driver's handbook says to always leave two car lengths, no matter what.

I do my best to be present, to offer to quiz her more on the driver's handbook, but honestly, all I can think about is Cara in front of the chorus room, hunched over her homework, alone. I sneak looks at Naeomi, trying to see if she's thinking about Cara too, missing her. Am wondering if she's blabbed Cara's secret to anyone else out of desperate sadness or as a way to punish Cara, but she just seems her same old even-keeled self.

So after homeroom I try to hurry to chorus to make sure nothing awful's happened in the last fifteen minutes, but of course it hasn't. What else worse could happen after losing your virginity and your best friend pretty much at the same time? What could my giving her an extra hug really do to make any of it better?

On the way to math, we walk together just like usual, only when she gets a little ahead of me at the crossroads I feel all of a sudden like there's some kind of invisible cord between us, connecting us to each other: this thing that she's done and then told me, this intimacy kind of, this revelation holding us together, making us both now a little responsible for each other. A kind of bond we have that nobody else even knows about. Kind of like, I can't help thinking, the thing connecting her and Michael now forever.

It's not a responsibility I'm sure I want. While I'm very glad Cara and I have gotten so close in the last year, we've each had other best friends for the really big stuff. Now all of a sudden she's bestowed me with this secret I can't even share with Morgan, or my parents, really. Just because Cara broke her fidelity to everyone but Michael, does that mean I have to break some of mine, too?

Not that I really want to tell Morgan about Cara, specifically, but she always wants to know everything I know the minute I know it, and not telling her this—just by virtue of omission—already feels like some kind of wrongdoing. But beyond that she's bound to notice pretty darn soon if Cara's never around. What will I say if she brings it up? There's no way I can fake ignorance. Not with Morgan. Unless of course maybe Naeomi mentions something first, which she might, at least offhand, but would she all the way? Naeomi isn't really the type to divulge big details about much of anything, but if she was mad enough. . . .

But it's not really Cara I want to talk about. The million weird things I'm feeling about what she's done I definitely could use some counsel on, however, and those are the things Morgan's likely to sense first, anyway. Also I can't stop wondering what Cara will do with her ring now that she's broken her promise. I mean, it's not like she can give it back to Jesus, or Walt, who gave it to her in the first place. But if she stops wearing it altogether someone will surely notice, and even I get uncomfortable, thinking about the explaining she'd have to do. And what would wearing the ring mean, if the promise it represents isn't there anymore? And what would that say about Cara?

Morgan would know what to do about Naeomi, too. While you should stick to your scruples, shouldn't sticking by your best friend when she goes through one of the biggest deals ever—even if it's wrong—be one of them? Since Morgan's so clear on right and wrong herself, hearing her opinion about it might help me figure out mine.

Mainly, though, I just need to hear her say there's no way she would ever abandon me like that, no matter what I did. That she'd stick with me through thick and thin, and help me wrestle with whatever demons set themselves on me.

The absence of any note from her after math makes me feel even more bleak. I wonder if she's already somehow talked to Naeomi; if she knows, and worse, if she somehow knows that I know and didn't tell her I knew. I go through PE, lunch, English, trying to concentrate on the stuff in front of me, willing myself not to hide in the bathroom between classes and text everybody just to make sure nothing major's happened without my knowing it. But that would be, on top of everything else, breaking one of the cardinal rules of school, and even though it's not clear how they really enforce it besides taking away your phone, I'm sure I'd be the one person in the whole school to get caught, and then Mom would definitely rescind any phone privileges she's thinking about giving me.

So, instead, I rush to Morgan's locker immediately after

English so that we can walk the whole way to biology together instead of just meeting outside class. She half smiles when she sees me, but slams her locker so hard I'm sure one of her Echoing Angels pictures must've fallen off inside.

"What's wrong?"

"Ugh." She holds up her hand like stopping traffic. "Don't even."

We make it about ten yards before she unleashes.

"Is everybody on their period today or something? I mean, Gah."

I stay quiet, dodging traffic around us, concentrating on the stairs, moving, biding my time, waiting.

"I mean, Naeomi I swear has got something up her *butt* these days at rehearsal. She won't give any input anymore and we totally need her because she's the smartest and the best, and Maverick Mayhem is, like, practically tomorrow. But no. She just totally shrugs when Dawn goes off on her stupid crossing-cartwheels thing, saying it doesn't matter to her, it's not important. *Not important!* As if! And I mean it, I totally think I'm going to break up with Cody. Now baseball's practicing on Friday afternoons, too, and he just doesn't *get* how that's annoying, but *beyond* that—" We cross the windowed bridge between the 300 and 400 wings and have to work our way around a slow-shuffling group of kids in Braves jerseys. I keep my eye on Morgan's shiny ponytail, praying she's not about to turn around and challenge me about Cara.

"—then! Oh, then!" *Oh God, help me, here it comes.* "We get our essays back in history today and I made a *C*. Can you believe it? I mean, it was a good essay. Martha Washington is, like, completely boring and I managed to make it entertaining, and did great comparisons to Mary Todd Lincoln *and* Jacqueline Kennedy *and* Hillary Clinton. I totally do *not* need another C in history. Do. Not. I mean, I don't know what I've done to deserve all of this lately, but it isn't good."

By that time we're at bio. Morgan stands over by the lockers across from our class door, huffing and practically stamping her foot. I'm sympathetic, I am. And usually at this point when she's upset I say soothing things: tell her she'll be able to bring up her history grade, that maybe I can help her with a revision, that Cody's just stressed about the spring games, and then try to make a joke. Except that yesterday, apparently, my jokes didn't go over well, I'm seriously relieved she hasn't mentioned Cara's Big Secret and My Not Telling Her as one of her things to be mad about, and I can't help thinking that her little string of "grievances" is nowhere near as serious as Cara's.

Still, she is my best friend. "Well, tomorrow's Friday at least," I try.

"And what's *that* supposed to mean?" she spits.

"I just mean that tomorrow's Friday." I'm chipper, relaxed, cool. "The week'll be over and you can start over and we can maybe go to the movies Saturday and bake cookies and you can sleep late and, you know. Reset."

I am hoping my face looks something akin to Mrs. Kent seeing us in new outfits.

"Oh," Morgan says, slouching against the lockers. She gives

a wan smile and at first I think it's at me but then I see Cody hunching down the hall.

"Hey babe," he drawls.

She turns to him but even our biology teacher deep in the classroom could look up and see she's not into discussing what, if anything, they'll do tomorrow night. I hang back, watching but not watching Morgan pout her way through it all. I'm waiting for the whole rescue thing I normally feel when Morgan's sad or angry: to want to do whatever I can to make her smile and giggle again. But right now listening to her sulk, all I can think about—still—is Cara getting ditched by Naeomi. *You're lucky all you got was a C today,* I want to tell her. *You're lucky the only thing you and your boyfriend have to mull over is weekend plans. You're lucky all you lost was your ring.*

Instead, after Cody waves to us both and tells Morgan to text him, I reach out and squeeze her hand, calming us both.

"You already need new polish," she says. We both look down. She's right.

"Do 'em for me on Saturday? I don't have to be at the Center." *And then I can tell you about my date, and we can act like everything's fine, and maybe by then it will be.*

She's maybe going to smile.

"We can work on your driving. Or your renewal service," I say. "Ours."

And now she actually does.

The bell rings, and she turns to go into class.

I follow her with my stomach full of ashes.

• • •

When school is finally over I have two texts: one from Morgan, one from Cara. Morgan's says, *So do u really wnt 2 slpovr Sat?* and Cara's says, *Want to ride this weekend?* I doubt, when factoring in the homework part of the equation plus church, I'll have time to do both, since Friday's already taken. But *depending* on Friday, I may need a double-infusion of girlfriend support. Manicures and cookies with Morgan would be great. And so would checking on Cara and being on a horse. I shut my phone and decide to decide later.

When Mom picks me up she wants to know how school went but seems okay with me simply saying it was all right and giving her a homework rundown as we drive the short but traffic-clogged distance to the Center.

Normally I'd be thrilled to see Lacey and get to talk to the sweet old ladies and gentlemen at the Center, but today it just feels like one of those things I have to get through. I suppose it's evident I'm distracted, because after med drop, while Lacey and I are changing the announcement on the bulletin board in front of the dining room for a sing-along viewing of *Singin' in the Rain*, she says, "You wanna tell me?"

"What?" I sound more irritated than I think I am.

She reaches down into her basket grabbing some streamers. When she comes back up she looks almost as irritated as I don't quite feel.

"Really, Lace, what?"

"Never mind." She flicks her red bangs out of her eyes and adjusts a photo of Gene Kelly that we touched up with glitter and puff paint.

I lean against the wall and sigh. "Are you still friends with your high school best friend?" I ask from nowhere.

"No way," she snorts, straightening a few letters. "We kept up through college okay, but I haven't talked to her in—gosh. Like, three years? I saw her when I was home once for Christmas. Gained twenty pounds, married, a kid. Totally different life from me. It was good seeing her but you could say we didn't really have much in common now."

This doesn't help. "Well, do you miss her?"

"I guess I did at first. But honestly?" She waves it off.

"That's sad."

She shrugs, scoops up the decorations. We head back to her office. I think about how much history Morgan and I have shared together, and Naeomi and Cara. Heck, even Priah and I have our own past. I can't imagine all of that becoming totally not important, something I get used to being without.

"What's going on?" She's not annoyed anymore.

"Just don't want that to happen with me and my friends, I guess," I say once I'm sure I have my voice.

"I'm sure you'll get it worked out." She gives me a careful look. "Friends are important. They keep you honest. And sane. But hopefully in your case not so sane that you forget to go a little *in*sane over Mr. So Fantastic I Forgot About Even Jesus For Fifteen Minutes. Deal?"

I can't help but grin. Even though this isn't about Jake at all, just the sideways mention of him makes me feel better. "Okay, deal."

chapter 12

After work and then almost an hour of struggling over my English essay, Mom and Dad call me downstairs for dinner. There are candles lit, and they're both standing by their chairs. We have place mats. There's a scroll tied with a ribbon next to my plate. I know immediately what this is about, but I try to go solemnly to my chair.

"What's going on?"

"Well," Dad starts as we sit down, "we wanted to reward your past discipline and adherence to the rules imposed on you out of love and affection from your only two parents, and to also honor what seems to be a new phase for our little family."

"And to put the kibosh on whining," Mom adds.

I unroll the scroll. It's one of our old cell bills. On the second page where it lists all the calls, Mom has blacked out about an inch worth of numbers and has written, in metallic gold pen, a bracket that says *Tabitha's new minutes*. There's an arrow down to the bottom of the page where it says in really big letters YOU NOW HAVE 200 MINUTES A MONTH.

"There are still limits on how late you can accept calls," Dad says.

"And every minute over two hundred you pay your father and I double for," Mom pipes in. "It's not just about the expense. Most of this is about trusting you to be responsible."

I try to remember to be earnest, that this is a big deal, both for me and for them, that two hundred is way better than none. "Really, thanks."

During dinner I make a big show of figuring out how to find out exactly how many minutes I've used by punching a few buttons on my phone, and how to put people on speed dial now that I can call them. It occurs to me I can give Jake my cell number, and not just my home one.

My only dilemma after dinner is to decide who to call first. If I call Cara we'll have to talk about It. If I call Morgan I'll have to not talk about It. I decide to text Morgan NEW PHONE PRIVILEGES 2NITE instead, and then e-mail her the details. Even if she doesn't get the e-mail until two weeks from now (she is horrid about checking her e-mail), she'll know I was thinking of her this minute.

By bedtime nobody's called, which I try to think of as silent meditation time, rather than the silent treatment.

When I get to Morgan's locker in the morning, everyone's there. Everyone except Cara. That Cara's absence has become "normal" gets to me for some reason. Maybe it's the melancholy of yesterday, the conflict I felt last night, but it gets to me.

"Where's Cara?" I ask, looking straight at Naeomi.

Priah whinnies. Morgan laughs, but in a dismissive way. Naeomi shrugs.

"Well, has anybody talked to her?" My eyes on Naeomi's.

"We've all been busy," she says, staring back at me, blank at first, but then I see her all of a sudden see that I know. I feel hot and cold at the same time.

"Let's hope she didn't get kicked in the face while fitting horseshoes or anything," Priah says.

Maybe there's a day when this would be funny. Maybe even Cara would laugh, if she were here.

"She works hard. We should be supportive. She's our *friend*." I'm looking at Priah—who's a little shocked—but really I want to be screaming this at Naeomi. The heat under my collarbones, my fast heart rate, the tingling at the edges of my eyes—it's overwhelming.

"She's got Michael if anything's really wrong," Naeomi says, even, cool.

"Well." I can't take my eyes off her now, her thinly striped gray shirt, her melon-colored shrug, her long brown hands. *How* could *you?* "Even when you've got a boyfriend, sometimes you still need your girlfriends. Right, Morg?"

"Um—yes?" Morgan's got What the Hey? Face and a little of Tab, Take a Chill Pill, Like, Right Now Face too.

"So did you get a whole new phone?" Priah butts in, honestly sounding excited. Morgan must've told her before I arrived. "You're so lucky. Parents who *get* you."

I can't tell—I can never really tell; one day I'll just have to ask her outright—if Priah's just intentionally planted one of her famous diversions, or if she's seriously been bursting with excitement this whole time.

"No, they just expanded my minutes." It comes out breathy, mainly because I'm afraid of how close I just came to blurting everything. "It's no big deal."

"Three-way marathons here we come," Morgan squeals.

"Yeah, well, not really. They capped me at two hundred."

"But that's hardly—" she starts, before biting her lip. "I mean, great."

"Yeah," I shrug, the buoyancy of false freedom evaporated. "It's better than nothing."

"Tab, I didn't . . ." Morgan sighs. "I mean, what's your pro—"

"What's your voice mail message going to change to?" Naeomi interrupts. "Now that you don't have to say, 'Gah! Call me at home instead!'" Her face is joking, seriousness, apology, and something else. It takes me a minute to process.

"I don't know—" I'm scrambling for a joke myself. "Maybe 'This is Tab's secretary, leave dictation'?" Not even I think this is any good, though maybe Jake would like it.

But: "Cool," Priah says.

"Cool," echoes Naeomi.

"Yeah—cool," Morgan chimes after a minute.

"Cool," I finish, just in time for the homeroom bell.

Pure

• • •

All Morgan's note says after math is What is wrong with you? Clearly we need to talk. So before French I risk it and dash over to the 400 wing to try and catch Morgan. I get to her English class three seconds before she does and twenty seconds before the bell.

"You wanna skip later and meet me for lunch?" is all I have time to say. She takes a beat longer than either of us can afford before nodding, "Okay." I squeeze her hand and start running back the way I came, making it to French sixty seconds late but in enough time to say "*Oui*" when Ms. Capriole calls my name for roll.

Unlike last year, when we had more classes together and our rotations turned out neatly, this year there are only a few times in the six-week term when I have lunch with Morgan. I've actually gotten kind of used to it, and take advantage of the homework time when I can, but this week it is completely not convenient. I would feel bad asking her to skip psychology right now, except that the psychology teacher is also one of the dance team coaches, which means she has a lot of leverage in a class that everyone takes for the easy factor anyway.

When I get to the Coke machine Morgan is already there, scanning the crowd of Second Lunch Losers, looking for me. I hug her tight.

"Hey," she says, eyes darting to tables. "Where should we sit?"

"Want to brave the wild outdoors?" I cock my head and my eyebrow at the same time, trying to be playful. It is still kind of chilly outside, but because of that most of the good inside seats are taken.

She nods, eyes going over again to a gang of band kids—
clarinets, by the looks of them—before following me to the
courtyard. We find a place in the sun and spread out our bagged
lunches: mine in standard-issue brown recycled, hers in Velcro-
sealed pale blue insulated nylon.

"Thanks for meeting me at the last minute." I straighten my
leftover stir-fry, yogurt cup, and organic pineapple-carrot juice.
She opens a Rubbermaid container: inside is chicken salad scooped
into clean sheaves of endive.

"Another film today." She shrugs. "And, anyway, you've been
kind of intense."

I look at my lunch, at the pale concrete faux-fancy table
underneath it.

"Things—" I start. What is it I really want to say? It seems,
now that she's here, like nothing and everything. "Things aren't
right."

Morgan takes a second, like one of those automated phone
things after you say "One" as loudly and clearly as you can. "I
agree," she finally nods.

I go carefully. There's all kinds of "not right" she might
think I'm talking about. But there's also the small thin sliver of a
possibility that she already knows, that her Shut Up Right Now
Face this morning was all about not wanting to let Priah in on
what Naeomi, like Cara, had already blabbed.

"I don't know what to do."

"I don't either."

I take this as a good sign, but still go slow. "I mean, of course, sometimes when you're friends, people go in different directions, and you have to adjust."

"Like in seventh grade."

I nod. "Like in seventh grade." In seventh grade when Erika Biggs and Briel Dunnedin suddenly stopped wearing matching outfits and instead went for I Will Wear Anything But What Would Remind You Of Her, which was funny because sometimes that meant they ended up matching.

"But sometimes," she says.

"But sometimes, people go, like, way off the path and you're not sure you know how to get them back."

"Exactly." She is eating now in earnest, but she's also nodding.

"Exactly. So, what we have to do is try to—we have to try to get past the temporary disconnect and get back on track."

"Right."

"Well." I open my yogurt. "One tactic is to just be completely honest."

"About the changes."

"Exactly. About the changes." So Naeomi definitely must've told Morgan. The iffy communication Morgan and I have had this week would be reason enough for her not telling me, and maybe she thought I knew already. Or, more likely—this is it—Naeomi made *Morgan* swear silence, which means she's been feeling all the weirdness and secrecy that I have too. Which then explains everything. So this is good.

"Maybe we should all just be totally open about it, then," I go on. "Maybe we should just get it out there and work together to sort it all out and make the bad stuff okay and get past it."

"But what if everything *isn't* okay? What if it's totally messed up now?"

"Well—I don't know. That's why I wanted to talk to you. To figure out what to do. To figure out . . . how to get them talking again. Because sure it seems unforgivable, but maybe it isn't. Maybe we just haven't figured it out. What's the best way."

I'm scraping yogurt from the sides of my container. Morgan's watching.

"Tabitha, what are you talking about?"

I look up at her. She's looking at me like maybe suddenly I'm talking backward Chinese. I have a weird sensation similar to the one where you take a sip of what you think is a glass of apple juice, but really it's iced tea.

"I'm . . ." *What else would I be talking about?* "I'm talking about Naeomi and Cara, is what."

"Naeomi and Cara?"

"Their fight. How they're not talking to each other. This morning. I mean, you know. They're not talking. Naeomi said. I mean, didn't she? But they're not. And—and it's bad. And we have to figure out how to make it right with them."

"Why isn't Naeomi talking to Cara?"

"I thought you—" A million bubbles of *Oh, crap* swim around me.

"Is it because of Michael? Because Cara totally needs to stop hanging out with him so much. It's gross how she has no life besides him and horses. I mean, ick."

"Well, she really—"

"Sure, Naeomi's totally way too obsessed with SGA and her GPA and everything and she's losing weight too, you can totally tell but—" Suddenly she looks at me and her neck, I swear, it lengthens about two inches. "Tabster—what are we doing? I thought this whole time you were talking about *you*."

"Me?"

"Yeah, you. And Jake. And your utter, like, total preoccupation and inability to think about anything else this week. I mean, late much? Every day? And hello what *up* with the phone thing? How come, after *years* of us both having phones and me being your best friend and everything, your parents 'suddenly' change the rules? Because of a boy? Because you couldn't beg hard enough for me, but now that a boy's come around you manage to wheedle it so you can talk to him all the time and completely forget your friends so much that everything totally goes out the window for this *guy*, which leaves everyone high and dry until they have to nurse you back to reality when you figure out that he's just like every other boy on the planet and only wants one thing and completely disses you once he finds out your ring is no joke? You mean, like that? Is that what you wanted to talk about?"

"I—uh—" *Uhhhhh* . . .

"I mean, you're going out with him tonight, not like we didn't all already know. And already you've talked to him, like, a zillion times, and you can't even *bother* to text your own best friend back, or, like, God forbid even give her a little grin or pep talk after pretty much an incredibly crappy week."

"I was—" Oh, no. I did ignore her this week. Not on purpose, though, and it was just about a ride. But still. I didn't answer. Because I was—*Ach. Gah.*—talking to Cara.

"You were *what*?" Her face is ice. I can't feel my hands. My tongue.

"I can explain. It—"

"And don't *even* start on your parents. It's so immature and tired, how you are always complaining about restrictions, blaming them for why you can't do anything. Why don't you just own up to the fact that—"

"Morgan, it's not about *me*." I have crushed my lunch bag into a ball. I stare at it, but only for a second. "It's about Cara, okay? And Naeomi. Our friends. Who right now are *not* friends. That's what I said. I'm not trying to—" I put my head in my hand, try to concentrate on the initials and quotations drawn in Sharpie on the table instead of everything swirling in my mind, how this all derailed so fast with my own best friend just because someone else ditched hers in a time of dire need. This will not happen with me. It won't. I pull my head up, level with her. If I can't make everything right, I'm at least going to keep *this* from going wrong.

"Look. It's really bad. This has nothing to do with you and me. You and me are fine. Maybe some things will change because of Jake, but honest I am so glad I have you to go through that with. I *need* you. And, besides, we can cope with anything, right? We have before. And maybe we'll have to now. Because Cara and Michael did it and now Naeomi isn't talking to Cara, and Cara's really upset and I'm not supposed to tell but I don't know what to do. And I need to talk to you about it, and I'm sorry if I'm weird but I don't really know all the ways how to even feel about it, let alone get my head around what I really think, and come on, they're our good friends and we have to do something and at least I'm talking to you about it now, so can you just help me try to—"

She stops me. "Cara and Michael *what*?"

I look at her. It feels like a long time before I say, "They did."

Her eyes go away from me. "And now Naeomi isn't talking to her?"

The bag is still in my fist. I loosen my fingers slowly, feel the crushed paper expanding against my relaxing palm. This is the main thing I'm aware of. That, and the fact that suddenly the courtyard seems very quiet. Morgan's still frozen in front of me. Crap. Okay. Well, then.

"No." I let out a long breath. "She's not. I mean, they're not talking. They had a big fight over it. About what happened on Saturday. I thought—I really thought you already knew."

"Well," she says. The concrete is cold under me; my bones feel hot and hollow at the same time, watching her actually say, "Good for Naeomi."

I feel like . . . I don't know. Everything is in total sharp focus: the sound of someone's corduroys as they pass us, the sun gleaming off the silver edge of Morgan's thermos, the hallway attendant up by the library doors with her ankles crossed, Morgan's pale gleaming lip gloss, one hand around the other, ringless. "Wait. What?"

"You heard me." She starts packing up her things. "Good for Naeomi."

"But Cara's her best friend."

"*Was* her best friend."

"What?" Green dots are swimming in front of my face.

"Cara made a promise. She made a *vow*. And, well, she broke it. Some curly-headed poet comes along and shows her the darker side of life, and she just laps it right up." Her face is full of disgust, but also righteousness. "So, good for Naeomi. Good for her. She stood up for what's good. What's *right*."

"But she and Cara have known each other since—"

"The love of Jesus is forever, Tab. *Forever*. It's hard to get your head around but that's the thing about faith. It expands beyond—"

"Yes, but even He said . . ." But I can't think of anything. In front of Morgan's superior rightness, I know everything else—no matter how right it might be—is wrong. "I can't believe you're being so . . . so . . ."

"So what? I'm being so dedicated? I'm being so *loyal*?" she hisses. "Frankly, Tabitha, I can't believe this is such a big issue for you. I mean, look at you, like you're wrestling over what side to be on. Is *that* what's wrong with you? Well, there isn't any choice about sides here. There's nothing to debate. You know what's right and what isn't. You know what the Bible says, what we all promised. I can't believe—I really can't believe that you're even hinting about waffling about this."

"So that's it? You just totally drop Cara and that's it?"

Her eyes level at me. "That's it."

"But, Morg, what if it was *me*?"

She doesn't even blink. And she's looking right at me. Right at me. "If you had it in you to do such a thing," she says, "if you could betray yourself and me and your vow to Jesus Christ like that . . . Well, I wouldn't want to be friends with you, either."

It punches me in the stomach. I can't believe she's said it, but she has and I can't bear it. I stand up, heft my book bag. I can't look at her.

"I understand that you feel that way," I finally manage. In two seconds I am going to cry, and the lonely realization comes: I don't want her to see. "I just hope, when you think about it," I choke, "you've got a little more faith in me than that."

"Well, let's just hope you don't test it," I hear her say behind me.

It's a stab in my back as I stumble into the building. The bell rings, and kids start pouring out of classrooms around me. I weave through them, past the crowded crossroads, past my locker and the counseling office, out the main doors and into the cold sunshine. My throat hurts from trying to hold in the crying. At first I think I'm just going out the front doors to get as far away from where Morgan might be, to get a deep breath, to clear my head a little, but instead I just keep going, deciding that minute that I can't stand trying to sit through the rest of school as though everything is normal. I turn right and head up the hill, my back tight and tingling, expecting a hallway monitor or, worse, Mr. Bell to shout, "Hey!" and come after me with a detention ticket, but none of this happens. Instead my feet go, one after the other, my shoes knocking into each other from time to time, my feet stumbling over roots, then sidewalk cracks, but eventually I'm past the school and heading to the square.

Once I'm out of eyeshot from any classrooms, I start crying in earnest. Morgan's words over and over, the immediate, easy look of disdain on her face, the feeling of wind being taken out of me. *"Good for Naeomi."* That Morgan turned on Cara, and then on me so fast and so easy is a shock I can't absorb. And Cara—Cara! What is she going to say now when she finds out that not only can she not trust her best friend, but now she can't trust me, either, me so stupid trying to take matters into my own hands, trying to fix everything, trying to do better than God.

I sit down on one of the benches in the square. It occurs to me as I dial—*oh, the irony*—that the first time I'm using my new minutes, it's for a call my parents would've approved, anyway. When Mom picks up, I start crying harder, which I didn't think possible, but it's mainly because I'm afraid she'll be mad at me for skipping school.

But she isn't. After I tell her enough of what happened, mainly that Morgan and I got into a huge fight because I stood up for Cara, she tells me to go home and lie down, drink some water or make some tea, maybe take a bath, and that she'll be home after her two o'clock class. She asks me several times if I'm really okay, and she says, bizarrely, that she's proud of me. She makes sure I have my keys, and says she'll let Dad know I'm going home early. When we hang up I feel completely wrung out and exhausted, and regret briefly that I didn't just ask her to come get me.

I do make it home, though. It takes me a while, but I get there. It's only after I shut the door behind me that I realize I'm still clutching my crumpled lunch bag in my fist.

chapter 13

Mom gets home around three thirty and finds me flung on the couch, staring at the TV, not really watching anything but not able to turn it off.

"Tabitha Gretchen," Mom says from the hall.

I don't look at her. She goes to the kitchen and I hear her pulling out the pot, opening the pantry, getting ready to make some curry corn.

"I don't want any," I growl.

She ignores me and I lie there, waiting for the four or five *pop-pop-pops* that mean the oil is hot enough and she can pour in fistfuls of kernels that will then explode in stovetop deliciousness. I focus on the sound of Mom sliding off her shoes, on the talking birds on the TV advertising some window cleaner, on the numb feeling in my face, because otherwise all the awful thoughts on the fringes of my brain will come crashing over me again and I may never be able to move from this spot.

But that only lasts as long as there are sounds on which to

focus. As soon as the activity in the kitchen has stopped, and Mom comes in with the curry corn drizzled with her special butter recipe, saying only "Twink," I start crying again. Amazingly, even after all the crying I did when I left school early and walked home, I can still cry about this a lot. Mom puts her arm around me. *Good for Naeomi. Good for Naeomi. Good for Naeomi*—over and over in my head, until I'm just too tired to keep going. I sit up, wipe my face, take a handful of curry corn. Mom reaches over to smooth my hair.

"Little better?"

I sigh. "You mean better than being stricken with a flesh-eating disease?"

She smiles a little.

"I guess so." I lean into her again. "But I don't think I'm up for going out. You and Dad staying home?"

It's astonishing how quickly Sympathetic Mom Smile can immediately transform into Disappointed Professor Look. Really, she could get a medal. "It's almost four, Tabitha," she says. "Jake's due here in an hour and a half. Whatever happened today, whatever's going on between you and your friends, it has nothing to do with him. And it isn't really very polite to cut out on such short notice. To back out on your commitment."

I just look at her. *Yeah, Mom. No kidding.*

"Come on." She hauls me up from the couch. "Let's go reduce some of this crying puffiness with a lavender shiitake mask and some of those soy-cucumber pads Meg sent me from California."

This is an obvious Mom carrot, but it works, especially since she usually hoards her expensive face gook. I take advantage of her pity—milking it, really. In her bathroom she fusses over me, though I'm still being as sullen as possible, just to keep her from getting too full of I Told You So.

But it's actually really fun and relaxing playing spa, and before I know it, Dad's home, which means it really seriously is five o'clock. I only have thirty minutes to fix my hair, do my makeup, and decide which purse to take. Suddenly I'm panicking and missing Priah horribly, both, so when my phone rings it's like Divine Intervention—maybe she can tell me what to do with my eye shadow—but under that I'm really praying, *Please let it be Morgan.*

But it's Cara's name and number flashing on my screen. My heart sinks and does an excited flop at the same time, which results in a flux of vertigo that I don't need. I stand there, holding my phone, looking at myself in the mirror and trying to think about what shade of lip gloss is going to work its best magic, while simultaneously wondering if she's calling to give me a pre-date pep talk, or cuss me out and disown me because she found out I told Morgan. I toss the phone on my bed.

Of course, two minutes later I listen to her message.

"Hey." Right away from her voice I can tell she doesn't know. "I just wanted to call and wish you luck and to say just be yourself because you're amazing and he's stupid if he doesn't know it already. Have a good time and really thanks for everything and call me as soon as you can. Okay, bye. It's Cara."

I sit there at my dressing table, looking in the mirror for a minute: looking at the mini-pleated neckline of my creamy silk top, my good-fitting jeans, my cascading hair, my glowing skin, my remarkable *togetherness*, and for a brief minute I hate myself. Why am I acting like nothing's happened? What am I doing, going on this date? How can I do anything but try to make things better?

Because Mom's calling up the stairs "Jake's in the driveway!" and I have to scramble into my closet and choose a purse as fast as humanly possible.

On the way down the stairs, I take a deep breath and say a quick prayer: a prayer for forgiveness and strength, for repairs with Morgan and Cara (and Cara and Naeomi), and, okay, for Jake to think I look really hot, too.

We manage to get out of the house relatively unscathed. Though Jake has to perch on our incredibly cool/incredibly uncomfortable angular white chair, my parents are fairly well behaved and unembarrassing, and Jake is the one who ends up emphasizing that I'll be home in time for curfew.

On the way to the restaurant, we compare all-time top movie favorites. (Him: the Bourne movies, Me: *Pride and Prejudice* and *Stranger Than Fiction*.) Perfectly normal conversation except that the whole time I'm saying to myself, "Wow. Look at me! I'm on a date! Is this what I'm supposed to be doing?"

Fortunately, once we get to Fritti there's plenty else to focus on, mainly the crazy pizza menu. The main deal here is about fifty (I'm not kidding) different individual-size pizzas, all with exotic names and even more exotic ingredients. Because we're in a hurry to make the movie, we decide as fast as we can (bacon-ham-asiago-ricotta for him; three-mushroom-gorgonzola for me) and then spend the time until our pizza comes making up our own pizzas: Oscar the Grouch pizza with sardine cans, moldy shoe leather, and wet newspaper; King Kong pizza with native-glazed bananas and barbecued Barbie heads. I'm having such a good time that it's like I'm on a completely different planet, like nothing about today really happened, like maybe I'm not even really *me*, until Jake looks up from his plate and says, "So your parents don't *seem* like Republicans."

I've just popped a bite of mushroom in my mouth. "What?" I say around it. "They're not."

Jake swallows. "This is good, by the way," he says, pointing with his fork.

"Mine too." I finish chewing. "But what made you think my parents were Republicans?"

He indicates my ring. "I just thought they'd be . . . more conservative."

Suddenly I can't look at him. Of course that means the first thing I see when I duck my eyes is my own hand, where my ring is suddenly Right There: so very sparkly and so very on my engagement finger. Not just a ring from my best friend, but a Symbol. Out of habit, I start twisting it with my thumb.

"I didn't know if you knew about these or not."

"'True Love Waits,' right?"

I'm surprised. I catch myself staring and have to look away. "Um, yeah."

I wait to see if he'll say anything else, but he doesn't. I try to cut my pizza again like everything's normal, but it's hard because the room has turned yellow and I feel like I'm in molasses. What am I supposed to say now?

"Your cousin's church go to the Ring Thing when it toured here?" I attempt.

"The what thing?" Now Jake is focused on pizza, too. He tries a bite of my mushroom trifecta delicious: "Dang, this IS good." Again with the pointing fork.

"I'll save you some." I watch him a minute, confused. "But, so, how do you know about . . . ?" I wiggle my ring finger a little.

He downs some water. "Um, online?"

"So you just . . . what? Recently made an investment in the diamond industry and your broker sent you some research?"

"No." He smirks a little, seeing that I won't let this go, won't start eating again until he tells me. He sighs and reddens a little. "After I met you at the hayride I looked you up."

My blush is outrageous. So he did see me on Facebook. This is enormously pleasing and mortifying at the same time. There are some pretty awful slumber party photos up there; I hadn't thought that *boys* would see my site. Not boys that matter, anyway.

"C'mon. You and your friends all had these glitzy rings on. I figured there was no way you could all be engaged. So I looked up a few things and, yeah, I saw you on Facebook, and then you and your cheerleader friend had all those links, so I read up on a few things."

It's embarrassing to hear him say it out loud like that, and part

119

of me wants to be on the defense, but most of me is tingling-happy down to the pads of my toes.

"Dance team, not cheerleading," I tell him. "And, you know, boys do it too."

He looks up, fork halfway to his mouth.

"I mean, not a lot of them, but they do." We both reach for our water glasses at the same time. He's so quiet I'm sure he's sitting there calculating some kind of excuse to take me straight home, skip the movie—and this whole him-and-me thing—altogether.

"Well, so what was it like?" he finally says.

And suddenly I'm completely relieved. I explain to him about the Ring Thing celebration, why Morgan and I went, and how afterward we got our rings. It's hard to look him in the face—or keep myself from sounding like a total Bible-thumper or complete prude, for that matter—but every time I do manage to sneak a glance at him, he's listening, and even once or twice giving a little nod.

"Cara and Naeomi, it turns out, went to the Ring Thing celebration too, and by the time we were all friends our freshman year, they'd each gotten rings from their families. Before long, Priah got her own ring and had made the promise too."

After that whole narration, Jake seems mainly interested in figuring out which friend is which, who knew who first, and how we all got together. This strikes me as incredibly nice, not to mention a good way to get off the ring topic. Once I've relayed my group's whole history (the short version, anyway), and had a chance to ask him about his own best friends (Paul and Sam), I take a deep breath. I've had to pee pretty much since making up Oscar the Grouch pizza, so I apologize and excuse myself.

During lipstick refreshing, I get a second to think about everything I just said. Talking about last year when we all met—how exciting it was for Morgan and me to find these other girls who believed the same things we did, who were cool and sweet and friendly, and who we could hang out with all the time instead of just at church, how that felt like some sort of affirming godsend—makes me suddenly incredibly sad. Only a few short hours ago I probably ruined all of that forever. Even before that, maybe all of it got shattered, back on Saturday when Cara and Michael—

It comes crashing around me again actually, all the stuff I pushed away to get ready for my date: the shock of Morgan's disdain, the awful pull I felt walking away from her at the table, my blind stumbling, skipping the rest of school and the crush of guilt that worsened with every step. That I was able to stop thinking about it over a date with a boy makes me feel even worse now. *How could I think getting glammed up for Jake was more important than making reparations with my friends?* Morgan would probably never forgive me for trying on jackets instead of trying to call her.

I look at myself, for real, in the mirror. My face doesn't look too sure about anything. But it also tells me I'm not going to be able to figure it all out here and now. I force myself to brighten up my eyes and put it all out of my mind, promising Jesus on the way back to the table that I'll spend serious prayer time when I'm safe back home.

But it's not so easy to stop thinking about Morgan and Cara

once I've started. Back at the table Jake's already paid, and he stands up and hands me my pizza box, suggesting we get going. He guides me out with his hand on the small of my back, and as we drive I wonder sadly if I'll get to tell Morgan how great it feels to be on a real date with a real boy: a boy who is funny and smart and interesting, who listens when you talk and who opens the car door for you, a boy who puts his hand on you just in this nice warm way, without making it feel like he wants it to go all over everywhere else.

Which then makes me wonder if this is part of Michael's appeal for Cara; this sort of nice, comfortable feeling, the feeling that maybe you could start to trust this guy and be open with him and have fun too. A guy who gets to be a friend and then some.

Before I know it we're at Midtown Art Cinema, looking for parking.

"Tabitha, did I say something wrong back there?"

"What?"

"You looked kind of weird when you came back to the table, and you've been super quiet since, so I just wondered if I messed up or something."

"No. Not at all. I—"

"I mean, I just want you to know that it's all cool with me. I mean, that I think it's cool. Your ring."

My thumb starts its ring-twirling again. "Thanks. Really. I mean, you know. Not a lot of—"

"Well, I just don't want you to—I don't know."

"It's really not that. Really." We're still circling the lot with no luck. The sinking feeling tries to grab me again, but I don't want to put *him* ill at ease. "Just a thing with one of my friends today. Well, actually two."

Jake sighs, but I think it's about the lack of parking. He is concentrating out the windshield and I'm getting a little antsy too, since the movie starts in three minutes.

"At this rate we may have to park over at Piedmont Park," he grumbles.

"Aw, I hate missing previews."

"Really?" This excites him. "Me too. Best part of the movie most of the time. I mean, we're going around and around and I keep thinking, 'We're missing the Twenty.'"

This makes me giggle. "I know, I know!"

We grin at each other and Jake stops the car to look me full on. "Tell you what. How about we just skip this. Hey, do you like milkshakes?"

"Milkshakes?"

"Or better, malts?"

"You mean, like, Ovaltine or something? From the fifties?"

His grinning hazel eyes widen and he rubs his hands together like a comic-book villain, plotting. "Ooooooh, my pretty, are you in for a treat." He heads us out of the crowded parking lot.

"Are you sorry about the movie?"

He shrugs. "Movie I can see anytime."

At the Creamery near Emory campus, I tell him a little about my fight with Morgan. Instead of divulging all the details and once again breaking my promise to Cara, I just say we disagreed about something Cara did—something I know about but Morgan wasn't supposed to—and that it was something I'm not sure will just blow over.

He scoops up part of his chocolate peanut-butter malt and holds it out for me to try. I feel myself redden, but lean forward to take a taste.

"Wow. That's good."

"No other food will ever taste good to you again." He smiles. I melt. "You'll crave this so much you'll be tempted to break in here at night and make one yourself."

"Yuh-umm," I assert.

He smiles and nods before frowning to think. "You and this other girl—you and Cara—good friends?"

I take a few spoonfuls of my own thick banana-and-Nutella milkshake. I picture being in chorus and having Cara looking straight ahead, instead of trying to sneak smiles at me; imagine her suddenly not coming to youth group; me never going horseback riding with her again; not getting to tell her about this date. I realize I'm nodding furiously to Jake's question. "I don't always think about it that way, but we really are."

"Then you need to call her and explain what happened, before she hears it from someone else. You gotta apologize."

"Is this some kind of—"

"Lacrosse thing?" He's sheepish. "Yeah. But also a responsibility thing. You mess up a game or someone else's shot or whatever, and you own it. You hit someone in practice? You shake his hand and apologize. It's a respect thing, but it's also just a smart strategy. See, you cut off their anger before they have a chance to think about it and get really pissed." He pulls loud and hard on his straw.

"So I should apologize before she gets wind of it?"

He nods, scraping the bottom of his cup with his straw. I get busy on my own half-melted shake, as well, thinking.

"But what if she hates me forever?"

"She hates you forever, you can't do anything about it. But at least she won't be hating you for trying to cover up your mistake."

I consider this.

"Ooo, but speaking of hate—" He checks his phone. "Your parents are going to put a pretty big hate on me if we don't start heading back."

When we get to my house, he unbuckles and gets out of the car, and it's only at the very last second that I remember to sit still and not jump out myself, so he can come around and open my door. In a rare moment I will probably never feel again, I almost hope my parents are peeking out the front window spying on us, just so they can see what a gentleman Jake is.

When I'm out of the car, he takes my hands. "I had a really good time," he says.

Gah, except all I did was blab the whole time. Some date. But then he's moving even closer, and all I can do is nod as he moves even closer. I had pretty much forgotten about the kissing part that comes next.

"It was good to just . . . you know. Hang out, kind of."

More nodding from me.

He leans in, knees brushing mine. I'm still nodding a little when our lips meet each other at exactly the same time. Again I'm helium balloons and hot prickles all over, kissing him.

But it isn't a long kiss. I guess the thought of my parents peeking out the window occurs to us at the same time.

"So . . . can I take you out again soon?"

I grin. Nod nod nod.

"Good. And see if your secretary thinks you might have a chance to come and watch some soccer polo next week too, okay?"

"I'll see what she says." *Yes! Yes! Yes! Yes!*

"Oh. Your pizza." He unlocks the back and hands me my box.

"Yeah, I was wondering if you were going to try to get away with snatching that."

"Well, if mine hadn't been better . . ."

This time I definitely see my dad pass by the living room window. Jake sees too.

"I better let you go. But really, I had a good time."

"Really, me too. And thanks for being so cool about everything, and listening. Sorry for all the drama. But you do give good advice."

He chuckles. "Call me tomorrow and let me know how it goes?"

"I have to confess *tomorrow*?"

As he backs away he holds up three fingers like a scout. "Honorable thing."

"Okay, okay." I start walking backward to my house: fast enough so my parents can see I'm heading in, not quite fast enough to make Jake feel I want to get away. "Thanks for the pizza. And the milkshakes."

"Hey, sorry about the movie."

"Rain check?"

He cocks a finger pistol at me and fires. "Deal."

I go up as far as my front door and turn so I can wave again, and watch him get back in his car and drive away. After he's safely out of sight, I lean against the door for a minute and close my eyes, trying to hold on to the buzzing swim of our kiss. It lasts for about thirty seconds, until my mom opens the door behind me, puts her hand on the top of my head.

"Okay, Cinderella. Pumpkin time," she says, but not with disapproval. We link arms and go inside.

chapter 14

Next thing I know, I'm going to the first day of a really important chorus rehearsal. We're getting ready for a huge concert in, I think, San Francisco or somewhere—a city we have to fly to on a plane. There's going to be some dancing, too, and I'm running to rehearsal because Lacey is doing the choreography and I'm totally stoked about seeing what she has planned.

Only, when I get to the chorus room (which isn't really the chorus room but is instead this giant old-timey theater) everyone has these cute cowgirl clogging costumes on already and they're expertly going through the routine as though for the eightieth time. Lacey stands at the back, snapping the beat.

"When did everybody learn the steps?" I try to ask Cara, but she just sort of doesn't hear me. Everyone else is absorbed in their fluffy skirts and practicing steps, unable to tell me either. Today is supposed to be our first meeting, but apparently everyone else has been rehearsing for weeks. I know I have a part, I just don't know what it is, and no one will stop and tell me. A few girls even ask me why I'm not in my costume yet, when I don't even know where to go to get a costume, let alone what I'm supposed to be wearing. When I turn down a hall toward what I think might be the dressing room, everyone else pulls me the other direction headed through this big door, beyond which is the stage. I can hear people clapping. I see the curtain going up, and then I'm awake, and sweating.

"It's weird, seeing your cell number," Cara says when I call her later after waffles and a shower. "I think there's some kind of emergency. I'm not used to it."

"Yeah well—" I want to joke, but can't quite.

"What's up? You coming over?"

"That still okay?"

"Me and Charley been waiting since seven."

And, like that, an hour later I am at the gate to Cara's, greeting the dogs who are pushing their big black noses at me through the front fence slats. Dad salutes happily before taking off, leaving me there in the pouring sunshine a moment. "We like Jake," and "Well, good, because I do too," was the majority of our family breakfast post-date conversation, which is slightly disappointing and a little weird, but mainly makes me feel giddily mature at the same time. And though the Rawlsons' horse farm seems like it's way out in the country, its only about fifteen minutes off the highway toward Stone Mountain, so there wasn't this big long gap of time in the car to fill with conversation either.

Not to mention, not much time to prepare for Cara. As I

near the house, she bounds out the screen door and I can't help smiling. "Morning!" she erupts, throwing her arms around me.

"Wow, you sure are in a good mood."

"Ah," she says, taking in a deep breath. "Pretty day. Pretty life. You know."

"You and Michael make up?"

"Never really fighting to begin with, actually."

"But I thought he—"

"Ah." She waves it off. "Just being protective, really. We're fine."

I wonder if this means they had, uh, *relations* again last night.

"You wanna ride?" She is grinning.

"Sure, let's go."

"'Cause, I mean, if you just want to sit here on the porch and bore me to death with every tiny detail of last night, I'm totally game."

I pretend to ponder. "Think I want you to try and drag it out of me first."

"Awesome. Let's go, then."

So then we're riding, and it's great. Once we get out into the field Cara goads her favorite horse Charley into a run, and Sunshine, the palomino, follows suit. We're too far apart to talk, but I wouldn't want to, anyway. Instead I just concentrate on my grip and let Sunshine do her thing without letting her forget I'm there. We cut diagonally across the whole property, a long stretch, and then bring them around across the back fence, before splashing through the creek and doubling back.

As we slow, Cara lets out a slow "Whooosh!" and I look over to see her grinning.

We slide off the horses to stretch out on the grass. "Oh, Gah, I was totally thinking of you last night!" She grabs my arm with an excited shake. "We were bowling with Todd and Wendy, and the whole time I kept looking at the clock going, 'Maybe they're straining for something to talk about at dinner right now. Maybe they're scooching elbows closer and closer at the movies. Maybe he's leaning in right now to kiss her!'" Her face goes kooky-wild with happy.

And it hits me, what a good date it really was, how good it is to be able tell her. All of it. Getting to dwell on every detail instead of acting as though boys don't matter.

"EEEEEEeeeeee!" she shrieks when I finish. "It is so, so great to have a friend who, you know, *gets* it!"

"Well, you know. It was still only a first date. There's no telling what will happen. I mean, we're certainly not you and Michael. . . ."

Her eyes shut down super-quick. "Yeah. Huh."

"Wait, I didn't mean—"

She pulls up some grass with her fist, twists the moist blades in her slim, dirt-rimmed fingers. She looks at her ring for a minute, then away from me, past the horses. "I put you in a spot," she says. "I mean, once Michael and I decided, I thought it was all so easy. But I guess . . ." She drops the grass. "I guess it isn't. I mean, not to everyone else."

"No, it's not like that." Except, looking where her eyes have gone, I know to her that must be how it feels. And, okay, if I'm honest she's sort of right. "Listen okay, yeah. It *is* weird. It's . . . this big, big thing, you know? The biggest. You seem really happy, so a lot of me wants to be happy for you too, but I—"

"You don't agree with my—choice." I see her swallow hard.

"Well—we . . ." I try to figure out what it is I'm thinking. "We promised."

It hangs between us. She sits up and drapes her elbows over her raised knees, hunching into herself. "My word is my bond," she murmurs.

"What?"

She looks at me. "My word is my bond. You know that—what is it?—Three Musketeers thing or something?" She shakes her head. "Thing is, Tab, I don't know anymore who I made that bond *with*. I mean, looking back I guess it was Walt I was promising, though now I don't see how my own body has anything to do with him or my other brothers. I don't even remember how it felt," Cara says, quiet. "Do you?"

"How what felt?" *You mean being a virgin?*

"How it felt to get the ring."

Immediately I do. Exactly.

"I mean." She lays back down next to me. "Maybe it's different because you and Morgan did it together."

"She got hers first."

"Still, you know? And Nomi's parents *did* invite her minister over."

I can't help chuckling.

"Shyeah." Cara snorts too. Naeomi's dramatic interpretation of her preacher's half hour blessing before the Sunday dinner when her parents presented her ring would get a million hits on YouTube for sure.

She rolls over onto her elbow and looks at me. "She still hasn't called me, you know. No e-mail, nothing. And I guess, I mean, it's awful, but I guess I can feel myself starting to get used to it. Kind of."

I can see she isn't really, though.

"And I think . . . I mean, I've had to think a lot this week, you know? And I think part of what made Nomi so mad was that I didn't tell her. I mean, that I didn't tell her any of it. You know how she was about Michael, and I guess even a long time ago I just sort of started not telling her things about him, because I knew she didn't want to hear it."

I realize I'm nodding.

"So there just kind of got to be this whole topic we avoided, so it didn't feel so . . . wrong. Wrong, I mean, not to tell her what he and I were thinking about doing. It wasn't like I was hiding it from her, really. It was just—"

"You just already weren't talking about it." The familiarity of this is upsetting.

She nods back. "That's what I meant about it being good to talk to you, even though I know you don't agree. Why it's nice, you getting it about guys. Because if there's anything I'd take back it's not telling her all along. I mean, if you can't share something with your friends . . ."

Her voice goes funny for just a second. She frowns, clears her throat.

"So I know I asked you not to tell Morgan anything, but I just keep thinking about what that might be like for you. I know this is a big thing to process, and I wanted to say that if you need to, you know, talk to her about it—talk to somebody else besides me—then I would really understand."

It feels like everything goes white. "I—I don't know what to say."

"Well, you can tell her whatever, you know? I mean, at this point it's not like she can blab it to Naeomi. And Pree I couldn't really care less—"

"No, I mean . . ." I sit up. My head rushes. "I mean, I really don't know what to say." Every part of my body is aware of the giant sky overhead, looking down on me.

"You already told her," she says after a minute.

"No, I—" I see her face and I can't stand it. "Yeah. Okay. Yeah, I did. But it wasn't like what you're thinking. I was trying to fix things with you and Naeomi, and she thought I was talking about me and Jake—"

She won't look at me, and the rescuing thing I get with Morgan comes over me. "Cara, I really was just sitting here, just now, trying to figure out how to tell you. It's why I came over. You just beat me to it. And I swear the only reason she knows is because I—"

"No." She faces me. "I meant what I said. She's your best friend. It's okay." She makes a noise like a broken toy laughing. "I mean, it's not like she and I were *best pals* before." This part is so poison, I wouldn't be surprised if the grass died around us.

"I'm sorry. I didn't mean to. I didn't just go and blab, I promise. It wasn't like that. I wasn't talking behind your back. It was an accident. And if it makes you feel any better, she isn't talking to me now either."

"Really?"

She's so honestly disbelieving I tell her all of it: my fumbled attempt at saving her and Naeomi, about Morgan's weirdness about me and Jake, about how it all came out in a giant horrible mess during lunch. How I left school early without even getting my books.

"Glag," is all she says when I'm done.

I realize Charley and Sunshine have disappeared, probably wandered back to the barn where they know they'll be fed. The shadows have shifted. I can hear the creek.

"Thank you for trying to make things better," she finally says.

I snort. "Yeah. Don't ask me to do it again, though."

She smiles, and it's a good one. "So . . . you mean now there's two of us drifting around, best-friendless?"

I'm not willing to give up that fast. I'm not sure Morgan won't come around, won't understand once she's had time to really think about it, but I'm smiling ridiculously, anyway, full of thanks. "Certainly neither of us can afford to lose any more."

She lunges and hugs me around the neck. I can't stop hugging her back.

chapter 15

Sunday morning, Mom drops me off for church and I settle into the clean, smooth pew, enjoying the families and couples, children coming in and taking seats all around me. I sit perfectly still, taking in the clean light, the cool crisp of the air, the echoey space up all the way to the peaked ceiling, high above. I hear the quiet greetings people give each other, the wood floor creaking when they slide into pews off the main carpeted aisle, the soft-as-possible footsteps of the choir entering in their two robed lines and moving to their seats at the back of the church.

The organ starts. Immediately something inside me feels straighter, calm. Serious but relaxed. I think the thing I like most about my church—the thing that attracted me even when I was seven—is that there's something about our Sunday service that makes me think of church at Walden Pond. There's just something very March family about the old sanctuary (built in 1807), the call-and-repeat prayers, the minimalist white lines and the giant organ with all its red velvet panels and Baroque pipes. And yet there's something counterculture here too: a kind of proactive energy running through the congregation that reinforces the Transcendentalist image: people working hard for a cause, a way of life, even if it isn't popular. It's a comfort almost stronger than Mom's curry corn, Dad tucking me in at night.

We stand for the call and response, the first hymn, and then the "Peace be with you," and exchange of handshakes or hugs. When I was little this was my favorite part, besides the singing, and I would enthusiastically hug everyone. Since going to church with Morgan so often, though, I realize not everybody likes to be embraced by strangers, so I just offer my hand, and hug only my old Sunday school teachers, Anna and Robert Westfall, who sit in the next pew.

Then it's time for prayers for thanks, forgiveness, and the world. Our ministers take turns saying prayers for different things (the soldiers, our leaders, other nations, members of the congregation who need special prayers, the poor, sometimes individual places or groups of people, forgiveness for our sins), and then there's some time for silent prayer before we say, "Lord, hear our prayer." I love the quiet, solemn chant of everyone around me, calling to God, praying for things both in and outside our own personal lives.

Today, though, I don't know what to focus on and my mind keeps wandering from good things to bad. Thankful? I'm thankful that my parents are trying to understand me, that they were cool about Jake, that I got to go on a great date and get kissed, that Cara is still my friend, that I—what? Am learning something? That it wasn't me who had to break my promise?

And forgiveness? What exactly needs to be forgiven, and where do I start? Do I need forgiveness for fighting with Morgan? For letting things get so off with her to begin with? For staying friends with Cara? For how things are changed with Naeomi and Priah?

I *can* pray for the world. I can pray for the people still fighting wars, for people dying, for victims of natural disasters or poverty or oppression. This I can pray for easily. But in my own life? My own world? Who needs me to pray for them most?

Before I know it I've barely prayed for anything, and we're already to the first reading. I try to remember what Marilyn said about prayer during our youth retreat to Ellijay last spring: that God understands, even if we do not, and the point is to continue to go to Him even when we aren't sure what we have to say— especially so then.

The next part of church was the most boring to me as a kid: a lot of reading and talking. This is the time I'd zone out, color my children's program, and only get excited when it was time to stand up and sing again, or to do the offering. I admit that even now sometimes I still let my thoughts drift, but more often I like to pay attention because it's fun to see how Pastor Tom weaves everything back together in his sermon.

Today's gospel lesson involves Jesus's parable of the Prodigal Son. This is a common story—one you go over lots in Sunday school, one we've talked about in youth group; today even Tom admits he has a hard time looking at it in more than one way.

Until, he says, he went on a neighborhood stroll with one of his friends from seminary, a man who teaches in New York. As they walked, Tom noticed a family walking together to the bus stop. The bus reached the stop before them, and everyone ran ahead to catch it. "Everyone," Tom says, "except the oldest gentleman with them." The grandfather of the rushing children. It wasn't that he couldn't speed up, Pastor Tom iterates, just that he didn't feel the need. Instead he walked patiently, even stopping at the crosswalk to look both ways, while the bus waited. Tom explains that it occurred to him then that you rarely see patriarchs—older men of position and standing—running for anything.

"And yet here Jesus says, 'But while he was still a long way off, his father saw him and was filled with compassion for him; he ran to his son, threw his arms around him and kissed him.' Here, the father—dignified, a property owner, past his prime—gathers up his robes, and even when his son is but a dusty speck down the road, the man *runs* to him." This, my pastor explains, is how God comes to us—running. Even just the sight of us coming down the road—seeking Him—overjoys the Lord so much that he runs to close the distance between us.

A sudden gush of relief comes through me then so fast that I start to tear up. No matter what we've done, God is running. Even if we squander everything He gives us, even if we break promises and make fools of ourselves and end up drunk in a *pigsty*, like the father in the prodigal son story—God is running. All we have to do is head in His direction.

I shut out the rest of the sermon and barely register the hymn and the offering afterward. Instead I pray. And this time I know exactly what I want to say.

• • •

After church I feel clearheaded and my whole body is loose, like after a good yoga class. I can't wait to get home, to call Cara and make sure she's coming to youth group tonight, to ask her if she's still been praying. I'm also going to call Morgan, I decide. If God can come running just at the sight of us, maybe my best friend can run back to me, so long as I head in her direction.

She beats me to it, though, my cell chiming immediately after I finish lunch.

"Hello?"

"Hey."

"Hey."

There's a quick quiet that feels long. Time enough to doubt.

"You just get back from church?" she asks.

"Mm-hmmm. Well, and we had lunch."

As though neither one of us knows exactly what the other one does every single Sunday. Already this isn't quite how I thought it would go.

"Going to youth group tonight too?" she wants to know.

I can't help but cringe a little. *You mean, am I seeing Cara?* "Probably. And then homework, you know."

"Yeah, we have some science." She sighs. "Chapter fourteen and then the questions afterward. I have notes, if you want to copy." This is a surprise, but a good one. Though I don't think either of us wants to go into why I wasn't there to *get* this assignment.

"Thanks. That helps."

"You okay?" She sniffs.

You mean post-date or post-fight or a little of both? "Yeah, I—"

"I figured you wanted to cool off a little."

I press my back into my bed frame. I want us to collapse now into *Oh my Gah I am so sorry we fought—I'm sorry, are you okay—I thought about you all weekend—how was your date—have you got your ring yet*—but she's stiff and weird still and it sets me on edge. Not that Morgan hasn't completely ignored fights between us before. It's just that she hasn't practically disowned me to my face before, and I'm a little on the defensive. But then again, maybe she is, too.

"Well," I go carefully. "Do you want to talk about it?"

"Of course I want to talk about it. I wanted to talk in biology, but then you weren't there and I figured you were mad so I haven't called until now."

My entire body relaxes. A rush of sweetness and relief comes over me and all I want to do is hug her. "Oh Morgs, I'm so sorry everything got so messed up."

"Yeah, I am too. Which is what I want to talk to you about. Priah's in but she's no help, and I tried calling Naeomi but she's total nowheresville this weekend—her phone isn't even *on*—so you and I have to figure out something for tomorrow."

"Tomorrow?"

"Figure out a way to make sure that it's clear that Cara is out and Naeomi is in."

That whitewashed feeling goes over me again. "What?"

A explosive sigh of disappointment comes through in full digital clarity. The peaceful good feeling I had after church has vanished. "Tabitha, don't do this to me."

"Don't do—?"

"Don't be dumb." The meanness in her is astonishing. "I thought after a couple of days you'd have come to your senses about all this."

"Come to my—"

"I swear to God, Tabitha—and in this case I really mean it— sometimes you amaze me. You really, truly, sincerely amaze me. Don't tell me that you're still thinking what Cara did was *okay*?"

"Well, it's—"

I see my talk with Cara yesterday: the way she listened, the way we were both honest. I think about the sermon today, about the total relief I felt, knowing God is there for all of us no matter what. But Morgan doesn't want to hear it. It's a completely disorienting feeling, with a little bit of "Oh crap" mixed in. This isn't just a fight. Something has *happened* between me and Morgan, and it freaks me out that the only person I could really talk to about this problem is the one who's causing it. There's a little part of me that wants to give in, but a bigger part of me—a part I didn't really know was there until now—isn't letting me.

"I'm not in sixth grade," I huff. "So stop talking to me like we are. Just because you think you have all the answers doesn't mean you actually do." I hurry on before she has a chance to interrupt me: "The truth is, Morgan, I don't really know what to think. I honestly don't. In a lot of ways I know what Cara did was completely wrong."

"Well, it's about time," she weasels in.

"But on the other hand I had hoped"—and here I start to

lose it a little—"that it would be something we could talk about. Something we could work out together. Help each other. But it sounds to me like you're not . . ." I have to take a deep breath. ". . . like you're not interested in much else than just shutting Cara out. Which I'm not willing to do yet. It's just not that cut and dry for me. So . . ." I start to fumble; my stomach quavers. "So I guess we still don't have very much to talk about. Thanks for the homework," I manage to mumble. "I'm sorry." And then I hang up on her.

I sit there for a second, completely surprised at myself, feeling guilty and really liberated at the same time. I wonder if she's as shocked as I am. For a minute I wait for my phone to ring again, for her to call back and cuss me out or maybe apologize and fix everything. But nothing happens. And I guess I don't blame her. Though I did it more out of cowardice, in her mind I've just done one of the rudest, meanest things possible in the middle of an intense conversation.

To her, I know, it might as well be a declaration of war.

I call Cara and tell her I'm skipping youth group. When she asks if I'm okay, I know she can tell I'm not, but I just say I have a lot of homework and I'll see her tomorrow. We decide to meet in front of the chorus room, and she offers to call later after youth group. I tell her I'm glad she's going, but to just fill me in in the morning.

Downstairs I check my e-mail. I have two new messages on Facebook: one a good-luck-on-your-date message from Priah on

Friday, and another one from Jake, simply wondering, "How was yesterday?" After talking to Morgan I'm pretty sure Priah's not my friend anymore so I don't answer her, but I do send Jake a quick e-mail, telling him that I followed his advice and it went well with Cara. I keep it short, though, because I don't feel like looking too long at my profile picture: me and Morgan grinning madly, our arms around each other's shoulders, holding our rings up for the camera.

But I guess that really *is* what I want to do, because after about an hour of reading the same paragraph of biology over and over, and then trying (unsuccessfully) to polish up my essay for English, the computer's a blur, and I find myself kneeling in front of my grandad's old trunk, the one I have at the end of my bed, filled with old diaries and paintings I did in preschool and a few tattered stuffed animals, my old binkie, and, most important, my scrapbooks. I lift out the big one for middle school: a fat, heavy one with a quilted-and-beaded cover that my aunt made for my eighth grade graduation.

I flip through the beginning quickly, passing dorky captions I wrote, pictures of me and Morgan and our friends, pictures of Mom and Dad and me on our trip to San Francisco and Seattle, birthday cards from Grandad and Granma before Granma died, Heart-O-Grams I kept from people I don't even know anymore, certificates for chorus and Beta Club and programs for my different shows, one big photo of Morgan from her first dance solo—page after page until I hit spring of seventh grade.

You can tell how important the Ring Thing was for me because

Pure

I made this huge section for it, filling the first page with only the photo of me and Morgan just before our special ring dinner, surrounded by a bunch of confetti and streamers I saved from the Ring Thing celebration. The two of us are standing in front of her fireplace; she's grinning directly at the camera and I'm smiling off to my left, where Dad was taking pictures too. Morgan's hair is much shorter than it is now, held back with a pale pink headband matching her ruffly, strapless pink dress. She's wearing her mom's pearls, and though it's not in the photo, she'd borrowed her mom's beaded pink clutch for the evening.

Next to her I'm wearing what was my favorite dress at the time, but looking at it now it's embarrassing what a giant bag it was on me. I'm wearing my mom's gold filigree earrings with blue beads hanging down from them, and a cuff bracelet of hers studded with real turquoise. Though you can't see in the photo, I know we both have on panty hose. I know Morgan's shoes are satin flats that match the ribbon in her hair, and mine are plain black pumps I'd had to get for chorus.

I stare at the photo a long time before flipping to the next page: more photos of me and Morgan around the fireplace, most of them less posed, then a shot of us waving from the backseat of her dad's Mercedes, and then the last picture Mr. Kent took before leaving us there together at the restaurant: us smiling and holding hands across the table.

It was our first time out together anywhere without parents, and still when I look at this picture I can totally feel the thrill of being in such a grown-up, fancy restaurant, being called "Miss" by the waiter, and knowing we could order absolutely anything—even just desserts all night if we wanted. I remember the whole time we thought people must be staring at us, wondering if we were famous tween movie stars visiting Atlanta for some secret TV shooting.

I remember giggling a lot, and mainly thinking this was a way-too-fancy way to make up for my missing Morgan's birthday slumber party because we'd had to go to Granma's funeral instead. Though the Ring Thing celebration had only been a few weeks before, I had no idea what she had in store for me.

I turn to the last page of the section, a picture I know so well I could draw it perfectly with my eyes shut. Mrs. Kent took it when she came to pick us up from the restaurant: a close-up of my hand resting over Morgan's, both of our rings glinting marvelously in the flash. Just in the background you can see the gold-rimmed plate, scraped clean of the strawberry cheesecake we'd shared.

She hadn't gotten down on her knee or anything embarrassing and dumb like that, but after dessert she had gotten all serious and even a little flushed, and took out this small pink box—the only thing in her purse besides some lip gloss. She got this really glittery, almost sheepish grin on her face as she slid it across the table at me.

"I used to be sad I didn't have a sister," she said, "but I'm not anymore."

I took the box then because I couldn't look at her. I didn't want her to see how jealous I had been about her ring, how grateful I was now to have one of my own. Inside, nestled in the groove of white velvet, was the prettiest ring I thought I had ever seen. My ring.

I put it on, and though it was a little loose, it fit. I remembered the Ring Thing celebration, the vows people had made down by the stage, some of them crying with happiness. I looked up at Morgan and her proud smile.

"I promise to be faithful," I said.

chapter 16

First thing Monday, Cara and I meet in front of the chorus room, and after I tell her about hanging up on Morgan, she gives me a hug and then works at making me laugh and telling me what I missed at youth group.

The rest of the school day progresses in its normal drone. Since the schedule rotated again, I actually have lunch with a few friends from chorus, and would with Naeomi too, but she's nowhere to be seen. I do see Morgan twice: once with Cody near the library, and the second time with Priah near her locker. I'm not looking out for her—not really—but if she's watching for me it doesn't show.

It's so sort-of normal that I almost expect her to be waiting for me outside bio, rolling her eyes, smiling, hugging me, and saying this is all ridiculous, isn't it? This, however, doesn't happen, nor does she look up once from her notes during the lecture, and when class is over I've gotten the message and just get up and leave.

Luckily now I have chorus last, so a day that starts with Cara ends with her too. After class we hug, say we'll call each other later, and she's off to the barn and I'm off to the Center, where, after med drop, Lacey has to do orientation with some new volunteers, so I don't get to tell her anything about everything else.

Rinse and repeat for Tuesday, except I don't have an English essay to turn in, PE is all about volleyball, I don't even try to make eye contact with Morgan in biology, and after school is yearbook instead of the Center. Extra bonus, Jake calls me the minute I get home, and we make plans for me to come see his lacrosse game on Thursday after school, plus a date together Saturday night.

On Wednesday morning, Mom's a little late and I'm a little harried, and we spend the drive to school in silence, both of us only half listening to NPR, consumed in our own thoughts. When we get to the drop-off circle, however, we look at each other, both with the exact same What The—? Face. Mom pulls along the curb, leaning forward a little to look. Standing there, in the widest part of the front walk, smack between the two drop-off circles (one for cars, one for buses), is Morgan, handing out flyers. She's shouting something, but with the windows up and radio on, we don't know what. Priah is with her, doing the same, along with two other girls: one from their dance team and another girl I've seen before but don't know.

I cock my eyebrow at Mom and hesitantly crack the window. In doing so I see Topher with them: tall and pale and freckled and gangly with vicious red hair. He's in Morgan's English class and has such a huge crush on her it's embarrassing. I can just imagine her approaching him about this. He is shouting the chant too with more enthusiasm than even Priah. His T-shirt is black with a white cross on the front, the top of it looped with a red crown of thorns. It is notable that he is here and not Cody.

"Pur-i-ty! Pur-i-ty!" they call, over and over. The other girls clap with every syllable, like this is a pep rally. I see Priah actually stick her fist up in the air to punctuate. Her T-shirt has a big white dove, and she smiles brilliantly at the crowd of morning bussers that pass, some of them accepting her flyers—most of them not.

"Umm. Tab?" Mom says next to me.

"Trust me, Mom. I have *no* idea."

When I look back at her she's smiling, though confused. "Well, good luck with that," she says.

"Shyeah." I kiss her quickly, deciding there's never going to be a good time to step onto that sidewalk.

Morgan must've spotted our car the minute we pulled into the circle, because when I turn from shutting the door, there she is with her blond ponytail, blue-and-white striped capris, and a T-shirt we used to make fun of: an outstretched hand pierced through the center with a big bloody spike. Across the top in Roman-looking letters, it screams: HIS PAIN YOUR GAIN. I can only imagine she borrowed it from Wedge, because it is huge and baggy and she's knotted it at her hip.

She sees me see her shirt and gives me one of her Miss Junior Yellow Rose grins. Her hand sticks out, shoving a flyer at me. "Come to our prayer group at lunchtime?" she chirps.

"You know I have first lunch this week," I growl at her. "What are you doing?"

"God listens to us no matter what time of day it is," she says.

"He is always ready to forgive us, as long as we admit we're wrong."

"Why are you doing this?" I glower. This is so not what Morgan's been about before. Besides the ring, she's always been like me, keeping church and school separate: loving God but not wanting to be all Look at Me I am a Cheerleader for Jesus about it, like some kids at her church.

For a moment the beauty pageant face is gone and her eyes go flat. "I decided I needed to try to do something to help keep people on the right path."

My mouth is full of things to say, all of them bad, so I move past her into school. I see Priah looking at me nervously, and out of habit I raise my hand to wave before she remembers and looks away again, picking up the chant with more fervor.

Cara's waiting for me outside of math. "Did you see?" She holds up the flyer. "Everyone's talking about this."

I take it from her to look closer, though it doesn't say much. Just:

PURITY!

PRAYER GROUP THIS WEEK DURING SECOND LUNCH

LOWER COURTYARD

There's a cross at the bottom, but Morgan's not the most techno-savvy girl when it comes to design. Still, the flyer and the chant and the pro-Jesus T-shirts took some coordination: She has obviously been working at this.

Cara reaches out to squeeze my elbow. "Sorry."

"About what?" I roll my head against the locker behind me.

"Sorry I corrupted you and turned your best friend into John the Baptist." Her mouth quirks into a smile, and her eyes twinkle with mischief.

Unfortunately I'm not ready to laugh about it yet. "Sorry. I just . . ." I sigh.

"You just suddenly realized you don't really know your own best friend at all?" she mutters. I can't do anything but nod. "Yeah, well—" But she doesn't have to finish.

Sprockett shuffles up to us then, and we step away from each other. "'Sup, Tab. Cara. Where you two been?"

"Standing right here, Sprock. Waiting for you." She gives him a high five.

"In the mornings, I mean."

Cara and I exchange a fast look. Ogling Priah must be a lot harder without an excuse for being at Morgan's locker.

Cara doesn't skip a beat: "Oh well, you know with the spring concert coming up we've been doing extra warm-ups in the chorus room. But thanks for being there for us. Can we e-mail you with questions?"

He moves from foot to foot, looming over us, shrugs. "Sure. Okay. Well, good luck with chorus."

"Thanks, Sprock." I pat him as he moves by us into the classroom, just as the bell rings. Cara and I swap another smile— this one genuine—and go in to brave geometry.

• • •

As soon as school is over I get a text from Naeomi, of all people: CAN U MEET @ JMNKY? I text back YES, change directions, and head toward the square, while calling Mom to let her know I'm not walking straight home.

It's weird, walking into the coffeehouse. Even though I was here—right here: challenging that very same counter girl and lifting up that very couch—only a week or so ago, I feel out of place, as though every head is now turned toward me, every face wondering, *What are* you *doing here?*

Fortunately Naeomi and I spot each other quickly, and I head to her table.

"Hey." As usual she is so flawless she looks cut out of a magazine. There is only the small frown in her eyebrows, the side of her mouth, that gives anything away.

"Hey."

"You want to get anything?" She is sipping ginger-pineapple juice on ice.

I shake my head, sit down. "How are you doing?" I watch her for signs as she shrugs and nods, says, "Okay."

"So . . ." I start, not sure if I'm supposed to say anything, or just listen.

"I can't stay long." She rushes. "And I probably should've just called you instead of making a big deal out of it."

"Big deal out of what?"

My interruption irritates her. "I just wanted to tell you I had nothing to do with this."

"I don't think I get—"

"With this whole"—she waves her hand in a loopy circle—"craziness this morning and at lunch. I don't know what you did, but she's really worked up."

"She hasn't told you herself?"

Naeomi takes a sip of juice, shakes her head. "Not exactly. But it doesn't take a rocket scientist."

I nod to that. It's why Morgan's so cranked that's harder to understand. Usually when she gets pissed off about something, she's all fire and temper tantrum for about an hour or two, but once she gets whatever it is out of her system (or just gets what she wants), she goes back to normal as if nothing happened. It took me years to figure out this pattern, but now it seems she's gotten a new one. That she was still mad enough about Cara and our fight to be this riled up days later? It says a whole lot. In a way, I'm actually kind of proud of her.

"But whatever. She can do what she wants," Naeomi goes on. "I'm surprised she got away with it, though. I don't even think it's legal."

"What? Praying? Isn't that, like, free speech?"

"Remember that school that got sued for praying before all their football games?"

Oh. I'd forgotten about that.

"Anyway. I just wanted to make sure you, and I guess Cara, knew that I want no part of her little revenge plan."

I have to pause. "You think this is about revenge?"

"I really don't care what it's about." She reaches for her purse under the table.

"Wait." I grab her arm and she looks at me, tired almost. "You want me to tell Cara?" Her eyes go away from me. "Nomi, why don't you just call her? She really misses you. She knows that you're mad she wasn't honest with you and she really—"

She snorts and leans back in her chair, crossing her arms. "You think this is because I didn't *know*?" Her eyes are flashing, her nostrils in that intimidating flare that is going to give her an exceptional advantage in the courtroom, or on the Senate floor. "I knew a long time before she did. Soon as school started and he kept coming around, instead of disappearing like we thought. Soon as she started carrying around Emerson and Rumi, writing in her stupid journal instead of doing her homework. I knew. I knew all *along*. You think I didn't *know*?"

"Well, then." I feel like her ferocity makes me stupid. "I guess I just don't understand why you—"

"Look, Tabitha. I appreciate it, but I tried to talk to her. I tried so many times. You don't understand. Michael—she can't see anything but him: not reason, not her friends, not her GPA. . . . Do you *know* how bad she's doing in school?"

I shake my head, trying to remember the last time Cara talked about anything school-related, really.

"Yeah, well, I do. Did. And she knew I knew. And she knew what I thought. And instead of even trying to listen to me, she just started lying. Making up that she'd be studying or working, when really she was with Michael or at least talking to him on the phone. I was sick of it already at the beginning of the year, but I kept saying, 'She needs you because she doesn't have anybody else talking sense.'"

It's weird hearing some of my own thoughts coming out of Naeomi's mouth.

"And then when she told me she'd gone ahead—" She doesn't say it, but I see her picture it for a quick second before her eyes go even harder: so intense it almost makes me want to cry. "I just couldn't—" She must hear how angry she sounds, because she unclenches her juice glass, leans back, looks around. When she turns back to me, she looks calmer, but also sad. "You think, I guess, that like Morgan I'm against Cara because she broke her promise to God."

I shrug, not sure what I think.

She holds up her left hand, wiggles her ring at me. "You know what this says to me, Tabitha? This ring?" She looks at it herself. "It doesn't say, 'I love Jesus.' It doesn't say, 'I'm better than all of you because I'm a virgin.' This ring, to me, it says, 'I give myself to God,' sure. And I do. But more than that? When I look at this ring?" She looks up at me again. "What I remember is my vow to my*self*."

She takes a breath then, and I do too, before she plunges on: "Morgan . . . she's making this into some kind of, I don't know. Some kind of holy war that's about choosing sides. I'm sorry the two of you are fighting, but if you ask me, she doesn't care one lick about Cara. She just cares about her statement. Which is her thing and I don't even want to get into it."

I can see her lips are pursed around all the things she doesn't want to get into, so I stay quiet.

"Look," she goes on. "I'm glad you're looking out for Cara. I'll warn you, though. It's like she's under a spell. And I couldn't watch it anymore, couldn't act like I thought it was all okay and great. It's not because she went back on her promise that I had to step away. It's because after everything we've talked about, after all that girl has been through to try and raise herself above her mule-class background, after all her hard work, she went right ahead and did the first and best thing that'll keep her on that farm with her jackass brothers the rest of her life. Because of some *boy*, she'll either fail school or get knocked up or both, and I just couldn't stand by and act like it was wonderful. She wouldn't be reasonable when I was there by her; maybe she will think harder now that I'm not."

She's so intense I half expect to be blinded by rays of truth beaming out of her eyeballs. I'm stunned, listening to that. Part of my brain knows she's completely right. It's a little mean, but it's true. The rest of me, though, is shocked I've never considered that what Cara's done could result in a lot more than a busted-up clique of girls, or a fight with her brothers. I got so focused on the promise part, I forgot completely all the trouble that our promise keeps us out of.

I don't know what to say. I don't know what to do. All I know is, I wish I could talk to Morgan even more badly than before.

"You understand me a little more now?" Naeomi finally says.

I feel myself nodding, realize she does need some kind of affirmation for all that. "I just don't know what to do."

Her face goes sympathetic. "I know. Believe me, this isn't easy for me. It's less hard, since I can focus on SGA and practice SAT tests, dance, my own church. . . ."

"She's still coming to youth group," I tell her. "If you want to know."

She nods. "That's good, I guess. And I do mean it that I'm glad that someone has an eye on her. I just knew it couldn't be me anymore right now."

I suddenly understand all the times people have said breaking up isn't easy on anyone, no matter who seems to be most at fault. "Are you ever going to talk to her?"

She shrugs, and it's so sad. "I don't know. We've all been changing anyway, you know? Maybe this was inevitable. We'll see."

"Do you want me to tell her we talked?"

Again, just a shrug of her slim shoulders. "I don't know if it makes a difference, really. She already knows everything I've said to you. Has heard it a hundred times. So . . . I guess, unless you feel like you need to, no. I just wanted to be clear with you, make sure you understood that what Morgan's doing has absolutely nothing to do with me."

"Is it weird with you and her too, now?" It hadn't occurred to me that the morning locker group may be reduced to really only Morgan and Priah.

"It's okay still at dance so far—we have a similar vision, and we do well together, so long as she doesn't get too bossy." She sly-smiles up at me, showing the front tooth-gap I love so much. This time I'm the one to snort. "But really even if things were okay with me and Cara, I'm studying so much, or at a meeting . . ."

"I think it's really cool, by the way," I'm moved to tell her. "How hard you work. I'm sure it's stressful but I really admire you. Sometimes I'll feel like not doing my homework or something—screw around on the Internet or watch TV or whatever—and I'll think, 'I bet *Naeomi* is doing homework right now,' and I'll go and hit the books."

She smiles a little. "I've got to go," she says, checking her phone for the time. "Really have to go. But listen—" Her hand covers mine. "I don't think all guys are evil, you know. And I hope Jake's being cool to you."

I grin at her, relieved. "So far so good. But don't worry; I won't get carried away."

She stands up, smoothes the creases in her seersucker pants. "See to it that you don't. I've still got your number, you know." And with that, she waves and strides out the door.

I watch after her for a long time, even when she's out of view. I realize that's probably the longest talk I've ever had with Naeomi, really. It makes me incredibly sad, since our first real conversation, after everything, might actually be our last.

chapter 17

On my walk home I try to sort everything out. On the one hand, I feel really good that Naeomi and I talked. On the other hand, I'm not sure how what she said affects how I feel about Cara. Or, for that matter, Morgan. If the ring is more about reminding yourself not to get bogged down in the world of boys and dating, as Naeomi suggests, then is it really a sin to stop wearing it? I mean, it might be a bad decision, but is it totally condemnable? Is it on par, for example, with murder? Or even stealing?

But maybe by even allowing for that doubt, for thinking the ring and my promise might be anything other than a holy vow, maybe I'm already sinning. Maybe doubting is just as bad. Maybe I am, like Morgan thinks, going down the wrong path.

Because, in the Bible, it *does* say that your body is a temple. So, defiling it in any way must be against God. But, it occurs to me, I'm not really sure what Jesus *actually* says about sex. I can't remember any passages, only other people attributing different things to Him. There is that whole weird Song of Solomon chapter in the Bible—what about that? I mean, it talks about kissing, and *breasts*. (I know this because looking at Song of Solomon for all the dirty parts was the main focus for my Sunday school classmates, before I started going to church with Morgan in sixth grade.) So, is sex—if you really love the other person—as awful as we're made to think? I mean, besides diseases and pregnancy, which, Naeomi's right, could be pretty terrible. But all that just takes me back around to wondering if, by even doubting, I'm somehow doing something wrong.

And then my phone rings. I get a little thrill, seeing it's Jake, but I'm also wildly embarrassed that the last thought in my mind involved the sexy parts of the Bible and getting pregnant. Still, it's a relief to be distracted.

"Tabitha."

"No, actually. This is Jake. The only Tabitha I know I think I'm talking to." We both laugh at what is, I guess, now our joke.

"How was your day?"

"Eh. You know. School. S'okay."

I wish I had so little a summary to give myself.

"Listen," he goes on. "I've got to pick up my brother and take him to piano so I can't talk long. Just wanted to see if you're still up for tomorrow?"

I grin. "Tomorrow?"

He hesitates. "Oh. Thought you might want to still come to—"

I can't torture him. "I know, I know. Yes, I can't wait to see you play."

"Cool. I'll e-mail you the directions later tonight, okay?"

"Sure." It strikes me how easy this conversation is, how not-nervous I am.

"Good. Look, I'm almost at the school and I can't let Austin catch me talking on the phone while I'm driving. He's ruthless."

"Okay. Well, tell Austin hi and have a good afternoon."

"Okay, you too."

"Later then."

And, remarkably, my grin lasts me the rest of the way home.

In the kitchen I grab some cucumber sticks and Wheat Thins and aim for a little homework, which is history, and which I detest. In fact, ten minutes into it I'm totally tempted to copy someone else's chapter summary tomorrow. But it's not just because I hate my history class. More it's that I have a rare hour or two until Mom and Dad are both home, and that whole "What did Jesus say about sex" thing is still lurking in my mind. If I knew for sure that Jesus thought it was unforgivable, it might be easier to understand why Morgan does. I go downstairs to the computer to see what I can drum up.

My first try, typing "abstinent" into the searchable online Bible site, brings nothing. Daniel in the Old Testament abstains from the king's food and wine, but that's it. Typing in "sex and marriage" (which makes me a little paranoid that somehow my parents will see I typed the S-word into the computer) yields nothing really, either. The marriage bed should be kept pure, is all. Which of course makes sense, though when I try "celibate," I get, "Sorry, no results for CELIBATE in your search."

I know this can't be right. There *has* to be stuff in the Bible, because otherwise where would any of us get this idea about the ring from? I decide to just go to Google and type "Abstinence in Bible." And, hooray, immediately a bunch of articles pop up. The first one I click on says that the Bible is clearly against sex before marriage, and it lists a ton of instances in the Scriptures to back this up. I feel a kind of bubbliness spread across my shoulders and into my hands. Finally some clear-cut answers about who is right and who is wrong. I can't believe, really, I haven't done this before. But, I guess, I also haven't had these weird questions come up before either.

I copy down the verses and then go back to my searchable Bible and type them in, but the bubbly feeling sizzles and dissipates. Over and over again, all I find are passages about "sexual immorality." Of course everyone knows that keeping the marriage bed pure means not coming to it with a spoiled body, but I'm surprised a little, I guess, that in a book where it talks specifically about how many people were in what family, or what kind of sacrifice to make when, and what exactly to eat, there isn't also a long laundry list of sexual sins, too. One passage I find condemns a man for it, though what he does is sleep with his father's wife (adultery, a no-brainer). Another one fills me with a small amount of hope—referring to sexual immorality and punishment by death—but when I click to read the entire Deuteronomy story, the man and woman at fault are stoned because she was engaged and so he, by sleeping with her, has essentially taken another man's wife (but if she wasn't engaged, would that matter?), and her death seems more about the engaged thing too, rather than the whole premarital aspect.

Maybe I'm not doing my search right; maybe if I talked to Pastor Tom, things would be spelled out more simply, but there's no chance to really explore this more on my own right now, since Dad will be home any minute, and I really don't want to deal with him razzing me about my little sex-in-the-Bible search. Finally, I click on the one link that comes straight from the Gospels, which I know will have something to do with Jesus. In a glance, however, I see that passage also just talks about not being sexually immoral, without really defining what, exactly, that entails.

I put the computer to sleep. I don't really need the Bible to explain to me what I know in my heart to be right, but I wish it had helped me understand a little more where Morgan's vehemence might be coming from. If there was something concrete backing her up—something really irrefutable—I'd know, at least, what inspired her anger.

I hear the garage door opening and Dad pulling in then. At least, for a little while, I can just concentrate on helping with dinner.

"Helping" is mainly keeping Dad company but staying out of the way. I kneel up on one of the high stools at the counter, leaning across to watch. He asks me about my day. When it comes back to me—Morgan this morning, Naeomi this afternoon—I'm not sure where to start.

"Dad," I try as he drizzles olive oil into a sauté pan.

"Yes, my child," he booms in Opera Voice.

"Do you know anybody who has really strong morals?"

He turns, hand to his chest. "You mean besides your wise and steadfast parents?"

"I'm serious." I snatch a piece of broccoli from the cutting board across from me.

"Well," he turns back to the oil, tosses in some chopped garlic. "We had a couple friends in grad school who were pretty serious about Tibet. Wouldn't buy anything made in China and things like that. Strict-o vegetarians. Pains in the butt, really." He shoots me a wink over his shoulder while stirring the garlic, which smells amazing.

Mom comes in from work then, balancing bag and laptop and an armful of papers. We help her with her load, kiss her enthusiastically. She shoves her shoes off under the table, rumples up her hair. "How was your day?" she asks me, pointed.

"Oh, that. It was—"

"We're talking about people with moral backbones," Dad interrupts. Mom's eyebrows immediately go into a question at me.

I shrug. "I was just wondering if you knew anyone who really believes in anything." At first Mom chortles. "I mean believed in stuff so much they'd be willing to, you know, stand up for it. Even if it was really tough." I see Priah's fist up in the air. Morgan gripping the flyer so hard it could burst into flames. Naeomi ignoring Cara's desperate calls. All of them having a clear idea of what to do, knowing—from somewhere—what's right and what's wrong.

"Of course I do," Mom says, semi-defensive.

I climb back up on my stool, looking at both of them. "Who then?"

"Well, my students are always getting up in arms about something," she starts. This time Dad laughs. "A lot of the time it's even something that really matters. They protest. They march. They write letters. They boycott."

"There's the Bushovens too," Dad contributes.

"And some of our other friends. Why, even your beloved mother has made an appearance at a march or two."

"Really?"

She nods. "But that's not who I thought of when you asked."

I snatch another piece of broccoli. Dad sees and swats me with his wooden spoon. "Who, then?"

"Well, I'm looking at her," she says, matter-of-fact.

"What?"

"Ah, Our Lady of Moldy Bath Towels," Dad says.

"Eliot, I'm serious."

"So am I," Dad says, mock innocent. "It takes a lot of moral fiber to withstand such constant resistance from doggedly oppressive authority."

"Da-aaad."

"No, really," Mom says, turning in her chair to face me. "You've been very serious about your beliefs, Twink. You've gone to church practically every Sunday since we took you in the first place, and you've stuck with it even though we haven't always been the most enthusiastic. It's something I really admire about you. And I'm sure it's not easy, considering most kids around here don't share the same feelings you do."

This certainly isn't what I expected to hear. It's nice, but it doesn't really help. "I don't think about it that way."

"Well," Mom pauses. "Maybe you should."

I change the subject then, making sure the details are all settled for tomorrow: Mom picking me up after school and taking me over to Jake's game, that he'll give me a ride home after, in time for dinner. I also ask them about going out with him Saturday night, suffering a rain of teasing from my dad while he rinses the pasta.

On the outside I'm the dutiful cool daughter, doing my best to entertain my parents and let them know I'm normal, while inside I'm divided. Mom says she admires me for sticking to my beliefs. The only problem is, my beliefs are suddenly on opposite sides, and I'm the rope being pulled between.

chapter 18

The next morning Morgan's outside again, with Priah and Topher and everybody from yesterday, plus more, including Cameron and his friend in the tutu at the dance. They're still handing out flyers for lunchtime prayer group, but today they're not shouting. Even if they were it'd be impossible to hear them over the other two groups out there: a gang of kids in all-black holding up a hastily made poster that says PUNKS FOR PEACE and chanting "All you need is love (and rawk)!" over and over, and another group of guys (most of them in the Golf Club), wearing ties and yarmulkes, reciting the prologues to all six Star Wars movies, in chronological order. They've got flyers too, and as I pass by one that's dropped to the ground I see it says, JEWS FOR JEDIS. FEEL THE FORCE AND MEET WHENEVER YOU CHOOSE. They're smart-alecks mainly: popular boys who loaf around in econ class and who take Spanish because (a) it's easy, and (b) Ms. Heermans, the Spanish assistant, is young and hot. I happen to know most of them aren't Jewish, either.

I don't stick around, but at lunch my chorus friends are talking all about how, probably not long after I walked by, Mr. Bell, the assistant principal, came through with one of the resource officers and broke everyone up.

"I heard one of the punk kids got expelled," Krista says, licking her fingers clean of potato chip crumbs.

"Don't be stupid," Amelia guffaws. "Nobody can get expelled for that."

I think about my talk with Naeomi yesterday, her suggestion that prayer during school isn't legal.

"It's obvious they all just want attention," Opal groans with poised judgment. Krista elbows her and looks at me. "Ooops," Opal says, holding her multi-ringed hand up to her mouth, only half covering her smile.

"I just hope everyone doesn't get really pissed at each other," Amelia sighs, "and they cancel Maverick Mayhem because of just a few stupid groups."

Everyone frowns. It isn't likely that the school's largest and most anticipated activity besides Prom and Homecoming would be cancelled—we do a full-page spread covering it in the yearbook, after all—but since Mayhem is just one big talent competition between the extracurricular groups and clubs who want to participate, I guess it could get ruined if different organizations started ganging up on each other. And if the competition on Friday night got messed up, it would ruin the Mayhem formal on Saturday, too. So maybe it could be disastrous. But after a minute Opal breezily insists they'd never cancel something as big as Mayhem, since ticket sales for it and the dance pretty much fund the entire football team.

While I'm at my locker between classes, Cressida, of all people, saunters over to me, bringing with her a nearly visible cloud of perfume and pride.

"You did the right thing, dumping her," she drawls, leaning against the lockers and cocking out her hip in order to expose her bony pelvis—and half her thong.

She's baiting me and I won't give it to her. "I didn't dump anybody. I don't know what you're talking about." I pretend I can't find my biology notebook, though my locker's so organized that my mom'd think I was somebody else's child.

"You know who I'm talking about." She smiles around her wad of gum. "She's a whacko. You should've seen her at lunch when Andy and Jeff decided to give her a dose of her own preachy medicine. She didn't seem to like the taste of it much."

I shut my locker, turn to her. "Cress, what are you talking about? I've got to go."

She shrugs, looks at people passing, her face full of judgment. She's not even carrying books. "Just did a little dance, sang a little song, you know." She acts bored but she's loving it. "I hear they're thinking of making it the Golf Club's Mayhem routine for her."

My cheeks are burning. I don't understand really what happened but I understand enough to know the Jews for Jedis are just being plain mean.

"She's allowed to express herself." I try to sound calm but I'm not.

"Whatev." She waves me off. "Just wanted to let you know you're better off. See ya." And with that she saunters away, those skinny hips swaying in her tight black jeans.

I hurry to bio class, partly because Cressida's already made me late, but also because I'm wondering if I might catch Morgan outside before the bell. When I turn the corner to our room, she's there all right, but so is Cody. Neither of them looks very happy. She sees me, and maybe I'm imagining it but her face gets a shade redder when she does. I drop my head, move to the other side of the hall to give them as wide a berth possible. As I pass them into class I hear Morgan say something about "you believed too," and, definitely, "I thought you'd back me up."

All during Mrs. Laboutin's lecture I keep trying to sneak looks over at Morgan. She's hunched over her notes, and won't look up at anyone—not me, not the teacher, not anybody. She doesn't even push her hair back away from her face. I notice other people in class are looking at her too, some of them smirking, and I suddenly feel horrible for her, want to tell everybody to mind their own business and leave her alone. *She's just sticking up for what she believes*, I want to say. *Even if you don't think she's right, at least she's doing something.*

It makes me think, all of a sudden, about Jesus and the people in His life: all of them watching Him do these amazing and sometimes dangerous things, listening to Him preach, thinking sometimes He's definitely talking with the voice of God, other times wondering if He should just be locked up like the Romans and Pharisees say. Being scared for believing in Him, and at the same time, afraid not to. Is Morgan more like Him then, because she's the one who's out there? And I wonder, if I'm not with her, does that make me—no matter what I say—that much less like Him?

I meet Cara at the crossroads so we can walk to chorus. I'm trying to figure out how to ask her if she still feels Christian, but she has other things on her mind.

"Did you hear?" she says right away.

"You mean about this morning? A little." We push through the crowd, banging books and knocking elbows.

"Lunch, I mean. They were all gathered in the lower courtyard, praying maybe."

I remember what Cressida told me. "Did you see them?"

"I couldn't help but watch. It's kind of fascinating, you know?"

Briefly I'm irritated. I wonder if Cara understands that this fuss is basically about her. Maybe she's even a little excited about it. I think of Naeomi and our talk yesterday.

"It wasn't a big deal at first. They were just sitting there. Almost normal-looking. No chanting or anything. Cameron had a Bible. And then the Jedi jerks come up, standing around the edge, acting like they're listening, at first."

We get to the chorus room and Opal's there. She joins us.

"You talking about lunch?"

Cara nods, goes on. "And then all of a sudden they just break into this stupid dance, singing that awful Roots song about the seed."

"Rich," Opal says, grinning. I feel an awful twinge, thinking people are *happy* Morgan's getting harassed.

"What'd she do?" I ask.

"Nothing. Just ignored them. But you could tell she was pissed."

"I'll say," Opal retorts. "Did Malik really tell them to quit?"

Cara nods. Malik is president of Reach, the Black History Preservation club at school. They do readings of Dr. King speeches and other Af-Am lit, and a few of them are on the Brain Brawl team for their specialty. Last year they did a re-enactment of a slave auction. It was pretty intense. Malik's also in the gospel choir, and in SGA with Naeomi. He's apparently really into the Masons, too, and wears a tie to school every day.

"I didn't hear what he said to them, but he did go up there."

Opal jumps in. "I heard he just said that in America, no one can be persecuted for their beliefs."

I'm impressed. "He said that?"

"'Swhat I heard." Opal shrugs.

I'm not hiding my worry well. Cara elbows me. "You okay?"

"We have to go in," I tell her. She frowns slightly and nods.

But after chorus she's over to my chair immediately. "Look, I'm sorry. I know this is all really weird. And hard. I wasn't thinking."

I sit back down in my chair while everyone else pools out of the room. "Everything is just so messed up."

"You still haven't talked?"

I shake my head. "I just don't know what she's thinking. I don't know what I'm supposed to do."

Cara's eyes go understanding. "You mad at *me*?" And for a minute I don't know how to answer this. On the one hand, yes, I absolutely am. If Cara hadn't gotten so swept up, hadn't broken her promise, hadn't done what she did, none of this would've happened. Maybe we'd *all* be going to Jake's lacrosse game together today, giggling and cheering, instead of walking wide circles around each other at school, divided. But on the other hand, in the last week I've also gotten a lot closer to Cara, and no matter what, she *is* a good friend. Like even now, she understands I don't know what to think, instead of getting frustrated with me for being unsure. And she's been there for me, more than Morgan, in my excitement about Jake. Besides that, things with Morgan *were* weird before all of this, anyway. So maybe it isn't really Cara's fault. Maybe Naeomi's right and something like this would've happened anyway; Cara just managed to be the reason. It could've just as easily been something Priah did. Or Naeomi. Or me.

"No. I'm not mad," I finally say.

"You sure?"

I look at her. She would never, I realize, drop one of us. She still doesn't hate anybody for what they believe. Not even Naeomi. Not Morgan either.

"Yeah, I'm sure." I purposefully look her in the eye.

"Good. Because you are going to be *late* to that lacrosse game, and you can't be, because after the game you're asking Jake to the Mayhem formal."

I'm surprised. "I'm *what*?"

"Michael and I decided we're double-dating with you and Jake." Her face is full of crazygrin.

"But that's, like, next weekend."

"I know!" She stands, hauls me up with both hands. "So we have to go shopping *this* weekend for dresses."

"But I thought you'd—"

"I haven't been to a single dance this year, Tab, and this is almost my last chance." She's pulling me by the arm now, toward the door.

"But—what if—" I'm fumbling but I have nothing. Only that the idea of asking Jake to go with me to a formal makes not only butterflies, but woodpeckers, kangaroos, and dancing circus horses tromp through my stomach.

"Just go," she says, smiling. "Ask him. And call me the minute you get home."

I promise and then hurry to the front of the school, where Mom's waiting.

"I can't believe I actually had to wait for you this time," she says when I climb in.

"Sorry about that. Had to wrap something up with Cara."

"She okay?"

"Yeah. She wants to double-date for the Mayhem dance." I'm still breathing a little hard from running the distance of the school.

"Not Morgan?" Mom says as casually as possible as we pull out. I realize I still haven't really clued either of my parents in on what's

175

actually been going on in the last week. Mom knows Morgan and I had a fight, knows about the rallies before school, but I've pretty much kept quiet about everything else. It isn't because I don't want them to know; it's just that once I start talking my parents will have all kinds of annoying questions and opinions that I don't want to deal with. I have a sneaking suspicion, for example, that my mom would have more than one thing to say about free-range praying in a public school, and Dad would probably want to join Jews for Jedis himself.

"Go right up here at the next light," I instruct.

"Tab, is everything okay?"

I pretend to be squinting for the street name. "Sure, Mom."

She makes Sometimes I Really Wonder Why I Had You Sigh. "Well, I'm glad Cara's all right, at least."

Paranoidly I wonder if somehow she knows. "What do you mean?"

"Some big crisis last week? Late-night hysterics?"

"Oh. Right. That." I forgot that whole thing. The part about my parents being involved, at least. "We're looking for a Kroger up here, I think. And then the left-hand lane after that."

"Well, I'm sorry about whatever's happening with you and Morgan. But I like Cara a lot. She seems like a really with-it girl."

This gets my attention. "What?" I look at her, then remember I'm supposed to be helping find the landmarks. "There. I think that's it. Okay, get over." Mom checks her mirrors, slides in between two cars.

"She just seems really easy in her own skin. Like she knows herself really well and actually likes herself. She seems—ah, grrr . . .

176

Is this it?" We've reached a big recreation complex with about a dozen baseball diamonds, some tennis courts, and at least three fields, where there is clearly some kind of sport involving lots of running, pads, and sticks going on.

"Looks like it," I say, barely registering that we're here. "She seems like what?"

Mom wrangles the old Volvo up the potholed drive and pulls alongside some other cars, one a station wagon with the back open. Two girls in short shorts and hoodies are sitting together, swinging their legs and drinking giant Frappuccinos. They look over and scrutinize me. I had forgotten there'd be other girls here too. Maybe even girls here to see Jake. I look back at Mom, who's trying to see over to the lacrosse.

"Ma." I try to get her to focus back on me, to finish what she was going to say. "Cara. You were going to say she seems . . . ?"

"Oh." She blows out a breath. "She just seems really mature for her age. You know." She looks at me for a minute. "More like a young woman. Instead of just a girl."

For some stupid reason this makes me, of all things, blush.

"Not that you're 'just a girl,'" Mom adds quickly.

I shake my head, brushing that off. "Looks like they started already," I say instead.

"You better get out there, cheerleader."

I snort. But it takes me a second to move. Looking at those girls—trying not to look—I somehow don't want to get out of the car. But he's expecting me, so I make myself lean over and hug Mom around the neck. "See you at home."

"See you at home," she agrees. As she backs out, she waves, but only through the windshield, instead of wildly out the window, which I appreciate.

I walk past the two girls in the open car, not looking at them looking at me. I concentrate instead on the field of green-and-gold jerseys, white helmets, white sticks, trying to remember what Jake's number is. I almost think I've spotted him but then as I get closer a whistle blows, and all the guys but three run farther down the field, changing places, mixing up, and I lose him. I climb up on the metal bleachers to about the fifth row, sitting near the end so I can be visible without being too obvious.

After leaning forward on my knees and pretending to be really focused on what's happening at the far end of the field, I sneak a look around at everybody else on the bleachers. There aren't really that many people here: a cluster of kids together up on the top rows, talking more than watching, a few moms down in front of me, clapping loudly and shouting encouragement, two obvious freshman boys wearing Seymour T-shirts. Everybody seems to know each other, but nobody, so far, seems to care about the Lone Girl Who Doesn't Belong, which makes me relax a little. At least no one's leaned over to ask me if I'm sure I'm at the right field.

There's some more running around, some lining up. I see Jake, smile uncontrollably and self-consciously, lose him again. Finally there's a loud long whistle and play stops. Either the game's over or there's some kind of break or something, because the team starts running over to the sidelines, grabbing water bottles and spraying them over their heads, into wide-open mouths. All except one.

Pure

One of them keeps going, headed for the bleachers and—oh—right toward me. It's amazing how fast everything else from today flies completely from my mind.

"Hi." He's smiling like crazy. And breathing hard. And very sweaty. *And, oh God, leaning up to kiss me now right in front of everyone; I'm not*—He is salty. And a little musty. And very, apparently, mine.

"Hi," I say back finally, trying to not look totally shocked that he just claimed me in front of all these people.

"I'm glad you made it. You understand what's going on?" He gestures to the field with his helmet.

I nod. "I mean, I think so."

"You meet anybody yet?" he wants to know. I start to shake my head, wonder who there is to meet, but his coach starts clapping hard and shouting what are, I guess, instructions.

"I gotta go," he apologizes.

"I see."

He is still—so—smiling. "So I'll catch you?"

Yeah, because I might pass out and fall off this bleacher. I nod. "Do good," I say.

He points his fingers at me like a gun and runs backward to the bench. "I'm glad you came!" he says again before joining the, I guess, huddle.

The whole rest of the game I see what's going on, but not really. Sometimes his jersey swims up out of the scrambling throng, sometimes I remember to clap once everyone else does, but mainly all I see until he runs up to me again after the game is his face coming pink and sweaty out of that helmet, and smiling and moving *straight at me.*

• • •

"You were supposed to call me as soon as you got home," Cara says when I finally call her after dinner.

"I know but we had to eat. I didn't get home until almost six."

"Oh-*ho*-ho!" she sings on the other end.

"No." I am blushing again. *Will I ever stop doing that?* "Not like that. One of the railroad crossings was closed because of construction and traffic was really backed up."

"Gave you plenty of time to talk, I guess," she teases.

"I guess," I tease back.

"So did you *ask* him?"

"About what?" I am horrible at feigning disinterest.

"Oh, nothing." She is equally as bad as I am.

But then I can't help plunging into the entire description, how I'd waited—my throat full of dry oatmeal—while he relayed his history class debate about whether or not the Founding Fathers had intentionally left out blacks and women in their Constitutional lingo, before I finally stupidly said, "Well, do you think they intentionally left out the part about you and me going to this formal at my school next Saturday?" How I nearly choked on the silence that followed, dying a little at the thought that he'd laugh—even if it was a good laugh—before he said, "I think it's actually in there. Article seven or something? But do I have to wear a tux?" How suddenly it wasn't a big deal at all but just something we were going to do.

There's a bunch of squealing and giggling and discussion about colors and when exactly we should shop. Friday I have to work at the Center, and Saturday Cara has a riding class to handle, and then we both have dates that night, plus homework and youth group on Sunday. I can't believe my calendar is so full really, even without Morgan.

"What about Sunday, before youth group?" Cara suggests, and a hundred Sundays spent with Morgan swim up before me. "Maybe we could meet at Perimeter? Grab some waffle fries and hit it?"

"Well . . ." It occurs to me that if I'm going to really be doing something different—not going to Morgan's, not getting my picture taken in front of that fireplace—I want to be doing something *really different*. "There's this vintage place in Little Five that Lacey really likes and I thought maybe—"

"That's so much more perfect." I wonder if she, too, wants to avoid the mall and too much nostalgia.

"Okay, it's a date, then." I realize I'm smiling. Incredibly excited, even.

"I'm so happy," she sighs. There's about a dozen things she could mean by this: happy we're going together, happy to be shopping at a cool and different place, happy we're friends, happy for me and Jake, happy about Michael—I decide to just accept happy though, and leave it at that.

"Me too," I tell her.

And even while I'm brushing my teeth two hours later after homework, getting ready for bed, I feel, deep down, that even after everything, I truly am. Happy.

chapter 19

Friday morning Mom has a meeting, so we're relatively early. When we get to school, it's apparent that a lot of other people made an effort to be early too: the drop-off circle is an absolute circus.

"Tab," Mom starts.

"I promise I'll tell you everything this weekend," is all I say, eyeing the crowd.

"Okay. Love you." I get out, we smile at each other, and she moves off into the line of cars.

The groups around the drop-off circle have expanded so much they spill down into the lower courtyard. Of course Morgan's group is there, loud as ever, and they've grown in numbers even since yesterday. Still, they've got a lot of competition. The Punks for Peace have doubled, and the Jews for Jedis have apparently recruited too. They've also had time to plan a cheer, mainly involving the word "Hail."

But that's not all. To my surprise, Cody, plus a bunch of the baseball team (including the less surprising Todd and Skip Rawlson) have also decided not to miss out on the pre-school action. They're mainly just standing around messing with people (not organized enough to have a cheer), but they're all wearing caps, belts, or T-shirts emblazoned with the Confederate flag. Behind them stands a quiet group of girls with a poster that says GIRLS FOR GANESHA, though they're just talking together like normal. I pass a throng of kids, including some I know from yearbook, doing a silly improv skit. One of them has a poster that says IMPROV IMPROV-ES YOUR BRAIN! JOIN NOW! The Amnesty International club is near the edge, trying to hand out flyers about Darfur. There are some other groups but it's hard to see what they're representing.

In a way it's almost exciting, and in another way it's a mess. Morgan's apparently decided not to be thwarted by the Jews for Jedis, and the two groups are basically having a shout-down match that you can hear across the courtyard. It's so crowded with groups or people watching groups that it almost rivals the crossroads in the middle of the day. When I finally get inside to the main hall, I find Cara standing there, looking out the windows.

"They're about to shut it down," she says, gesturing behind us to the main office.

"Can they do that?" I ask, watching Cody's gang start to sing what looks like "Sweet Home Alabama."

Just then Mr. Hammersley, our principal, along with Mr. Bell and Ms. Bruton, plus our baseball coach and a resource officer, all come out of the main office, none of them looking very happy.

"Come on," Cara says, pulling my arm. I don't want to be a

rubbernecker, but I also kind of want to know what, if anything, they're going to do or say to Morgan. Since she started this, I'm worried she'll be in the most trouble.

When we get back out to the courtyard even more kids are standing around. I spot Sprockett, hanging near the back but definitely keeping his eye on Priah, and immediately I'm swallowed by wishing I'd told her, weeks ago, to stop worrying about what Morgan and the dance team might think, to go ahead and let herself like him back, even if he is three feet taller than her. Though I'm sure she's not sad to be Morgan's new best friend, even if only by proxy, I wonder if she misses me at all—if she's struggling over the disbandment of our little group. This makes me think of Naeomi, too, and I look to see if she's anywhere out here. If she is, I can't find her amid all the other faces. Instead there's Cressida and her posse—a look of utter vengeful glee on Cress's face.

"Okay, okay, everybody," Mr. Hammersley says, holding up his hands for attention. He barely has to raise his voice to get everyone to stop. Mr. Hammersley ("the Hammer") is taller than even Sprockett; his hands are probably as long as both of mine put together, so whenever they go up they're more like flags. As principals go he's pretty good, actually, with an equal propensity for kindness and harshness, mercy and strict discipline. I think part of why we all go quiet is that we want to see which one he'll dispense today.

"Now we know you all are eager, this week especially, to show your club spirit, and we appreciate your right to express yourselves and your views, but you all are creating quite a disruption here now, and there are people trying to get to school. We can't have this kind of commotion out here, keeping students from their academic routines. Just as you have the right to assemble and to speak freely, other people have the right to go about their business without being harassed by you all."

I see Morgan huff immediately at Priah, their heads close together.

"Yo, Coach," Andy shouts out. "You wanna be our mascot?" His friends, plus a few of the baseball players, start to laugh. It even looks like Coach Allen will laugh, but he just looks back at Mr. Hammersley and frowns.

"Now you all need to calm down and move along here," the Hammer says. "We can't have the entrance blocked like this. People need to get to their lockers, do their studying in peace. So I'm going to have to ask you, out of respect to your fellow Mavericks, to break this up now."

At first nobody does anything, and I see Andy conferring with his group, possibly getting ready for another cheer. Morgan is talking to Topher, keeping one eye on Andy the whole time. But then Mr. Bell and Ms. Bruton and Coach Allen turn to the nearest students around them, and the Ganesha Girls start to roll up their poster. Cody and Skip high-five each other and split. Andy flashes a peace sign to Coach Allen and moves his gang toward the parking lot. Other kids start to dissipate too, and even Malik and his friends leave their watchful post. It's kind of unremarkable, actually, though I don't know what I was expecting. Total upheaval? Revolt? People getting expelled?

"I guess that's it," Cara says as the courtyard empties. But we still stand there, watching as Mr. Hammersley shoos off a few more students and heads over to a guy in khakis and a sports jacket who looks surprisingly like a reporter. They talk briefly, with Mr. Hammersley slowly—but clearly—walking farther away from the school, leading the reporter away from any lingering students.

"He's in an awkward spot," Cara says. "Can't make it look like he's silencing anyone, but can't endorse them either."

I nod, but mainly I'm watching Morgan, who's left her prayer friends and is standing a short distance behind the principal, watching the reporter guy like a hawk. Finally Mr. Hammersley shakes the man's hand, and then firmly, but nicely, gestures for him to leave. Morgan sees her opportunity and darts after him, but gets stopped by the Hammer. Not getting to Witness to the student body is one thing, but, judging by the way she glares at Mr. Hammersley, losing a chance to preach her message to the larger public is something she'll not easily forgive. It's actually kind of amazing, watching her stand up to the principal, clearly giving him a piece of her mind, and that odd feeling of pride comes over me again. To his credit, Mr. Hammersley even pretends to listen, though he's also looking over her head, making sure everyone really is breaking up and moving on. He makes a motion to the main office, as though inviting Morgan in for a cup of coffee and a chat, and her face goes scarlet. She turns on her heel and marches back to Priah, who immediately hugs her. Over Morgan's shoulder we catch each other's eyes, and for a brief moment I think she's even giving me a sorry smile, before she lets go and focuses back on Morgan.

• • •

That isn't, apparently, all Mr. Hammersley has to say, however. With the reporter gone I guess he figures he's safe, and during homeroom there's a special announcement straight from the Hammer himself.

"This week we've seen a lot of activity from some enthusiastic groups," his deep voice starts, "and while we encourage diversity and dialogue, there have been complaints. Things have gotten out of hand. As a result I'm afraid we're forced to request that all organizations not previously affiliated with the school refrain from meeting on school grounds during school operating hours, unless given written permission by the administration."

There's a burst of comments around me, everyone mainly going "What about Quill & Ink? What about Civettes?" and things like that, which is kind of dumb since they're all, as Mr. Hammersley just said, already affiliated with the school. He must be anticipating the hysterics, though, because he reiterates: "All previously school-sponsored, supervised organizations may continue to meet, after all academic classes are complete," he says. "But any unauthorized groups congregating on school grounds during school hours are prohibited." Prohibited meaning punishable by detention, or maybe worse. Wow. Someone must have *really* complained.

At lunch everyone's still buzzing about it: Krista heard that right after Mr. Hammersley's interference this morning, there was a fight in the parking lot. Someone else says some girl wearing a "Jesus Wasn't a Christian" shirt got asked to turn it inside out.

Our second baseman, Tripp, was maybe asked by a teacher to put a jacket on over his pro-Confederate T-shirt and belt. Another rumor is that the reason everything got busted up this morning was that a Muslim kid's mom wrote to the principal. Opal wonders aloud if she's the same one who clued in the reporter.

When we meet at chorus, Cara says she talked to Todd, who said he heard a couple of girls dropped out of the dance team because of everything that's going on, particularly that Morgan's been pushing everyone to pray before practice. I doubt this is true, since Morgan's not even captain, but I do think again of my talk with Naeomi on Wednesday, and wonder how she feels about all of this now. How Morgan feels is absolutely a mystery to me; in biology she acted as though my side of the room was completely invisible, and didn't even turn her head to look if someone in my row was called on for an answer.

"This is so out of control," I say.

Cara sighs. "At least we know we'll have a fun weekend."

And we will, at least, have that. Which is what I try to focus on as we warm up, and then sing—not our best, since it's the last class on Friday, and everyone's distracted—though my head is still kind of spinning, wondering how in the world my best friend went from sunshine sweetheart to vengeful zealot.

Saturday morning when I come downstairs for breakfast, Mom and Dad are there, drinking coffee, still in their pajamas, the newspaper scattered around them.

"So what're we doing today?" I ask, going to the cabinet for cereal since apparently this is not, to my chagrin, a Waffle Saturday.

"You're looking at it, kiddo," Dad says without looking up.

"What, no errands? No weeding?"

"Well, and you'll finally clean your bathroom of course," he says.

I ignore him, though good-naturedly, and think about what time I will start getting ready for my date with Jake tonight.

"Thought we might actually have a family meeting," Mom says, watching me as I bring my bowl and banana over to the table.

I feel a wild tremor and glance at the newspaper. "It wasn't in the paper, was it?"

"It was in the *paper*?" Mom says, reaching for it.

"What was in the paper?" Dad asks at the same time.

I'm still sleepy. They're staring at me. My granola is no help. "Uh . . ."

Mom puts down the Living section and scrutinizes me. "Tabitha, could you please tell us what is going on? I think I've been more than respectful about your personal life and your privacy. But I'm starting to feel like I live in an after-school special."

They don't make after-school specials anymore, Mom, I want to say, but I know better from her face and her tone.

"What was in the paper?" Dad says again, looking from her to me and back.

I sigh. "A reporter was at school on Friday. But it isn't a big deal," I rush. As nonchalantly as possible, because I have no choice, I tell them about the rallies. I tell them about the craziness that's been going on at school this week. I tell them Morgan started it, that she's been kind of on a rampage lately, but that it backfired and everyone's been in this weird upheaval since, but that the principal put a stop to it and everything should be normal next week. I flip carefully and slowly—trying to hide my worry there actually will be something—through the Local section with them, relieved to see that the nosy guy on campus did not, apparently, get enough quotes for the paper. Yet.

"So, see? No big deal."

Dad leans back in his chair and doesn't say anything, but I can tell he's going to.

"Does this have anything to do with Cara?" Mom wants to know first.

I feel my body temperature go up. "Why would you say that?" The first bite of my granola is suddenly very, very important. Even still, I can feel Mom's Come On, Give Me a Break Face. When I finally look up at her, it's still there.

"I don't want to talk about it," I try. Sometimes this works.

"Why not?" Dad insists.

"Because . . ." I stall. "Because it's personal." It comes to me. "To Cara, I mean. So I don't want to go into it."

But Dad's already shaking his head. "I ought to go give that smug Bob Kent a piece of my mind," he grumbles. I'm not sure who's more surprised: me or Mom. "No, really," he insists. "Clearly he's encouraging his daughter, and not in a good way. Public school is no place for this kind of conservo-Christian conversation.

And I should call the school administration while I'm at it. They should've put a stop to this much, much sooner."

"Eliot, I think—"

"I really don't need you to be peeved about this right now, Dad," I say over Mom. "I told you they made her stop. Made everybody stop. And besides, it didn't work. You don't have to worry." I feel the anger coming up in me fast and unexpected. I can't get out of its way. "The world is still safe from too many stupid Jesus freaks. There are still plenty of nonbelievers out there. Your ability to have an intelligent conversation with someone is still intact."

It seems like even the refrigerator goes into a stunned silence for a minute.

"Tabitha, that's not what I meant. It's just that people have the right—"

"Oh, believe me, I know what you think, Dad." I stand up, wanting to get as far away from him as possible. His precious intellectual high horse is so totally not the point. "That people who believe in God are just idiot brainwashed zombies. But to some of us, it actually does mean something: Something really special and important we can't talk about except in certain places and with certain people, because otherwise everyone thinks we're freaks who're all out to recruit more zombies into our coven. So go ahead and call the school, Dad. Call Mr. Hammersley and all my teachers on top of that. But when you do, do it to thank them. Because in spite of what Morgan tried to do, she got stopped. She can't do it anymore. And neither, for that matter, can anybody else, whether they believe in Allah or the Purple Donkey from Kathmandu. Okay? Now nobody can talk about religion at school at all."

I'm breathing hard. I can't really believe what I just said. I didn't know I even thought half that stuff until I was saying it, but standing there in my pajamas, waving my arms and practically spitting at my father like the crazy religious nut he thinks I am, I know it's all true.

"I'm not hungry anymore," I finish. "So excuse me. This," I say to Mom, but pointing at Dad, "is why I didn't want to talk about it." I flee upstairs to my room.

My heart's still beating a mile a minute, though, and my brain is racing. Still trembling from adrenaline and needing to do something, I snatch up my iPod and put in the earbuds, turning it up as loud as I can stand. Though it's a relief to feel the conviction of my beliefs, I need to let off some steam. I decide to take out some of my frustration on my, okay, I admit, very dirty bathroom.

Cleaning therapy is so effective that when I kneel back up out of the increasingly less-grimy tub, I nearly have a heart attack, seeing Mom there, sitting on my you-could-drink-from-it toilet, watching me.

"Gah, you scared me." I jerk the buds from my ears.

"Pretty scary watching you go at that mildew, actually," she says, smirking. I just shrug, hitching up my baggy pajama bottoms. She comes down from the toilet, turns on my bathtub faucet, starts scooping clean water along the sides of the tub. We both watch the soapy water slide up, and back down, and spin itself a few times before plunging down the drain.

"You know when I first went to your dad's apartment, it was so clean it was weird."

Dad's neuroto-perfections and their early intelli-romance aren't really what I want to be discussing right now, so I say nothing and keep rinsing the same spot over and over.

"He feels awful," she finally says.

"So why isn't he up here telling me that?" Rinse. Rinse. Rinse.

"Because he knows you don't want to talk to him."

"And he thought sending you in as diplomacy ambassador would help?"

"Not all of your dad's ideas are good ones," she admits. "But really I kind of wanted to get away from him too."

This is a surprise. When I look at her she's leaning back on her heels, dangling her wrists over the tub's edge, staring at nothing.

"I can't run interference for you two, and I don't want to. For the record, though, he absolutely does not think you are stupid. He just gets really worked up over people trying to legislate—" She sees my face and, thankfully, stops. "Mainly I just wanted to make sure you kept in mind what I said earlier this week. That I really admire you sticking to your beliefs. Even more so, now that I understand what you've been going through."

The water is still running but I've stopped rinsing and am just holding my hand under the clear gush, watching the splashes. I can't look at her. She doesn't even know the half of it.

"It must be really hard," she goes on. "I think when I was in high school all my friends and I ever fought about was who stole whose boyfriend or clothes."

I snort. "I doubt anyone was fighting over checkerboard jackets and giant socks."

She chuckles. "No, it was the mirrored plastic accessories that did us in, really. I'm still not on speaking terms with Courtney Richman, actually."

This does actually make me smile. I turn off the water and sit on the floor with her.

"Do you worry about it?" she wants to know.

"Um, which thing?"

She swallows. "Do you worry about sex, I mean."

I don't look at her, but at least I'm not blushing this time. Where she got this from I don't know, but okay. "It's funny," I start. "I didn't used to think about it at all. It's like all of us having rings kind of kept that stuff at bay. And now suddenly it's everywhere. Like it just leaks in."

She nods like I've given the right answer to a test question. "Does Cara talk about it?"

My head snaps in her direction. Her thin smile says, *I'm not as unobservant as you think.* Her ducked chin means she's uncomfortable about it, but trying not to be.

I have to clear my throat to answer. "Mainly she just gets this big, mystical grin on her face."

"Well, that's good, at least." Which is weird for her to say, but also not.

"Sometimes I want her to be sorrier," I admit.

She looks at me a minute. "What about you and Jake?"

I start twirling my ring with my thumb again. "What do you mean?"

This time she is the one to break eye contact. "Have you—talked about it?" She swallows.

"You mean about my ring?" I know what she means, but I decide to help her out a little. "He knows about my promise. He thinks it's cool."

Now she clears *her* throat. "I guess that ring of yours has protected me and your dad from some hard conversations too. I don't know if we've always—"

"I like that you and Dad are honest with me," I reassure her. "I mean, most of the time." I gesture to downstairs, the kitchen, Dad, if he's still there. Mom's lips press together. "It helps me," I go on, "be honest with other people. And myself."

She rests her hands on my knees and squeezes, looking at my face. "How'd you get to be so wonderful?"

"I'm adopted, remember?" And then we hug.

She pulls us both up off the floor and we stand there, admiring my bathroom, ourselves in the now-streakless mirror.

"What're you two doing tonight?" she says, back to normal.

"Dinner and a movie." I try to sound cool about it.

"I miss the movies," she sighs, examining her taut jawline.

"You and Dad should go to one tonight. Then we can compare notes about our dates."

"That would be nice." She stares hard at her reflection for

another minute, tousles up her Peter Pan hair—maybe, like me, trying to picture how she'll get ready for her date. "I have work to do first. You got homework?"

"I think I need some breakfast first." I grin.

"Good deal." She starts to leave but then turns back. "You know, if you do have any questions you can always—"

"I know, Mom." I nod. And can't help but smile. "I promise I'll go straight to Cara."

The rest of the afternoon is fairly quiet. I don't know where Dad's gone, but Mom and I don't discuss it and instead work together, she on the computer and me spread out on the couch with French flash cards.

Around three thirty I find myself getting anxious about tonight and so go up to my room to start fussing. My toenail polish is chipped again, so I concentrate on removing it and then repolishing. I have to correct both my big toes twice because I'm so sloppy with the brush, and I try not to think about how much easier this is with Morgan.

It doesn't help that my hair's not working well either. I decide on hot rollers, but either the humidity's bad or I just left the curlers in too long, because when I pull them out everything's poofball and refuses to lie down. Finally I just jerk everything up into a sort of messy twist and stab it with one of my lacquered chopsticks.

This is a mistake, though, as I decide I hate my top, and have to take everything down to change. I tug off the pink Naeomi-style shrug and go for my closet again. *Why don't I have any cute tanks besides this one? Where are the frilly tops I want?* "In Morgan's closet, dummy," I tell myself out loud, and it nearly makes me cry. I'm quite sure Priah's helping herself to that closet—*my closet*, I think—this very moment, she and Morgan giggling and fixing each other's eye shadow, getting ready for some fantastic BFF night out together. I sit down in my jumbled closet and throw a shoe, just out of spite.

There's a knock on my door. "Don't tell me he's here already!" I panic, glancing at the clock.

"No, just me," Dad says, sticking his head in.

"I can't find anything to *wear*," I moan from the floor. He glances at me and raises a finger, showing me to wait. When he comes back he's holding up his absolutely giant, holey Florida State Seminoles T-shirt—a really old one with the un-PC mascot.

"I knew you were going to do that."

"Well, it is lovely." He smiles, looking down with prim admiration.

I sigh. "I know in the grand scheme of things it doesn't really matter . . ."

"No, it does matter," Dad says, going over to sit on my bed. "This is your second date. You want to feel pretty. You want to make sure Jake doesn't think he made a mistake. That all your shine and sparkle wasn't just for first impressions."

This is abnormally insightful and understanding on Dad's part. I'm not even sure Mom or one of my friends would be so articulate.

"You married to the skirt?" he wants to know, cocking his head to examine me.

I look down at it, unsure. "Yes?"

He twists his mouth, assessing, and I watch him mainly out of curiosity. Though we aren't talking about this morning's incident, this is, apparently, a kind of truce, and I want to see where it goes. Not to mention what kind of outfit I'll wind up in.

"What about that black one with all the pockets?" he tries.

"I look like a plumber in that skirt, Dad. Plus, something's weird with the bottom so I have to take really small steps."

He nods, considers, comes closer. "Well . . ."

I look at the clock again. "Dad, he'll be here in, like, twenty minutes and I still have no makeup and my hair's crazy."

"I think it looks nice."

"Not *help*innnnng," I sing.

"Okay. Okay. I get it. Time is of the essence. Well, then—" He comes fully over to my closet and stands at the door a second, as if gathering his strength—as if trying to pretend this is a normal thing for him to do instead of being the first time. But then something happens in the set of his shoulders and he steps into the forest of my clothes, pushing hangers aside like branches. "Your first date was sort of done-up, right? Really sharp? So how about something"—he searches a moment, then pulls out a green jersey wraparound dress that's shoved between two fancier ones. I'd sort of forgotten I had it, actually—"a little softer."

I consider. Long, dangly earrings will go well since apparently I have to wear my hair up. I take the dress from him and examine it, trying to remember if I've even tried it on. "You think it goes down too low?"

"I think your *turtle*necks go down too low."

"That's just what you're supposed to say."

He gives me Heartbreaking Adoration Face.

"You're not, like, picturing giving me away at my wedding or anything sappy like that, are you, Dad?" I joke, partly to reassure him, partly to get him out of my room.

He chuckles. "No, just sorry I pissed you off earlier. It must've sounded horrible, what I was implying."

I move past him to my dressing table to dig for my earrings. I don't want to start thinking about anything too heavy ten minutes before my date is supposed to show up. "It's not like I don't know what you think."

"I think, unfortunately, that intolerance too easily goes both ways. That's what I was thinking today, anyway."

I look at him in the reflection of my mirror. *Why can't you just be boring, normal parents? Why do you have to* think *about everything all the time, and then* talk *about it on top of that?*

Dad sees and holds up his hands in surrender. "I know, I know. You need to get ready. Bad timing on my part. I should've come up sooner."

I try to make my face a little more forgiving. "I'm just nervous, I guess."

"I hope we'll talk more. I want you to know I do understand."

How can you understand when you don't even believe in the first place? But he's trying, so I should too. I go to hug him, since mainly that's what will end this fastest.

"Thanks for helping me," I say into his shoulder.

"That Purple Donkey of Kathmandu thing was brilliant, by the way," he laughs, stroking my hair.

"Dad." I can't help pulling away. "Hair."

"Sorry. Right. Well, we'll stall him downstairs."

"Gah, that's the last thing I need." I fake an exasperated eye roll.

"That's just what you're supposed to say." He smiles, but a little sad.

When he's finally gone I hurry into the dress, slather some lotion on my legs, shove my feet into my strappy sandals. It only takes three tries to get the chopstick back in my hair in a softly-messy-but-together way, and the green-and-pink sparkly earrings —birthday present from Priah— are perfect. Makeup happens in five minutes, and remarkably there's actually a little bit of time for me to sit, staring into space, taking deep breaths, trying to compose myself for the sound of the doorbell, and the arrival of the lacrosse player who may quite possibly be my boyfriend.

"You like tapas?" Jake wants to know when we escape my parents.

I try to remember what country tapas is from. "Um. I think so. Tiny food, right?"

He grins. "Lots of tiny food, yes. You're good with the whole breaking-things-down-into-sensible-parts thing. I like that about you."

Incredible blushing and grinning. The whole Driving with a Boy to Dinner and a Movie is still overwhelming enough—*Is this still really happening to* me?—let alone his noticing my little personality quirks and actually *liking* them when I'm not even trying.

"You're so polite," I say, meaning it.

He shrugs. "Mom's influence. She figured if she was going to be stuck with boys she'd do all she could to turn them into gentlemen."

"But when you're at your dad's it's all chest-pounding, right?" We haven't talked a lot about his parents being divorced, and I can't tell yet whether that means he's cool with it or isn't.

"Mostly at Dad's it's grunting at each other and a lot of *SportsCenter*."

I realize there are still a lot of essential things I don't know, even though it doesn't feel like that at all. "How old were you when they got divorced?"

"I was ten. Austin was in preschool."

I think about who I know whose parents are divorced. Strangely, it's not many. Not in my close circle, at least. It feels odd to feel like this is, actually, odd.

"Was it hard?"

He squints a little but that's the only clue I get, even though I'm watching his face intently. "It wasn't fun, I guess, but neither was knowing my mom was crying and angry and trying to pretend she wasn't."

He's quiet for a minute and I think the divorce conversation is over, which is okay, but then he goes on. "It's manageable since Dad made sure to get a place nearby—schools being important to him."

"That's cool he's worried about your grades, I guess."

We pull into the small parking lot and, luckily, immediately find a place. When he stops the car, Jake looks at me. "Not grades. Lacrosse."

"Ah," I say, getting a big piece of him, his life, in just three words.

The restaurant is small but not very crowded since it's sort of early for Saturday dinner. We debate the menu together with lots of "Do you like this?" and "How about this?" and the pleasant discovery of each other's tastes: me, vegetables; him, interesting meats. We end up ordering what feels like dinner for twenty, but when the first plates come I see that the food really *is* tiny and involves just a couple bites per person. The conversation in the car got us going on our histories a little, I guess, because we spend dinner talking about our families, telling background stories, filling in more sections of each other's bigger pictures.

Again he pays for dinner, so I insist on getting our movie tickets. Waiting in line he holds my hand and I add up in my head all his boyfriend behaviors so far: calling me consistently, kissing me at the lacrosse game, saying yes to the Mayhem dance, complimenting me all the time, talking seriously but also joking with ease. I wonder if, in his mind, I'm adding up too. I wonder how many equations it will take before either one of us decides on an answer.

At least I know enough not to bring it up.

When we get to our seats we have to laugh that we only catch the final wrap-up of the Twenty, both of us bringing our fists down on our knees in mock frustration at the same time. After the obligatory Silence Your Cell Phone messages, the lights go down and Jake immediately takes my hand again, and I feel it all over: the pressure and warmth of his fingers on my knuckles, the heel of his hand against mine, even the dark hollow place where our palms curve in and don't touch, all of it sends a swirling heat almost to my shoulder, which is already buzzing from where it meets his.

It's so overwhelming I think I'm going to faint before the previews are even over, and when he leans to murmur, "Want to catch that one?" close to my ear I practically do. I feel myself nod, feel him looking at me still, and I have to swallow back gorilla-size butterflies before I look at him to smile. *What movie was that for again?* I can't remember. There is his face. His eyes are on me, saying something, I don't know what, only feel crazy sparks along the outline of my face when he reaches up to touch it and then pull me a little forward to put his lips on mine. Somewhere around us is the noise of another preview: some crashing, some angry soldier shouts, but really it's like everything else has just dropped away in this dark floating, and when I open my eyes again it's a little jarring to see people sitting not far from us, several heads in the row in front. The way I feel is so unfamiliar and out of control, and what's scarier is I don't want it to stop. So I make myself. I smile at him and then concentrate, hard, on the screen.

But then I can't. Once I've decided not to think about how great everything about Jake feels, that's all I can pay attention to. Even the tiny shifting of his fingers, his knee slowly drifting over to touch mine, the involuntary clench of his forearm muscle when he sits a little straighter in his seat. Before when we were at the hayride, and even at the dance, I was hyperconscious of him too, but this is different. At first all my bonkers feelings were mainly about being nervous and wanting him to like me.

Now, sitting here trying to pay attention to the complicated spy plot unfolding in front of us, it's not the stuff I don't know about him that's making me practically vibrate out of my chair, but the stuff I do: that he takes his brother to piano lessons. That he gets really, really sweaty when he plays lacrosse. That he hates math too. That his mom wants him to be a gentleman. These things I know and adore about him don't calm me down, they stir me up even more. I'm bouncing ping-pong balls inside and have no way to let it out.

I squeeze his hand and press my palm flatter against his. He squeezes back. I squeeze again, this time for longer, and when I stop he pushes my fingers open with his and starts to stroke my palm. I do the same to him, and then our fingers entwine and press together, this happy tumble of interlacing. I look at them, our hands, and it makes me so happy I have to look at him and smile. And then he leans and I lean and I'm not going to make myself stop because I am so full of bubbles and this is the only way to spill them.

We kiss. We kiss and kiss and kiss and keep kissing. Our hands are still squeezing together and we kiss some more.

"Tabitha." He whispers it so soft it's not like a name at all but more like part of his breathing. His forehead is pressed against mine, our noses crossed, his mouth still warm and close. I smile a little, hearing it, feeling wild and bleary. I move to kiss him again, lightly—*mine, mine, he is mine*—but he says it a second time, my name, this time not so breathy. He clears his throat. Our hands are holding with our elbows bent, arms pressed up between us. "Tabitha, we have to stop."

The warmth drops out of my face, replaced by a stunned prickle. Embarrassed, I turn away from him, back to the movie, try to sort out who is who and why they're in what looks to be Morocco now, instead of D.C., where they just were a few minutes ago.

Jake gives my hand a little shake. "Hey," he murmurs. But I can't bring myself to look at him. I'm too mortified by the fact that I just got told to slow down, that I let myself get so carried away he had to tell me to put on the brakes.

"Hey," he tries again, leaning toward my shoulder. My hand goes loose in his. I'm so stunned I barely register him straightening up next to me, shifting around a couple of times and tugging on the knees of his jeans. He clears his throat, goes back to holding my hand. I try to squeeze back, to enjoy just holding hands—*we're just holding hands!*—though it was "just holding hands" that turned me on in the first place.

After the movie we take the chance of me missing my eleven o'clock curfew and go by the Creamery for takeaway post-movie malts. Standing in line under the fluorescent lights I watch Jake secretly, trying to see if he's uncomfortable at all with what happened in the theater, if he isn't right now formulating his Maybe This Isn't a Good Idea Speech. Of course, when a boy is primarily driving and/ or paying for a malt, it's sort of difficult to tell what he's thinking. He does reach out to touch me a couple of times as we wait near the counter, but he did that plenty of times before so it's not really any kind of indicator, and maybe he's just trying to make me feel better. Or does it mean I should say something? Does it mean I should forget it?

At least, when we get to my house (In time! Five minutes before eleven!) I know that the kissing can't go anywhere crazy, because we're right there in my driveway and either of my parents could take a peek anytime they wanted to.

Jake turns off the engine and looks at me. "I'm really sorry about earlier."

He's not supposed to be the one to apologize. It's so surprising I cough a little.

"I just got carried away I guess and I'm sorry," he goes on.

I pull back. "Are you kidding? It's me who's sorry."

Now we are both looking at each other like the other one is crazy. Simultaneously we burst into nervous laughs.

"No, really, *I'm* the one who—"

"No, no *I* am. I'm the carried-away one."

"No, me! It was me who—" Both of us insisting on top of each other, louder and louder and more ridiculous.

Finally he slides back in the seat and lets out a laughing breath. "Man, I really thought you were pissed at me for losing—"

"I was just embarrassed." I can't look at him but it is good to say. "I haven't really ever—" I have to swallow. My blush I think could strangle me. "I haven't ever had to think about, you know—boundaries before."

Jake shakes his head and reaches for my hand. "I never knew a girl I just wanted to *be* around so much, you know?" he says. "Even just talking to you I get really—"

I can look up at him then. I'm nodding. "I know what you mean."

We smile together. And then, even around the awkwardness of seat belts and stick shift and milk shake cups we are kissing again, and smiling with our faces close, keeping our hands linked and squeezing. And it's a good kiss, a tingling thing that just is what it is: neither a stop nor a go but a contented little idle.

"So, basically, you're saying," I brave, "all we really have to do is just *be* together? And you're, like, all elated and stuff?"

"Cell phone works too. E-mail. Whatever." He fakes aloof.

"And the rest of it can be just, like, icing?"

He smiles. "Really, really delicious icing that you want to scoop directly out of the bowl, even though you know it will make you sick."

"So, then we—"

"We keep doing what we're doing." He shrugs. "Baking ourselves a cake."

And he kisses me again on top of both our smiles.

chapter 20

STNDG O/SIDE WHR R U?!! A text from Cara beeps on Sunday, just as Dad parallel parks in front of the vintage store, Stefan's. I'm excited about shopping today, but Cara's clearly *really* excited: Once she sees me she bounces up and down on her toes and waves her hands out at me like a two-year-old wanting to be picked up. I tell Dad I won't be home until after Youth Group, and then head over to hug my giggly friend.

As soon as we hit the store I can see that Cara is like me when she shops: all business. She immediately attacks a rack frowning with concentration, flicking hangers aside quickly, stopping only occasionally to pull out a dress or two. She stares it down, fingers the price tag, and then puts it back to flick through the rest. We work opposite each other, from time to time holding up one dress or another for the other's opinion, neither of us afraid to turn a bad choice down. Unlike shopping with Morgan, when Cara's ready for the dressing room she has only two or three serious contenders she wants to consider, instead of a giant pile of whatever caught her eye.

We take separate stalls, coming out to show each other the best of the lot. For me it's a sleeveless emerald-green cocktail dress with a nice flaring skirt that has lots of big pleats, and another off-the-shoulder creamy one made out of something like taffeta. For her it's a sleek black one with a low-draping back and a big rhinestone buckle in the front, and then a sleeveless coral one with a high collar and fluffy skirt. After try-ons, we go back through the racks one more time to see if there's anything we missed. I find a blue lacy shift that Cara shakes her head no to, and a black one she thinks I should add to my pile, but she comes up with nothing, and I figure she knows, like I do, the scoopy-backed black one is the one she'll get, though she insists we still have to eat first.

We get settled at a small table on El Myr's screened-in porch, smiling and satisfied, consulting the menu while the waitress brings out some chips and salsa.

"It's so nice to be *out*." She stretches, grins, and reaches for a chip. "Seems like I've been cooped up either at the barn, school, or my own head so much lately."

"You and Michael went out last night though, didn't you?"

She shrugs. "Just the movies, you know. Nothing big."

I think about my own experience at the movies.

"What?" she says, munching.

I squint a little at her and grab a chip too. "Was it weird for you at first with Michael?"

"What do you mean, was it weird?" She hunkers down, leans closer.

I'm not sure how much I want to tell her, what I really want to ask.

"You mean was I completely nervous as all get-out and had no idea what to do, how much I wanted to do, what he expected me to do, what we'd end up doing, even though he was cool with the ring? Like that?" she helps.

I grin. "Yeah, kind of."

The waitress comes and we order our burritos. When she goes, Cara's nodding and leaning in again.

"Morgan always made it seem so easy," I start, but then I remember her outburst right before our gigantic fight, when she talked so angrily about boys only wanting one thing, and how they'll dump you in a minute if you don't give it to them. I wonder if it actually was all that easy for her. "I mean, I guess she didn't ever seem very confused."

"She always makes sure to pick boys who won't confuse her," Cara says simply.

I frown, thinking.

Cara pushes back her hair, takes a sip of Coke. "What I mean is, for Morgan everything is very cut and dry. She doesn't like gray areas. She doesn't like things messy, because then she might actually have to think about them." She glances up at me quickly. "I mean, not to sit here and slam her or anything, but from what I know of her she works really hard to keep things very straightforward and simple. She chooses boys carefully based on how complicated they are, and if she ends up being wrong—"

"She drops them," I finish. We look at each other across the table then, both of us knowing we suddenly aren't just talking about Morgan's boyfriends.

"Tabitha, I'm so—"

But our burritos arrive then; I pick up one bulging end, considering it. "This whole week I've felt so messed up," I say. "Thinking about everything, questioning it. It's been awful, not talking to her, not knowing what she thinks, but maybe . . ." I try to step outside myself, all of my feelings about Morgan, all our closeness, our history. "Maybe in reality, she isn't thinking anything. Maybe, for her, there just really isn't anything to think about."

Cara's eyes are sympathetic. For about the hundredth time this week, I feel grateful to be with her. "You never know," she says. "Maybe all of it is a big defense mechanism, you know? Maybe there's more going on in her than any of us has any idea."

I finally take a cheesy bite.

"Or maybe you need me to just change the subject and ask you whether or not you are finding new shoes to go with that awesome green dress."

I can't help smiling. "Maybe I'm not *getting* that green dress. What about that?"

"You're not getting that green one like I'm not getting that black one, and we both know it so why don't we eat up and get our fuel on for the really hard decisions we still have to face this afternoon, like shoes and earrings and will I wear my hair up or down?"

"Oh, definitely up," I say, taking a huge bite of beans and rice.

"You know it," she says back, snatching another chip.

• • •

After lunch we go back to try on the dresses again, just in case. Then we sling our long plastic bags over our shoulders and head to Abbadabbas, where we find a lot of adorable flip-flops and tons of rubber clogs, but no appropriate heels. Not ones we can afford, anyway. So Cara grabs my hand and we run across the busy street over to the Junkman's Daughter. I tell Cara I'm not looking for any polka-dot knee-highs or navel rings, but she moves swiftly to the back of the store where there's a staircase. Apparently before I've been too busy looking at Girl Friday action figures and candles in the shape of the Buddha to notice that there is, actually, a small shoe department upstairs.

"Perfetto," Cara mumbles, and moves over to a pair of chunky-heeled black patent-leather pumps. When she slides them on, they're a combination of Forties Femme meets Future Forward, and we squeal aloud in tandem when we see they're sixty percent off.

"That leaves you, missy," she says. Aside from a bunch of clear plastic ankle boots and some neon-blue wing tips, there isn't much to choose from, so Cara pulls me out the door again and back down the street to Rag-O-Rama.

I don't ever find any good shoes (there's a pair of gold flats I like, but of course they're too small), but thanks to Cara's Eagle Bargain Eye, by the time Todd comes to pick us up I'm loaded down with a bunch of new T-shirts and tops (a lot of them in a kind of vintage style I've always admired but never really gotten for myself), plus two new skirts and these big fake-emerald earrings that go perfectly with my green dress. Jake's been texting me the whole time too, so by the time Cara and I get to church for youth group I'm giggly and floaty in a ginger-ale way I haven't felt in a long time.

Evie's all over us like an untrained puppy first thing, wanting to know where we went shopping, what we bought, moaning that we're so lucky, but Cara and I manage to derail her a bit by asking what movies she saw this weekend, swapping small smiles at each other behind her broad back when she launches into her reviews.

There's a medium-ish group of us tonight: Evie, me and Cara, Aaron and his friends Ted and Forrest, two freshmen girls, and a few of the seniors clutched together in their gossipy knot. When Marilyn and Greg arrive we herd around them, curious about what we're doing.

"I know you were all eager to get going on our next project," Marilyn says. "But an old friend of mine is playing tonight, right down the street at Grace Methodist, and they've invited us to join them. After the performance we'll walk back here, but if some of you want to get picked up over there you can call your folks on the way. Show's starting soon, though, so let's get going. Greg?" Greg looks up from playing thumb war with Ted. "You want to stay here and bring along any stragglers?" Greg nods and salutes, tells us all to be on our most exemplary behavior, being guests at another church. Ted, Aaron, and Forrest all beg to stay behind with Greg, and I guess Marilyn must really want to see this friend of hers, because she actually lets them, just so we can get going. As we head off I pull away from Evie and the rest of the chatter, and fall in step with our youth group leader.

"Could've used you last week in team-building games,"

Marilyn says once I'm beside her. Her voice is gruff but her brown eyes are twinkling. For a minute I can't remember why I wasn't here last week, and then it comes back to me: Morgan wanting to blackball Cara, my hanging up on her. Possibly the last time, I think, I'll ever talk to her again.

"Your week go okay?" Marilyn asks, neutral. I make a noise that indicates some good, some bad, and she nods.

I watch our feet for a minute: hers in white sneakers with little white tennis socks, my flowery brown flats peeking out from the low hems of my jeans. I try to clear my head and still all the babbling voices inside. Next to me, Marilyn waits. In my mind I see vindictive smiles and cold stares; I see talking and not listening; I see everyone with their own different answer; I see myself, in the dark, with Jake.

"How do you know what's really right?" I finally say. "I mean, how do we really know what God wants us to do?"

We've stopped at the curb to wait for the light to cross the street. I can see the tall white steeple of Grace Methodist Church, people waiting outside. Marilyn's eyes are on the cars passing us, then on the rest of the group as she turns to make sure no one's straggling too far behind. I watch her face, knowing she's thinking about my question even though it doesn't look like it. I know she feels me watching her, waiting, but she doesn't say anything until we've started crossing the street and moved a little ahead of everyone else again.

"That's the question of the ages, though, isn't it?" she says. "What we're all struggling to figure out."

"There's just so many different . . ." I hesitate. "Rules. Sources. Voices talking, you know? How do I know which one I'm supposed to . . ." I trail off, shaking my head. We're only a half a block away from the church now, and I realize this is way too complicated a question to be asking, especially since I don't really know what it is. The closer we get to the group outside Grace, the more foolish I feel. People see us coming, a few break away to greet us and when they do I see Seamus Kittridge from school: tall, hot, soccer team, and, more recently, a Jew for Jedis. He doesn't notice me because he's only half turned in our direction, talking to a bunch of other girls from his youth group, and even if he did see me he probably wouldn't know who I was. I flush with something like shame and something like indignation, anyway.

Marilyn reaches to touch my arm gently as we stop and wait for everyone to catch up. Cara exchanges looks with me while pretending to listen to something Amy's telling her, and I just give a little shrug. Once everyone's accounted for, Marilyn moves me a little off to the side and gives me a gentle smile.

"I'm sure there are a lot of people who would like to think there's an easy answer to that question," she tells me, watching my eyes. "And there've been times—not many, but some—when I've felt close to a real answer myself." She elaborates: "Pray, listen to God in your heart, mainly. Follow Christ. But—" She cuts me off from asking which *part* of following Christ. "I think maybe what might help you to keep in mind," she says, moving toward the sanctuary entrance, "is how much struggle there is in the Bible, even in Christ's life, to address that very question. I think you yourself can come up with more instances of wrestling with God than there are of really straightforward answers."

"Even God changes His mind," I say, laughing a little, thinking about Old Testament God versus the New Testament one.

This isn't the answer I wanted, though it's not her fault, and it's too late now for me to explain what I mean. I swallow my disappointment with myself as we move into the yawning narthex of our neighbor church, kids filing around and behind us, people murmuring and jostling each other, giving sly smiles and giggling. I see Seamus and his gaggle huddled and laughing together as far back in the church as possible, and I wince internally, though it's clear they're laughing at each other and not us. Yet.

Marilyn guides our group to the right side of the middle section, where we can get the best view of the singer, who is adjusting the microphone and watching everyone come in. She's a tall woman, long and thin everywhere, and she's wearing loose drawstring pants and a kind of wraparound batik top. She has about six different silver rings on each hand, and they make small metal scratching noises against the strings of her guitar. With her up front, making his own final adjustments to a set of bongos, is a handsome black guy with thick dreads hanging past his butt. I'm not sure which one is Marilyn's friend, until she raises her hand in a tiny wave, and the woman with the guitar breaks into a big grin and nods, so obviously glad to see her that some of the people around us turn to see who she's smiling at. Marilyn smiles a little herself and then leans her head to whisper to me: "If He didn't love us for our failures and frustrations, if He wasn't pleased somehow with our attempts to find meaning, rather than inherently knowing it all already, I think God'd be a lot more pissed off with us, don't you?"

"Maybe He is really pissed off with us," I mutter back, thinking about the war, all the crazy diseases in the world, the terrible way we treat the environment and each other.

But Marilyn shakes her head as the lights in the church dim and everyone makes shushing noises around us. The woman with the guitar steps up to the microphone to greet us, strumming a few times and smiling. "If He was," Marilyn whispers, "I don't think He'd keep giving us so many beautiful things in the world, would He?"

Immediately I look past Evie and Amy to Cara. She sees my head move and looks over, and we both smile and make faces at each other. I think about all the beautiful things that have happened to me, even in this awful week, and I feel a kind of pressure break open and go away. *No, come to think of it, I don't guess He would.*

chapter 21

Even though the Hammer shut down the rallies, Monday morning on the drive to school I suddenly wonder if things will still be going on, perhaps with even more fervor. Maybe the appearance of the reporter encouraged Morgan, and the chants will be even bigger and wilder and more aggressive than anything last week. There isn't really a whole lot to base this on, but seeing as I didn't expect any of the other stuff either, this morning my mind runs away with me. Maybe she spent the whole weekend contacting parents, raising community awareness, and getting more backers. Maybe there will be TV cameras and even national news. Maybe school itself will be shut down, there'll be so much disturbance. Maybe Morgan's prayer circle will handcuff themselves together in protest, insisting on their right to pray at school. I even allow myself to picture some kind of re-enactment of the crucifixion, with Morgan casting herself in either the role of Jesus himself, or perhaps, more likely, the weeping and benevolent Mary.

Of course, none of this happens. In fact, if Mr. Bell and Coach

Allen weren't standing around watching everyone coming in, I'd think last week had never happened. It's a relief, but it also makes me shake my head a little, realizing how quickly even the biggest dramas in the universe can dissipate after a couple of days.

Still, I know better than to try and approach Morgan's locker, and I aim for the chorus room, where Opal sees me and breaks away from the girls she's talking to.

"Did Cara find you?" Her face is genuinely worried.

"I just got here," I tell her.

"You'd better go find her," she says. "She seemed pretty bad."

I'm aware that "pretty bad" to Opal could just mean Cara had a pimple. "Do you know where she went?"

"Maybe the bathroom? She looked like she was about to cry."

I thank Opal and head to the nearest bathroom. I check in the three stalls but there's no one. I also turn on my phone. If there was anything *really* wrong, Cara'd have called me, and besides I just saw her not even fourteen hours ago: It's not like that much can have happened. Maybe another mini-fight with Michael, but I've already seen how fast she gets over that. When my phone stays blank after a minute or so, I meander to the library, anyway, wondering if maybe yesterday's shopping meant she didn't study and is freaking about a test.

I look down each aisle of books like a lost kid at the grocery store, feeling stupid. Maybe she's waiting for me at the drop-off, I figure; maybe she discovered the reason her dress was so cheap was there's a big hole somewhere we didn't catch. I turn down the first corridor by the library without thinking, and then nearly stop myself, but turning and going around would take too long, since the bell's about to ring. Instead I duck my head and go to the far side of the hall, right past Morgan's locker. She's pretty much facing me, but I don't look up and I don't pause. There are more kids hanging around than usual—her prayer group, I think—all of them talking over each other about their weekends, enough so I can pretend I don't hear Morgan calling my name.

It rattles me, the sharp urgency of her voice, so much so that when I turn the corner again I nearly careen into two seniors leaning against the door to the guidance office. "Sorry," I yelp, hurrying past the main office, into the front courtyard and up to the drop-off circle. I stand there, searching faces, and take out my phone, text RU OK? to Cara's cell. When there's no response, I decide to double back to the chorus room one more time, in case she went back to look for me, but halfway there the bell rings and there's nothing to do but give in to the tide of people and make my way to homeroom. Maybe I'll swing by my locker, see if she left a note, since the schedule's rotated and I won't see her until the day's pretty much over.

After first period, Naeomi is waiting for me by my locker, and from the tenseness on her face I know she's talked to Cara, and I know, whatever it is, it isn't good.

"Did she talk to you yet?" she asks me right away.

I feel a sinking in my heart and shake my head. "I couldn't find her this morning."

"She found me first, I guess. I'll tell you everything later but mainly she's completely grounded. They took her phone and everything."

An awful feeling comes up in me, wondering if we weren't really supposed to go shopping yesterday, if it's me who got Cara in trouble. "Is she okay?"

Naeomi just shakes her head once, her mouth grim. "I have to get to class but I'll try to get online in western civ. Go to the library at your lunch and maybe we can chat."

I nod and give Naeomi a quick hug. "I'm glad you talked to her," I say. She nods and goes quickly, her eyes a combination of worried and, somewhere in there, mad, leaving me to fill in all the gaps in between.

All through English I'm nearly sick to my stomach, trying to displace my own selfish disappointment with thoughts of how distraught Cara must be, if grounded means not getting to go to the dance this weekend, but on top of that being in such trouble that her parents would take away her cell phone: basically her lifeline to Michael in between weekends. Maybe one of her teachers called about her grades. We do have report cards coming out right after spring break—maybe Cara's academics are even worse than Naeomi thinks. Since Cara's essentially the smartest of all the Rawlson kids, finding out she's been slacking would tick her parents off in a severely damaging way.

I'm so wrapped up in being worried about Cara that I forget this week is science for lunch, which means I'd normally eat with Morgan. I think briefly about her calling to me this morning as I sink in front of a library computer and sign in to MavChat.

Naeomi's already writing: CAN'T STAY ON LONG. PRETENDING TO RESEARCH. I watch as more messages appear on the screen, one after the other.

SHE GOT HOME FROM YG.

THEY LET HER DO ALL THE CHORES

BEFORE THEY CONFRONTED HER

ABOUT WHAT SHE DID WITH MICHAEL

THEY ARE FURIOUS

SHE ISN'T ALLOWED TO SEE OR

TALK TO HIM.

omg, I type. how?

SHE DOESN'T KNOW.

THEY SAID

SHE DIDN'T DESERVE

TO BE TOLD THE TRUTH ANYWAY.

I picture Mr. Rawlson thundering in the kitchen, her mother yelling and maybe crying at the same time, her brothers standing and sitting around, their arms crossed in judgment. *Oh no-no-no oh no how did they find out oh no oh no.*

I HAVE TO GO

WILL TRY TO CALL MICHAEL AT LUNCH.

u thnk he knows?

But Naeomi's already signed off by the time I'm finished entering even that. I want to throw up. And then I want to try and find Cara now, give her a hug, tell her everything will be okay, even though I know she's ensconced in PE, and the best I can hope is that they don't have to play dodgeball or something hideous like that. I take out a piece of paper, write a note to tell her that I talked to Naeomi and I am so, so sorry that I wasn't there for her this morning. I start to say we'll do something fun in our new dresses once all this blows over, but to be honest I can't imagine her parents ever getting over this, and wonder if I'll ever do anything fun with her again. It's all so awful I can barely come up with anything comforting to write, so I just end by telling her I'm there for her, whatever she needs.

Then I just have to sit for a second, processing, waiting for the adrenaline to quit coursing through me. *Dear God, how did they find out?*

I position myself to dart down the hall as soon as the bell rings, ending first lunch and beginning second. When I reach the gym I see Cara; I call out to her but she doesn't hear me, so I push past a few kids and grab her by the arm from behind.

When she turns to look at me her face is so white it's almost gray. "There you are," she says quietly, and we just stand there and I hug her as hard as I can. She's stiff as a board, not saying anything, but I just hug her and hug her and I can't even say it's going to be all right because, seriously, I don't know.

When she finally looks up her face is not crying but obviously keeping a lot of crying at bay. "Well, at least Naeomi and I are talking again," she says in a thick voice. I tell her that I know, ask her about a hundred times if she's okay. She nods but we both know she isn't, know if she talks about it more right now she completely won't be.

"I'll see you soon in chorus," is all I can say, hugging her again.

She nods into my shoulder and I give her the note I wrote, even though it pretty much says everything I just said, which isn't much to begin with.

On the way up the ramp toward the science wing, I see Priah coming from the other direction with a bunch of her dance team friends, and all I notice is how easy it is for us to ignore each other.

In bio we're starting lab again, and I'm grouped with Claire Bonneman, one of the ponytailed cheerleaders who can hardly stand to admit she's doing anything academic, let alone acknowledge my existence. But being ignored by Claire is a lot easier than being ignored by Morgan, even though I've got some practice with that now too.

Except when we all stand up to get our equipment and go to our stations, Morgan's not ignoring me. Instead she comes over and says, "Do you think we can talk?"

I'm so stunned it takes me a second before I can say all I think, which is "Why?"

She looks at her toe, which is drawing a small circle in the floor. The corners of her mouth go down. "I just think we should, you know . . ."

I just look at her. The truth is, in my heart of hearts I think I secretly know what she wants to talk about; I just want to imagine for a little while longer that I don't. There's no good reason for such a low blow to Cara, and I can't listen to her pretending there is.

Behind us Mrs. Laboutin claps her hands and tells us to hustle up so I get up and move away from Morgan toward my unwilling lab partner. "Maybe after your practice?" is all I concede—I could be wrong, I could—before fully turning away, though not quickly enough to miss her sad and ashamed and—*no God please God no*—guilty face.

• • •

In history I'm a robot. I don't care about history. History doesn't matter. What matters is right now, and right now my friend is falling apart and I'm worried about her and who cares about anything that happened before? That's all I can think as I copy down everything Mr. Schwenke says in order to promptly forget it all. Maybe I'll regret it when test time comes on Friday, but even if I fail eventually my history grade will be history, so what does it really matter?

I practically run to chorus, getting there before Cara, even though my class is farther away. Of course, as soon as she sees me, Opal tries to come over and find out what's going on, but I dodge her by saying something about Cara's period—Opal thinks anything even suggesting menstruation is vile—and she leaves me alone. The whole time I have my eye on the door, watching for Cara, worrying maybe she'll skip, but just as we're standing for warm-ups she shuffles in, grabs her music folder, and goes to her place without looking at anyone, even me.

We warm up and sing. The whole time I keep sneaking glances over at Cara, watching to make sure she doesn't collapse, which, of course, she doesn't. In fact she does her solo better than ever, even though her face is still that weird ash color.

When the bell rings, Cara waits for me outside the door, leaning against the wall and making it clear she does *not* want

Opal to come over and ask how she is. Thankfully Opal takes the hint and sweeps off in her scarves and her cool twisty hairdo and her perfume.

We don't say anything; we just walk. Down the long corridor past the band room and gym. When we get to the crossroads and its teeming throngs of people, I feel Cara stiffen next to me—all those faces: possibly Skip's or Todd's in there—and I reach for her now definitely ringless hand to keep her close. She hangs on to me, hard, and I wish like anything we could stay this way, with me protecting her and pulling her through whatever lies ahead.

When we break through everyone and are safely in the 600 wing, Cara says in a small voice, "I'm so sorry about this weekend."

"You don't have anything to be sorry about," I say firmly. "This is not"—and here my heart starts to beat faster, my nostrils flare— "your fault." Although okay, yes, technically it *is* her fault. All of it is her fault, the whole thing; every bad time we've had in the last couple of weeks is specifically *her* fault and Michael's, but I'm already way past the point of being condemning anymore.

I see her about to start crying again and I tell her firmly to stop. "If you start crying now I will too and we have to get through math. It's the last thing you get to do before you have to go home again and face your family, so you'd better get in there and enjoy it." I quiver-smile through my fake-angry voice and the tears of frustration I feel pricking around my eyes. I put my hand on her shoulder and give her a firm shake. "Okay?" She takes a deep breath through her nose and blows it out. She nods once, and then again with more confidence.

"If I'm lucky," she says, stretching her eyes wide a few times to get rid of the tears, "we'll even have a pop quiz."

"That's my girl," I say, and together we move into class.

Sadly, in the first half of geometry we actually have to concentrate. Mr. Outif is showing us a harder version of proofs (not like they aren't hard enough) and we're all furiously taking notes. The second half, though, he has us move into groups to do some practice problems. During the part where we all stand up and shift our desks around to face one another in clumps of four or five, Sprockett sways over to me. I can tell he has something on his mind because he's stooping even more than usual.

"Need to sharpen your pencil?" I say to help him out. He smiles quickly and we both fish pencils out of our bags and go to the back of the room near Mr. Outif's desk, where he keeps one of those beyond-nerdy old-fashioned pencil sharpeners screwed into the wall: the kind with ten different pencil diameter possibilities on a dial, and a crank. I stick my pencil in and turn slowly, looking up at Sprockett's face.

"I wanted to ask you," he says, low and polite, painfully shy, leaning in over me, "if you think—" Here he looks around at the class to make sure no one's listening. I suddenly panic, wondering if I had it all wrong and it wasn't Priah he was dropping by in the mornings to see.

"Sprock—" I speed up on the sharpening to help drown out his barely audible voice.

He finishes in a rush: "If you think I should ask Priah to the Mayhem dance."

I'm so surprised I stop sharpening my pencil. "You haven't asked her *already?*" To cover up my semi-stunned face, I swap places with Sprockett so he can fake sharpening his pencil next.

"I mean," I whisper, "isn't it a little late? Don't you worry someone else has already asked her?"

He shakes his head. "Her Facebook says she isn't sure if she'll even go. I mean, you guys talk and stuff, right?" He blushes a little, realizing he just admitted he's basically stalking Priah online.

Mr. Outif clears his throat, gives us a warning look over the tops of his glasses. "Your peers are awaiting your input, Miss McAbe and Mr. Brockett." Sprockett gives me an eyeball-enlarged panic glance and speeds up his sharpening.

"I just don't think it's a good idea, Sprock," I feel myself whispering, fast. I look away from him so I can't see his crushed expression. "I mean, you've seen how serious Pree's been taking the whole Christian thing lately. And her commitment. I think she'd probably be insulted actually if you even asked her. I mean, I think it's pretty clear she's not interested in boys right now, right?"

He gives me a confused look, trying to remember, I'm sure, what he last read on Pree's blog. I've read that blog too, though not lately, and I know pretty much what it says. Though Priah's not stupid—she knows everybody reads everybody else's blogs—

and wouldn't put anything up there that was truly personal, if she confessed not having a date yet to the Mayhem dance, she must be pretty desperate.

"Look, she's my friend, right?" I say, patting Sprockett on the shoulder as we head back to our desks. "Don't you think I'd know?"

I can't tell if he sees I'm lying or not, but knowing Sprockett, he probably thinks I'm just protecting him from an even bigger letdown: that I happen to know Priah doesn't like him. That part I feel awful about, for Sprockett's sake. He might be a bit of a lunking dork, but he is really sweet. He and Priah would actually make a great couple. And the truth is, I *am* Pree's friend, and I do know. Or was and did. If he finally worked up the nerve to just ask her out, she'd be so thrilled she'd forget to be worried about what anyone thought.

She doesn't deserve you, Sprock, I think angrily, glancing at him one more time before trying to pay attention to the scramble of symbols and exponents in front of me. Besides, there is no way in you-know-where that I'm going to help *Morgan* go on a double date if I can't, even if it does hurt Sprock's feelings for a little while.

Whatever guilt that lingers during math completely disappears when school is over, as I walk Cara to her locker. I wait while she considers what she needs to bring home. Resting atop her jumble of books and crushed papers there's a neatly folded note, and Cara picks it up gingerly. Her face relaxes visibly seeing the handwriting. I wonder if she knew Naeomi was going to call Michael during lunch.

"She's been great, by the way," Cara says, gesturing with the note. But watching her read, her face goes whiter than it was before. She crushes the paper in her hand and throws it on the ground, storming off without even shutting her locker. I slam it for her, pick up the note, and run after her, calling out.

"I have to go," she says without stopping, her voice tight.

"Cara, wait a second," I holler, my bag slamming against my thighs. "Just wait."

"I have to *go*, Tab," she chokes out, spinning toward me. "Don't you understand?" And then her face goes from angry to sad and her eyes are full of a kind of worry I know I have no way of understanding. "This is all so messed up," she whispers. "This is all. So. Messed. *Up!*" She kicks the wall next to her. "Look, I'm sorry but I really have to go. They're waiting." She gestures toward the front of the school.

"I'm worried about you," I finally say, still holding the note. I offer it out to her.

"No, just read it. It explains better than I'll be able to." She looks like she's about to cry again, but doesn't. "I don't know what I'm going to do, but I'll be in even more trouble if they have to wait."

"Okay. Well, call me if you—"

But she's already on her way down the hall. She only stops to give me this awful destroyed little shrug. "I can't," she says simply, before pushing her way out one of the side exit doors.

I stand where she left me and uncrumple the note. Inside is Naeomi's perfect grandma handwriting:

C—I know I didn't ask if I could, but I had to try to do something on your behalf so I talked to M. for you. He said to say that he loves you, so there's that. I also need to tell you that you were right to worry about your brothers: They already paid him a visit. I know you won't be able to talk tonight and I'm sorry I can't meet you, because of practice. I'm sorry about all of this, really. Love, N.
PS: Meet me at the library first thing tomorrow. That's an order!

This is absolutely worse than . . . I don't even know what.

On the walk home I think about everything I know about the Rawlson brothers. Truthfully I haven't spent much time with them, since Skip and Todd are too cool to be bothered with us at school, and they all make themselves relatively scarce whenever I've been over to Cara's house. But pretty much everybody knows that if you see their beat-up truck pull in at a party, someone's going to get their butt kicked. Each of them has been in legendary trouble: Mack, the oldest, for supposedly punching a teacher back when he was at school here; Walt for failing tenth grade twice and eventually dropping out; Todd for spitting on umpires and starting fights during baseball games; and Skip, a grade above us and definitely the meanest one of the bunch, for about sixteen kinds of vandalism, especially over at our rival school. Cara's their baby sister, and you can imagine what they might think about a boy who is the president of his school's Poet's Forum, even if he *wasn't* touching her.

My imagination's whirling with all kinds of horrible things they might've done to Michael, but I have to wait until dance-team practice ends to find out what "paid a visit" really means. I pace between my phone and the computer, hoping somehow the impossible happens and Cara manages to call, checking my e-mail obsessively even though I know the only computer in the Rawlsons' house is in her dad's office— definitely off-limits. I'm pretty much driving my mom crazy, and when I say at five fifteen that I need to make a call, she waves me to the back porch and all the privacy I want.

"Hey," Naeomi says after one ring.

"So he talked to you?"

"Not for very long, but yeah. He's pretty freaked out."

I picture Michael with a broken arm or face. "What'd they do?"

"Took a tire iron to his car. Smashed all the windows. He said he couldn't even open the driver's side door."

"Oh. My—"

"They said they were going to castrate him like a horse."

"He *talked* to them?"

"Spray painted it on his car."

"So he'd know who did it." I picture scrawny Skip and his can of spray paint, Todd spitting through the broken windows into the seats, Walt whamming away with all he's got, and Mack maybe pouring sugar in the gas tank or shredding the tires.

"I don't think there was ever any doubt about who did it," she mutters. Then, "Hey, Dad" away from the phone. "Look, I have to go," she says back to me, "but listen, she is going to really need some support. He's totally freaked out. I couldn't bear to tell her—I'm sure she kind of figures—but he thinks they should take a break."

My heart sinks and turns cold at the same time.

"Thank you," I finally say. "For doing all this."

"Yeah," she sighs. "I'll call you later tonight if I can. But that's the story."

We hang up and I sit there for a while, staring out at my backyard, watching the trees, looking at my mom's herbs, following the dark spots of birds flying randomly from branches to the ground and then back again. *This is all so messed up*, is exactly right, I think. *So, so, so, so.*

My phone startles me when it rings again in my hand, and for a second I think a miracle really has happened and Cara's found a way to get through. But it's not her name that appears on my screen: It's Morgan's. In all this, I'd forgotten she wanted to talk.

I push IGNORE, watching the screen go blank as I turn my phone off.

I know it was Morgan who told the Rawlsons about Cara and Michael. I *know* it was Morgan, and I am never, ever, ever going to forgive her.

chapter 22

The only good thing about the Rawlsons knowing about Cara and Michael is seeing it bring Naeomi and Cara back together. I almost don't want to interrupt when I find them Tuesday morning in the library, but as soon as I walk in Naeomi waves me over.

"Hey," we all say in the same quiet, low tone.

"How are you?" I want to know.

Cara sighs. Her face is still a weird shade, and I can tell she hasn't slept much. She gives a weak smile. "You'd think, after so much yelling and storming around on Sunday, that the silent treatment would be an improvement. Take it from me, it isn't."

"So what happened?"

"Basically they said I've completely destroyed their trust, so until I earn it back—essentially, when I'm old enough to move out on my own—I get nothing. No friends over, no cell phone, no movie nights, no nothing. School and the barn: That's it."

"What about youth group?" I try.

"If I can convince Skip or Todd to come as my chaperone, maybe. In, you know, the year 2015."

I can't help it: I was secretly hoping maybe somehow she'd get to go to the dance, even if just with me. Hoping so much, in fact, that I didn't have the nerve to call Jake back last night, in case I got better news this morning. If they won't let her go to youth group, though, the dance is completely, definitely out.

"Have you been able to talk to Michael?" I say to detract from my selfish disappointment.

Cara's mouth makes a straight line and she doesn't say anything. Naeomi looks at me, gently shakes her head, once: *Don't ask.*

"What can we do?" I try again.

Cara's laugh has a crack in it. "Pray?" she says, her eyes rolling to the ceiling.

I wonder briefly if this is actually what God *wants*, if Cara's being punished for breaking her promise. Maybe there really *is* a clear-cut rule about abstinence buried in the Bible somewhere, and once you cross that line you're on your own. But then it strikes me that this punishment isn't from God, but someone who'd like to *think* she's God.

When the bell rings we head in our different directions, none of us feeling much better. As I leave I catch sight of the freshly filled newspaper baskets just outside the library, and it's hard not to groan out loud.

A RIGHT? OR JUST WRONG? the main headline accuses, just

above a photo of Morgan shouting for purity. I snatch a copy and try to read it on my way to homeroom.

> Last week several members of the student body were disturbed to begin what they thought would be just a normal day, only to find themselves accosted by several loudly opinionated groups, many of them of a religious persuasion. Though it was against school policy, several students chose to take their beliefs outside the private realm and make them disturbingly public.

I skim a bit, reading what I already know: In response to the prayer group, others were motivated to "advertise their own affiliations fervently and obnoxiously" as well, resulting in "eventual interference by school administration."

I make it to homeroom and slide into my desk.

> While the separation of church and state is essential to our Constitution, these students—ignoring this eparation—forced everyone to listen to their proclamations, regardless of their beliefs or background.

Here the student reporter quotes a few kids who also think religion should be kept off school grounds, though to her credit she does include one girl who thinks it's great that people aren't afraid to say what they think, so long as they don't try and make everyone else believe it too. It's notably bad journalism that Morgan's not interviewed at all, but I happen to know the author, Lightsey, and I know objectivity's just something she gives lip service to. She's hated Morgan's guts ever since not making dance team this fall.

The article ends with a dramatic statement:

Even if religion is put back where it belongs—in private gathering places—one must wonder if it hasn't already permeated our classrooms and our psyches in an irreversible way.

Not a very good article, really. Beneath it, though, is an interesting student poll (I never know who answers these polls—I certainly haven't ever contributed) that asks, **SHOULD WE DISCUSS RELIGION AT SCHOOL?** 53 percent of respondents say no, 31 perecent yes (more people than I would have guessed), and 16 percent "don't care." I stuff the paper in my bag to show Dad. Right now, though, looking at that article makes me picture the five of us analyzing it together in an alternate universe where we're all still friends, and I'm just not up for it.

After first period Naeomi's at my locker again. While I'm liking this whole me-and-Naeomi-talking-more thing, I'm not so crazy about the reason, especially not seeing her face now.

"I'm so pissed," she says right away.

I hurry with my books so that I can walk down the hall with her a bit before we have to separate. "About which thing?"

"Michael," she says, her mouth full of disgust. *Oh, right. That.* I follow her down the hall. "She's totally worried about him still, says he needs comforting after what happened and she's devastated she's not there to give it to him. She says with her whole family against him, he needs her even more, and it 'kills her' that she can't talk to him."

237

She's walking so fast. "But you said he thought—"

"Exactly. He's so spineless. I mean, even in the few minutes we spoke yesterday, I could totally tell he's not sure this is worth it. It's all I can do not to tell her."

"You can't tell her." I stop. "She'd die."

"I know. Which is why I haven't. Yet. But as soon as she gets her balance back, I'm going to have to."

"Maybe he's just scared. Maybe he just needs some time."

Naeomi's You Know So Much Better I'm Not Even Going to Respond Face is almost paralyzing. But the idea that Michael— after what they did—would dump Cara so quickly, would break his own promise to *her*, is just too hard to believe.

"Okay, I hear you," I finally say. "Just don't tell her yet, okay?"

She glances at her watch. I realize Naeomi has a lot going on in her life too, not to mention rigorous practice this week for Mayhem, and dealing with her own possibly even-more-very-strained relationship with Morgan. I wonder if members have really dropped out, realize I haven't asked her. Haven't asked either if she's glad to be dragged back into things with Cara or not.

"Hey, are *you* all right?" I'm as sincere as possible, considering we both now have ninety seconds to get to our next classes.

"I'm the one who's hard as nails, remember?" she says.

There's not time to focus on debating that, so I just give her back one of her straight-mouthed, firm nods, and let her jet off to class on her own.

• • •

Pure

In English it becomes painfully clear that somehow, in all of this, I've gotten behind in my reading. I fake my way through discussion, nodding like I know what my peers are talking about and even taking a huge risk by raising my hand to be called on (thank you, Jesus, I'm not), to try to camouflage my slackdom. This coupled with a B on my *Pearl* essay shocks me into remembering that I do, no matter what else is going on, have school.

During lunch I go out to the track and find a bleacher where I can read as much as possible uninterrupted. I'm so engrossed and it's such a pretty, clear day, that I debate skipping biology to keep reading—Dickens being much easier to handle than facing Morgan—but then I remember that I've already skipped biology recently, and Mrs. Laboutin isn't the type to take pity. Still, when the bell blares loud enough to be heard all the way in the parking lot, I wait a full two minutes before packing up my books and walking, as slowly as possible, over to the science wing, hoping I'll be able to go straight to Claire and our petri dishes, without having to interact with Morgan at all.

And in fact this almost happens. Mrs. Laboutin calls roll and briefs us on today's necessities (write ev-er-y-thing down) before we're let loose on the mold cells we combined yesterday. Supposedly they'll have turned orange, and we have to take the orange parts away from the remaining black parts and then bind them with something else, but before all that we have to, of course, get our goggles and aprons. Since Claire's utterly uninterested and defenseless to boot, I'm the one who has to go, and it's here where Morgan accosts me.

"I tried to call you last night," she says, while I'm trying to reach behind Doug Quo without actually touching him.

I pretend I don't hear. It's reasonable to think I don't, since Mrs. Laboutin has decided, right then, to tell us the fit of our aprons is, contrary to our beliefs, the least important aspect of this assignment. I manage to grab two aprons and pull, knocking poor Doug in the shoulder in the process. Next I make myself very busy with lunging for goggles. I can feel Morgan standing there, just by my left shoulder.

"Tabitha," is all she says when I turn—my eyes *not seeing* her sad face—to make a beeline for Claire and our lab station. For a brief moment I glimpse a version of myself, who would have some sort of tart and cutting thing to say, but since I'm just me and not that person I watch myself duck past and say nothing instead.

As Claire and I scrutinize our petri dish, my heart is racing and my hands are shaking so much I can barely hold the scraping tool. I feel like I just ran a marathon. Like I've been on trial.

Double ugh that I don't even get to go home after all of this, or to the comfort and jocularity of the Center. Instead, no. I have yearbook after school. More time filling in clever quips about clubs and SGA, more focus on superficial school spirit. Yeehaw. After math Cara and I hug and I wish her luck, tell her I wish we were neighbors so we could at least send flashlight signals from window to window. It's a lame joke but she does smile a little, and I notice she's got her arms filled with books, which is at least a good sign.

When I finally get to the yearbook room I'm surprised to see everybody's gathered around the big round meeting table in the middle of the room, talking.

Yuhn waves me over. On the table are a bunch of photos—pictures of last week's "rallies." Cal, our photo editor, picks up a photo every now and again to examine it, while Lydia talks at him from across the table.

"It'd just be wrong not to include it," she's saying. "We still have room in the Year in Review section, for example. I mean, if we have to pull all-nighters in order to get Mayhem and Prom in there we can certainly do it for this."

Cal holds up a photo: Morgan in a pink T-shirt with a Sacred Heart Jesus emblazoned on it, her mouth open, yelling. "Rebecca won't like it," he says to Yuhn.

"Well, you can pick a different one. One that shows more people."

"Who's Rebecca?" I whisper over to Yuhn. She writes on the edge of her notebook: Girl who runs devotional group before school. I'm unable to hide my surprise. Yuhn nods, smiling like a sphinx. Every Friday. Completely legit. I stay shocked. I had no idea a prayer group was already meeting on campus, just like a regular club. I know Morgan doesn't know about it either.

Cal leans back in his chair and crosses his arms, looks over at Lydia and Peter. "You want to do a sidebar on it?" he says, thinking out loud. Mr. McClellan comes out of his glassed-in office to listen.

Mena goes to get some of the layouts we've already done, and spreads them on the table. "We could move What's Hot, What's

Not," she says, pointing. Cal looks up at Mr. McClellan, seeking advice. While everyone debates and makes suggestions, I decide to get a little more information from Yuhn.

"Where do they meet?" I try to whisper.

I watch her pen, as she writes that Mrs. McCarthy, the AP English and creative writing teacher, holds the meetings in her room.

"I didn't know McCarthy was religious," I say.

"She isn't," Yuhn whispers back.

Immediately, for some reason, I think of my mom. "Why didn't they participate last week?"

Yuhn shrugs. "Rebecca's not into all of that. It's more personal for her, for them. They don't want to make a scene. They just want to be able to gather and discuss. A lot of them are Quakers," she adds, as though that would explain anything.

I wonder how they must have felt last week, especially after Hammersely got involved and had to shut everything down. Probably more than a little pissed at Morgan, who's now made anybody with an ounce of pride in their faith suddenly ashamed to admit it—especially after Lightsey's flaming article today. But maybe an even bigger group resented, as the article suggests, that they had to discuss or think about faith at school in the first place, that it didn't stay in the secret corners it was already in. Maybe, much as I hate to admit it, my dad was kind of right.

I try to focus on the discussion at the table, which is moving more to design than content. I realize how self-absorbed, how microcosmic I've been, focusing on my friends and myself, instead of the bigger picture. There's a lot I've missed out on. I mean, maybe I'm not totally all on my own, wondering what's right. Maybe there's a place right here at school where I can find some answers to the questions going on in me lately—or, if nothing else, find the guts to actually ask them.

Later Jake calls me after his lacrosse practice. I hadn't planned to, but when he asks how I am I end up I telling him everything about Cara and Morgan and Michael. It still really bugs me how easily Michael seems to be just giving up on Cara. In a way, I want to know Jake wouldn't do the same thing.

There is quiet for a long time on the other end when I finish. "You there?"

"Yeah," he sighs. "Wow, that's harsh."

"Pretty much." *And here's the part where you say it's a terrible thing to do and you would never even think of backing out on your girl at a time like this.*

"What kind of car did he drive?" he wants to know.

"What? Um. A Toyota or something?" It's hard not to sound annoyed.

"Sorry. Just trying to picture it. Wow. He must have really freaked."

"Yeah, the Rawlsons can be pretty scary, I guess. But Cara—"

"No, no, of course. I'm sure it's much worse for her. I mean, I can't even imagine. I guess that's why I asked about the car. Easier to visualize."

Suddenly I don't want to be talking about this anymore, to have to think, on top of everything else, how *Michael* might feel. "Just visualize a really big emotional crisis, and no access to anyone who cares about you, I guess."

"Hey, are you okay?"

Grrrr. Duh! No! "I'm really worried. And I can't do anything. Usually I can do something to help or cheer up my friends. But in this case I can't. And I hate it." I start picking at my toenail polish. Suddenly, I hate *it*, too. "Listen, I'm really behind on my homework and I—"

"Hey, wait."

"Yes?" I can't believe it. I just sounded *exactly* like my mother.

"We're still going to the dance, right? I mean, do you want to?"

I try to picture going and not feeling guilty about Cara sitting at home, alone, wondering if she'll ever see her boyfriend again. I'm also, stupidly, glad Jake still wants to, even if I don't.

"It just feels weird, going when she can't," I have to admit. "You know? I really want to but I feel, I don't know, not right about it."

He is quiet enough for me to think he's mad. Then, "Something else? Mini golf?"

I sigh. "I'm sorry I'm just kind of heeberdeederb right now. Can we talk tomorrow?" *Please, please don't break up with me, too.*

"Wish I could bring you some Ovaltine, make you feel better."

"Rain check?"

"Deal."

Okay, this is amazingly better. "Thanks for being cool."

"Okay. Well, call me or e-mail me or something if you want to later."

I smile. "I might."

"Okay, cupcake. Well, I'll talk to you later maybe then."

"Okay then."

When we hang up it takes a full ten minutes before I can stop grinning. Even though five minutes ago I was completely annoyed with his dumb boyness, now it doesn't matter: I just got my first sweetheart nickname that didn't come from a girlfriend or my parents.

chapter 23

Suddenly it is Friday and it is five thirty, and Mom has just brought me home from the Center, and Dad is coming in from the garage and booming about solving some kind of problem with a storage closet, and I'm all anxious and irritated. I guess I've just been in a fog this week: mainly avoiding anywhere Morgan might be and praying she won't come near me in bio, which works. I've done homework, removed my toenail polish, eaten and not eaten, thought about things and then pushed them away. I've talked to Cara some, mainly telling her I feel too weird going to the dance without her, or even Mayhem itself. She argued a little, but then let it go—understanding my unsaid desire to avoid watching Morgan be fabulous, or getting stuck remembering last year and how fun Mayhem weekend was for us. But now it's Friday and I've snapped out of it and am all edgy. When Mom calls me on it, I realize my problem is that I seriously *do* want to go tonight. It starts in less than two hours, but the idea of missing it makes me want to die.

"I can't wait until you can drive," Mom sighs, leaning against the counter.

It occurs to me I could call Jake, but I know he's planning on taking his brother to the movies tonight. "I'm sorry but I didn't know how important it was until just now."

Mom rolls her eyes to Dad.

"Well, are parents invited?" he says, eager-eyebrowed.

I consider this. On one hand, I don't really want to be one of the dorks who shows up with parents in tow. On the other hand, I don't want to be one of the dorks who shows up *alone*, either. I do a quick mental rundown of who I might see there: not Cara, obviously. Naeomi and Priah and Morgan will be busy performing, and all their parents will be there, anyway. Sprockett will be there, of course, but he doesn't really count. So will a lot of other people, but as I check my mental list of attendees, I realize *they* don't count much either.

"Sure you can," I say slowly. "If you want."

Mom and Dad exchange a complicated series of looks, but finally they say okay. I decide not to look a gift horse in the mouth.

When we get to the gym it's almost seven thirty and the bleachers are jammed. We have to climb past people nearly all the way to the top, and even then when we get a seat we have to keep our hipbones practically locked together. Sprockett and some other guys from the basketball team are sitting near the judges' table. Yuhn and Mena and Peter from yearbook are also near the front on the other side: covering Mayhem instead of actually being in it. Tashara's roaming around taking pictures already, especially over near the table across the gym, where the DJ is set up with his laptop and about a dozen giant speakers. Cressida's over on the far left side, surrounded by her girl posse and five or six boys who are mostly shoving each other. I haven't spotted the Kents or Naeomi's parents yet, but right before the cheerleaders all come bouncing out along with the school president and Mr. Hammersley, I see Krista, Amelia, and Opal not too far away. A brief feeling of letdown crosses me: They could've asked me to go. On second thought, though, I realize they probably figured I'd come with Cara. Cara, who can't be here. Cara, whom I don't want to think about.

"Good evening and welcome," Mr. Hammersley says into his microphone. Immediately everyone in the audience cheers and whistles, including my dad, while the cheerleaders shake their pom-poms at us.

"We're glad to see you all this evening, showing your support for our school and the students who are about to perform for you tonight." More cheers, more whistling from the audience, and the Hammer glances at a small index card he's holding in his giant hand. "Tonight you will see just some of what our students are capable of doing when they gather and work together around a common cause. Though this is a competition, though it is intended to amuse and entertain, I want each of you to keep in mind the hard work and dedication of all our student organizations throughout the academic year, whether they chose to participate this evening or not. I want you to remember that, regardless of who leaves this evening with the Mayhem Mace, we feel all our Mavericks are winners."

More clapping and cheering from the audience (which seems to have grown even in the short time our principal was talking), as well as a burst of simulated trumpet fanfare from the DJ as Mr. Hammersley hands the microphone over to our school president, Bobby Ware, who explains the history of Mayhem and the rules. Bobby is smart and handsome and popular, but he already dresses and talks like the boring lawyer he's destined to be, so I shut him out a little.

I look over the audience, wondering what's going to happen, my hands forming tight little fists around the hem of my hoodie. I don't know what I'm so nervous about, really. The Mayhem Mace is basically just a baseball bat covered in glitter and ribbons in the school colors, and the winning club gets to keep it for the next year, bringing it to pep rallies and games, carrying it around during Spirit Week and brandishing it every other chance they get. It's not like a million dollars. Or six weeks of straight A's. So why are my knees jouncing, my head turning at every peripheral movement?

Below me Bobby morphs into professional wrestling announcer mode, jumping up and pointing at the DJ, the audience in one big motion, screaming "Are you ready for some May-HEMMMMMM!" as the pep-funk band suddenly pours out of both locker rooms, playing a jazzed-up version of our fight song. The cheerleaders bounce and kick, sparkly pom-poms waving. My hands are clapping, my feet stomping—whatever's going to happen, it's about to.

The first routine is Flag Corps: enough said. After them comes Bright, the sugary all-girls club that does lots of community service involving animals, baked goods, or knitting. They've all got these awful unitards on, waving gymnastic ribbons in rainbow colors and flitting around to some folky-sounding music. It's mostly vomitous, but I do notice one of the girls has on what looks like a purity ring. If it is, I wonder if she got it before or after Morgan's increased visibility.

My anxiety tweaks again when Bobby screams, "Give it on up to the rafters y'all for the priceless girls of Platinuummmmm!" and the sleek hipsters of the cool girl clan come out wearing old prom dresses and tiaras, their fake eyelashes and over-glossed mouths sparkling with glitter. When Jews for Jedis leader, Andy, swaggers behind them wearing an all-white tuxedo and a black tie, I scoot even farther on the edge of my bench.

The music starts. It's a fifties' doo-bee-doo song, and Andy's lip-synching like an old-style crooner. The girls start in a big circle around him, and as he sings they all drift closer with these dreamy looks on their faces. Finally as the violins swell, there's this huge record-scratch sound, and Andy freezes with his microphone stretched up in one hand over his head. Immediately the music completely changes into this jungle bass mash-up of "Nasty Girl" with "SexyBack." The girls pull away their dresses like snap-on basketball pants and then they're all in lingerie of varying degrees of trashiness—knees, hips, and collarbones all gyrating around Andy in an extremely coordinated (and extremely dirty) routine.

Everyone around us is going nuts, and I'm uncomfortably aware of my father sitting right next to me. Besides the dirty factor (okay and the jealousy factor, because Platinum girls are so enviable—rich and pretty like the cheerleaders but too cool to go for the squad), I can't help being sensitive to the whole message they're sending, about Good Girls Who Go Bad.

When they finish, there's what feels like about two minutes of screaming and clapping and whistling. I see Mom raise her eyebrows at Dad, but he just winks and does one of those loud fingers-in-the-mouth whistles he's so good at but I somehow just cannot learn.

After Platinum has scooped up their dresses and blown saucy kisses to the audience, a bunch of guys from ROTC do a line dance in their cowboy hats and boots. They're followed by Model United Nations, who from their internationally authentic costumes alone should totally get mega-points.

But the dancing part is great too—really diverse styles melded together—and when they're done *everyone* is on their feet, including some judges. The energy stays high for the pep-funk band, and when the gospel choir comes out to join them, the gym is practically trembling with the strength of all that sound.

A pretty tough couple of acts to follow, which makes my palms sweat and my heart jump again when the first few beats of the dance team's theme starts. Before I'm ready, there they are. Just like during the basketball games, they stream out of the locker room, full-on smiling and toes pointed as they run. Mom reaches over and gives me a little squeeze on the knee but I barely notice. Instead I'm watching Priah, Naeomi, and Morgan as they move into their different positions. They tuck their heads down so I can't see their faces until the music starts again with a jolt and all their heads go up at once, dance team grins intact.

I don't really know what I was expecting, but watching them start in on a pretty standard routine, I realize this wasn't it. Though they're good—they're always good and fun to watch—they don't seem to be doing anything beyond what they usually do, and even their song is standard.

I feel my anxiety dissipating, even as I'm watching Naeomi's face for a sign of tension between her and Morgan or Priah. She's all stiff dance girl smile, though, and when they clasp each other's shoulders for the line kick, Naeomi's there right next to Morgan, kicking away and beaming. They're finished before I know it, flawless and waving and pointy-toe running off the gym floor. I feel almost a little let down, on top of incredibly relieved.

As soon as they're off, a droning, monkish chant starts to play and the Golf Club comes out of the locker room single file, wearing choir robes. My stomach completely drops. *This* is what I've been afraid of: the Jews for Jedis and whether they're really going to call Morgan out tonight, like Cressida said. I flick my eyes over the audience, only to see Mr. and Mrs. Kent, smack in the middle of the top middle row. *Oh please, God, don't let them humiliate her in front of her parents.* My hands are sweating again. I keep myself from looking over at Cress and watch the guys in their robes lip-synching to some boys' choir song now playing over the chanting. They've got their hands open and their eyes cast heavenward, faces pure as the driven snow.

Is it better or worse that next, out from the center aisle between the bleachers, comes Tyler Eberly, this tiny freshman guy, all dressed up like the Devil: red shiny tights, red leotard, red silky cape with sequined trim, and red sequined horns. Someone's painted a twirly-ended mustache along his upper lip. A pathetic little tail dangles from his rear. I can't take my eyes off him as he totally milks it, hunching his back and raising up his knees in this crazy goat walk, creeping toward the choirboys, who are pretending to look nervous while they're also trying not to laugh. The DJ starts to mix in this scratchy electronic noise when Tyler jumps onto the back of one of the tallest choirboys. The others fall to the ground in a fake faint while the tall boy whirls around in circles, little Tyler clutching him in piggyback.

Everyone around us is laughing, but when Andy, Seamus from Grace Church, and two others all appear at the four corners of the gym, they absolutely lose it. Each guy is dressed up as a religious figure: Andy a Hasidic rabbi (complete with fake curls dangling by his ears), and Seamus in a white robe and this over-the-top pope's hat made of cardboard and lots of glitter. One of the other guys is a Buddhist monk, and the last guy has a turban and this crazy long fake beard. Also, they're all wearing superhero capes. Even I have to crack a smile, while my brain is zooming, trying to figure what they'll do with all of this.

Superman's theme starts playing, and the four religious guys rush out and attack Tyler, throwing fake punches at the devil. In the chaos, the pope ends up hitting the rabbi, and the rabbi retaliates by fake-kicking him in the groin. The Buddhist goes to defend the pope and hits the rabbi, while the Imam keeps struggling with the devil. The choirboys on the floor are all still lying there, trying desperately not to laugh, while Tyler still clings to his victim who is whirling around, first knocking down the Buddhist, then clocking the pope.

It doesn't seem like anything more is going to happen— and, okay, yeah, this is funny—until Natalie Shallenberger (the supremest Platinum girl) comes out of the locker room in a white leotard and angel wings. She goes out and circles everyone, frowning and shaking her finger at them. Slowly the whole Golf Club straightens up, staring google-eyed at her, and then Natalie snaps her fingers: "One two three four" and the music becomes an old disco classic, launching everyone into their ultra-synchronized *Saturday Night Fever* line dance.

It's pretty hilarious, and incredibly cool, and a warm feeling goes over me as my spine relaxes. I'm not making fists anymore. I have to say, they're actually good: costumes, dancing, and, considering what they could've done, even the message kind of rocks. Everyone's fighting the devil and each other, but in the end it's all about getting down. Even Morgan has to appreciate this.

But the night's not over. After the floor is cleared of sinners and saints, Bobby yells out, "They need no introduction— Reeeeeeeaaach!" Though their routine totally kicked last year, Reach only won second place, and you can feel how everyone is hyped with anticipation, seeing if they can top themselves and win tonight. At first everyone is screaming like crazy, but then quiets down quick when Reach files out, all of them dressed in black. The music is an executioner's march. They're so serious it's mesmerizing, and the previous goofiness has completely evaporated.

When the whole group gets to the middle of the gym they all split up, forming two parallel lines with a circle in between. The ominous drumming picks up at once, and they all start this one-two-hitch thing with their feet, shifting back and forth, hands behind their backs, faces totally blank.

The music's so loud it's like your heartbeat. People around

us are rocking back and forth, practically vibrating the seats. All there is is this rhythm. The dancers in the center circle pull out long pieces of red, yellow, and orange silk, furling and flapping the fabric, likes the flames of giant fire.

With the fire dancers undulating back and forth, the line dancers slowly lift up books covered in black paper—big white letters spelling out THE BIBLE or MLK SPEECHES or MAVERICK MOMENT or THE CONSTITUTION across them. As they dance forward, each member throws his "book" into the "fire," before joining the line again and continuing the dance. When the last dancer flings his book, the empty-handed members of Reach file out, leaving just the "fire," the discarded books, and the only booming lyrics: "Time to think. Time to think for yourself. Time to think. Time to. Think."

Before they're finished everyone—everyone—is up clapping and screaming and stomping. All I can see are hundreds of hands slamming in applause that goes on and on and on. When it seems like things might die down, it's just so everyone can get in the same *clap clap clap clap*, even my parents next to me.

It doesn't take the judges very long after that. The audience is still clapping when Bobby and Mr. Hammersley step forward, carrying the Mace. They both hold up their hands to quell the applause, which only barely simmers down. Even though what Reach has done is controversial, it was clearly—clearly—the best and most thoughtful performance of the night. There's no way the judges can pick anything else. Unless they want a riot.

"Ladies and gentlemen, we want to thank you all for coming

out tonight, for showing your support for our clubs and your general school spirit. I have to say this is one of the finest evenings of performance I've seen, and I am proud to serve and lead a student body with such unified diversity. I hope you are all proud of what you've accomplished as Mavericks, and will join me in celebrating this year's Maverick Mayhem winners—" Here Mr. Hammersley pauses just long enough for me to get nervous. "The members of Reach!"

There is immediate, deafening cheering. I mean, deafening. You can barely hear Mr. Hammersley say "second-place winners, the Model United Nations, and honorable mention, Bright." But it doesn't matter. Reach comes out of the locker room, all of them smiling. Malik shakes Mr. Hammersley's hand and accepts the Mace from him, and instantly there's a huge surge from the bleachers and tons of students, even parents, rush the gym to get a chance to go hug and congratulate the winners.

I'm so full of—something—I have to just stand there a minute, watching. As parents and students make their way down the bleachers, I see Tyler the Devil squeeze a boy in a cowboy hat. A Reach guy high-fives a prom queen. Two girls from Bright—still in their unitards—jump up and down, hugging a girl in a Dutch costume. The dance team bobbles around the cheerleaders, and you can hardly tell them apart. After a really divisive week, I stand there and watch my schoolmates all being sincerely happy for themselves and each other. Right now, everybody thinks everybody else is cool, and everyone's cool with it.

"Good show," Mom says, breaking my spell. Dad takes her

hand and we inch toward the bottom of the bleachers, thrumming groups of students only slightly parting to let us by. I want to find Naeomi in all of this, to at least tell her she did a good job, even though I'm sure her parents and half the school are trying to do the same thing.

At the bottom I get stuck. Mom and Dad slip ahead of me, and when I try to push past a group of gospel choir girls I'm stopped by someone grabbing my hand. I expect to see Naeomi or even Yuhn, caught up in the excitement and maybe wanting to ask me to go for pizza afterward, but when I turn there's Morgan: smiling, sweaty, glowing, and breathless. She's happy and she's right there and her hand is clenching mine.

"Your parents came," she says, eyebrows going toward Mom and Dad. "I saw them right away. Before my parents," she gushes, flushed. "It was nice."

I am looking at her. I don't know what to say. My hand in hers feels electric. I want to keep it there. I want to jerk it back.

"You guys were good," I manage, wondering if Priah might show up now with one of her famous diversions. Instead I lock eyes with Natalie Shallenberger, who squeezes by us and even smiles as though she might have some small idea who I am.

"I tried to—" I hear Morgan say, her eyes distracted by people surrounding us. "I wanted to talk."

There are warm bodies everywhere: touching my back, shouts going off near my ears, everyone still excited and yelling. I can't believe how friendly, how open, everything feels. I could see Andy and probably hug him right now. Tonight, he'd probably hug me back. And then there's Morgan, and my hand still in hers.

"I didn't mean for . . . it . . . to happen. I mean. About Cara." She focuses on me for real. "It's not like you think."

I stare, feeling everyone around us, everything between us. My heart is racing. I don't know from what. It's completely inappropriate, her trying to bring this up now, and yet it's also the absolute best time.

She shakes her head and her hand goes loose. I want not to let go.

"I didn't mean to hurt her," she says finally. I must be half reading her lips. "Or you. There's your parents." And suddenly she's dance team smile again, Mom and Dad suddenly there, giving her congratulations hugs.

I hear them say, "Good show." I hear her thank them, hear her tell me she'll talk to me later. I'm aware of Dad's hand on my shoulder as he steers me out of the gym and into the back parking lot, where the air is cleaner and cooler and not nearly as buzzing or loud. I hear them ask me what I thought, say to each other it was impressive and they're glad they came; I hear myself talking about how amazing it was; hear them ask me about Morgan—I see and hear all these things around me, and I know I'm reacting, but as we get in the car and drive away together, mainly all I can really feel over and over again is Morgan's hand, grabbing mine, out of the crowd.

chapter 24

Saturday morning I spend a large portion of time in my pajamas looking at Tashara's website, reviewing pictures from last night's performance. I enlarge photos of random people hugging and smiling, people from totally different clubs with their arms around each other like they've been friends forever; I decide I'll say in yearbook on Tuesday that this, above all, should be the message we use to close the year.

Of course it's not lost on me, everyone acting like they've never had a beef with anyone, combined with the still-shocked feeling I can sense in my hand from where Morgan grabbed me. Though sleep has made the whole thing feel farther away, I keep my phone close by the computer, and later, on my desk while I'm studying, just in case.

But she doesn't call. Not that I know, really, what I'd say if she did. Still I jump when, at around four, my phone does finally ring. I'm both happy and only very mildly bummed to see that it is Jake.

"Tabitha."

"Yes, actually."

"Glad I got it right this time."

We both snuffle-laugh. I ask him about the movies; he asks about my night.

"My night was . . . my night was interesting."

"So interesting that the idea of going to a party tonight pales in comparison?"

"I don't know. Is it a clown party?"

He's quiet for only a beat. "Would clowns be a bad thing or a good thing?"

"Definitely bad."

"Okay, then no."

We make plans for him to come and pick me up at eight thirty and go over to his friend Paul's house "to hang out." I have no idea what this means and so when Dad asks later if there'll be parents present, I say yes because it doesn't occur to me until right that second that there might not be, doesn't occur to me that, if there weren't going to be, Jake wouldn't know he needed to point that out.

As I get ready I try a lot not to think about the fact that I'm supposed to be getting ready for the formal with Cara. I've shoved my green dress way out of sight so I don't have to think about how lame it is that my only real chance to wear it is at a fake wedding in front of a bunch of Alzheimer's patients, since Lacey asked me to be the maid of honor this time. I also don't think too much about poor Cara *never* getting to wear her dress, and maybe never seeing the boy she bought it for again. I also take extra time to curl my hair in order not to think about Morgan and Priah getting ready for the formal together right now, posing in front of the white fireplace for a photo.

On top of this I am very much not thinking about this party and meeting Jake's friends for the first time; not thinking about whether he will introduce me as his girlfriend or just as Tabitha, whether the girls will sneer at me and think I'm not good enough while the boys all try to check out my butt.

I'm so busy not thinking about all of this that it takes almost four tries to get the right outfit, and Mom hollers up the stairs that Jake's here before I've even started my makeup.

Nevertheless, we do get out of the house. On the way to the party Jake tells me a winding story about a campout he once had with Paul and some other friends, how somehow a possum became significantly involved.

And then we're there and we're out of the car, up the front steps, and the door opens and Jake is greeted by everyone—and I mean *every*one. First, Paul's mother, Pam, gives us both these giant squeezy hugs and practically pushes us into the kitchen, where a bunch of kids are standing around the table eating from a giant bowl of tortilla chips and nuclear-orange cheesy salsa dip. There's a ton of food, including a crock pot full of mini sausages in gooey brown sauce, a platter of cheesecake brownies, a tray of mozzarella sticks, and another plate of those soft pretzels next to a bowl of brown-flecked mustard.

Suddenly a big, tubby kid with merry eyes and pink cheeks (this must be Paul because he is just a big-boy version of Pam) comes to give Jake a tremendous bear hug. With me he politely shakes hands and looks at Jake approvingly. As this happens about six more guys appear from the den, where people are apparently having an intense Dance Dance Revolution smackdown; I'm introduced to all of them, and they all seem to be named Sam. As I'm smiling politely and all too aware of Jake's hand on my back, a herd of girls appears from somewhere else (the bathroom? Did they really all fit in there?) and there's another round of smiling and nodding and reciting their names to myself. *The girl with the shiny hair is Caroline. The curly girl is Eliza. Gemma has braces.* Finally I nod and smile at the folks originally standing around the table, not even trying to keep names straight anymore. Meanwhile Paul's huggy mom brings in two more people from the front door. It's about fifteen minutes before Jake and I can look at each other instead of everyone else.

"You wanna eat?"

I nod and we gather snacks onto small paper plates (Jake insists I try the creamy crab artichoke dip and the honey mustard chicken niblets) and then go into the huge comfy den to squeeze ourselves onto the leather couch with Sam and—Eliza? Everyone is eating and wiping greasy fingers and guffawing at Sam and Sam and some other kid not named Sam who are trying to make their characters break-dance without much success.

"So, is it Paul's birthday or something?" I whisper to Jake.

"Nah," Jake says around a wad of pretzel. "Pam just really likes to see us eat, and she'd rather everybody hang out here where she can keep an eye on us, instead of do doughnuts in some parking lot somewhere."

"You do doughnuts in that car?"

Jake's eyes glitter at me sideways. "For me to know and you to find out." He presses his knee against mine and again the warm feeling shoots up from where our bodies touch. I glance up to see if anyone notices and catch Braces Gemma's eyes flick away and back to the screen. This both embarrasses and pleases me greatly.

After a lot of eating and the arrival of more people and several rounds of very silly dance-game playing, Paul claps his hands and says it's Rocket Time. Immediately everyone climbs up from the deep pillowy furniture and starts to mill toward the sliding back door. I shoot Quiz Eyes at Jake; he goggles his eyebrows and leads me outside.

Where there is, unbelievably, this giant patio with an even more giant grill and a big fire pit with a fire already in it, and then beyond that a smooth sloping yard and then—a lake. Down by the lake are some benches, and most of the girls aim straight for them. I hang back and watch as Jake goes to help Paul and a few Sams with Rocket Time: jamming bottle rockets into the ground and lighting them, watching them shoot their loud spark lines into the dark water beyond.

It's actually kind of redneckish, though I guess since Jake is officially sort of a jock, it's okay. Cute, in fact. The goody two-shoes in me can't help glancing back at the house to check if we'll be in trouble, but all I see is Pam moving platters around the big table, so I figure this must just be what they do. I take it in, trying to observe it objectively instead of under the lens of We Are Supposed to Be at a Dance Right Now with My Friend. The boys are bending and lighting, clapping as the rockets hurl off across the water, and the girls all look at them, talking together, a little bored but laughing. I try to decide what I think about all of this, try to picture myself three parties from now when I'm not the New Girl and manage the nerve to Dance Revolution or light a bottle rocket myself.

I'm thinking it might actually be great (the Sams are all nice, anyway, and Paul and Pam) when one of the girls from the bench gets up and heads straight for me. It's Braces Gemma. We make line smiles at each other and I feel myself not being able to tell if this is going to be friendly inclusion or an ambush.

We stand there together a minute just watching the boys who are now making bouquets of rockets in the ground and trying to light them all at once. It doesn't take her long to get to her point.

"So, are you and Jake going out?"

I feel myself stiffen. "We met at this hayride in February," I say, dodging. She nods, and I let her do the mental math herself.

"That one's mine," she points. The Sam in the denim jacket.

I nod. "He's nice."

"He's a goofball, is what," she says.

I feel myself relax. At least Gemma's not official competition. She reaches for my wrist and pulls my hand out of my armpit, where I'm trying to keep it warm. It's both friendly and invasive. "I like your ring," she says evenly.

"Thanks," I say as evenly as possible back.

"Is it real?" she wants to know.

I feel my thumb moving for my ring, wanting to twirl it around. She feels this and lets go. "Real crystal," I tell her, trying to sound coolly sarcastic instead of defensive.

"Where'd you get it?" she keeps going.

"My best friend," is all I say.

"She have one too?"

I look at her for real now, trying to catch what exactly it is this girl is digging for. Is she just interested in things that sparkle? (Possible.) Is she being nosy about my relationship with Jake? (Even though she's taken, she could still harbor a secret crush.) Does she know about purity rings already? (Fifty-fifty chance. Maybe sixty-forty.) If so, is she truly interested or is she one of those mean girls who gets off on making other girls admit they're virgins, or trying to bait me into some kind of religious debate? (Not likely, though I don't know any of these people, really. Mean girls lie in wait everywhere, even possibly at an innocent little party of my—boyfriend's?—friends.)

I realize again how my little circle of ring friends has protected me, how I've been able to just take for granted that having a ring is something that's normal (at least with us) instead of something you have to explain, something other people might have opinions about. When we were all five together we were a group and everyone knew it. Even if people didn't know why we were wearing them, it didn't matter because we all had them and everyone assumed they meant something to us, even if they didn't know what. It was our thing and that was that. Not even Opal asked me about it until I'd known her for almost six weeks.

Now my circle is broken—maybe forever—and I'm going to have to start explaining. Which means I'm going to have to be sure on my own. I'm going to have to, like Reach's routine said, think for myself what wearing this ring is really about.

"It's a purity ring," I say, more firm than I thought.

Gemma reaches for my hand to take another look, and I give it to her. "Really?" she says. "You mean, like, no sex?"

I nod. Her eyes sneak over to Jake. *Here it comes.*

"Is it engraved?"

It takes me a second to realize what she's said isn't what I was expecting. "Mine isn't, but my friend's is. Actually two of my friends' are." Or, were. Cara's had GOD BLESS YOU AND KEEP YOU engraved on the inside; and technically it still is engraved, even if she's not wearing it.

"Your friends all have them?"

"Five of us." That we aren't really friends right now isn't something Gemma needs to know.

She looks at me a second and her neck straightens slightly, like a bird's, before she says, "Cool."

Suddenly everything in me is two degrees looser. I test a joke: "Well, you know how it helps to have workout buddies?"

Gemma laughs in her throat. "We certainly don't get any help from them." She rolls her eyes at the boys, who are lighting the last of the bottle rockets and playing at shoving each other into the lake next. I laugh with her, but watch Jake (who is picking up a squealing Paul and staggering toward the water), smiling secretly to myself and letting the warm feeling slide over me. *Well—some of us do.*

"Did you have a good time?" Jake wants to know as we pull out of the driveway. I tell him I did, and am glad to really mean it.

After some stupid boyshoving around the water—one of the Sams actually falling in and needing to go up to the house to change clothes—we'd mostly stood around the fire pit and tried to out-gross each other with stories of things we'd seen on Japanese sites or YouTube. Gemma'd actually stayed with me and brought a couple of her friends to stand with us, and by the time we left, it seemed like they might genuinely be happy to see me again.

"Your friends are nice. It was cool meeting them."

"They like you. Sam said my girlfriend was hot."

I look at him. He actually used the word. In a sentence! About me!

"What?" His fingers go up from the steering wheel, defensive. "You totally are. Wait. Do I need to kick his ass?"

"Just make sure he knows I have a boyfriend," I say, trying to make the word as loose as possible and not giggle.

"No doubt about that."

The only thing, I think, that makes me giddier the whole night is getting to my driveway and hearing him murmur, "Icing time," as he turns toward me in his seat.

Sunday morning means Palm Sunday, and while Passion Week has all my favorite stuff from the Bible, and sometimes it's fun to watch the little kids file into the church waving their palm fronds and singing "Hosanna" in their sweet little voices, I decide to snuggle under my covers and stay in bed late. I tell myself it's to give Mom and Dad a chauffeur break, but really I'm hoping if I stay up here long enough, I'll eventually catch the scent of waffles.

Lucky for me my parents take the hint, and after warm syrupy goodness, I even help with the dishes. It's a nice lazy McAbe family Sunday, with Mom and Dad and their paper and even a good romantic comedy on TV.

By three o'clock, however, I'm listless and bored and trying very hard to avoid my phone, which is somehow silently calling out to me from my dresser upstairs. I ignore the screaming desire to check it for three reasons: One, I don't want to be looking at it while it sits there not ringing and it not being Morgan. Morgan, who made it seem like she really would be calling, like, any minute now. Two, looking at it makes me want to pick it up and call Cara and tell her about the party last night and how Jake Officially Called Me His Girlfriend, but since she's under martial law, I can't. Three is that I very badly want to call Jake for no reason just to see if I can get him to refer to me as his girlfriend again, but even I know that is needy and ridiculous and Naeomi would kill me.

Instead I try to study some more (though I studied a lot yesterday and it is getting pretty old), and then for the heck of it change my Facebook profile from "single" to "in a relationship." I stare stupidly at my new ranking for a while, debating whether or not I should move Jake up a little in my friends list, until the screen beeps at me and I see that Priah's just logged in. I sign out real fast as though she would even care.

It's a pretty boring Sunday, actually, and though I'm not crazy about going to youth group without Cara, it's definitely better than sitting around watching more stupid tennis with Dad, counting each hour that Morgan hasn't called.

Pure

When I get to the church Evie rushes up as usual, and I dodge her curiosity about Cara's absence and the Mayhem dance with the Homework Shrug. Marilyn and Greg arrive with snacks and we help unload them, then move the folding chairs into semicircle rows to listen to our guest speaker from Emory, talking about building green, in order to kick off our new project on the environment. It's pretty cool and I should be excited since this summer our mission trip is probably going to help the Green Home Society install solar panels in new houses for mothers leaving abusive relationships, but I already know a lot of what she's saying, since one of Dad's claims to fame is that he used a lot of green stuff in his projects way before it was cool.

Even circle prayer at the end has a bit of drudgery about it, as I realize there isn't anything really to pray for except for Cara to be okay and God to appear on my doorstep and tell me exactly what to do about my friends (okay and maybe for Morgan to call me?), but those are specifics I don't want to air out in front of the group.

As I'm giving Evie a last hug and saying good-bye to the other girls, Marilyn calls me over from where she's putting away the final chairs. I help her finish up and she motions me over to her backpack, where she bends down to remove a book.

"I thought about what you asked me last week, kiddo," she says, "and this might be a more helpful response. It's helped me, anyway."

I take the book from her: slim and square with a photograph of the ocean on the cover, and the word *Desiderata* in silver script.

"Hang on to it for a while," she says. "Maybe something will connect."

I thank Marilyn and hug her, squashing the book awkwardly between us. I want to ask her more about it, but she's already steering me toward the door, turning out the lights, ready to leave.

Dad's waiting in the car outside and when I climb in, of course right away he wants to know, "What's the book?"

I show him and he nods. "Ah, yes. That's a good one there."

"You know it?"

"Read some for me?" is all he says.

I open the cover and turn to the first page, a black-and-white photograph of a crowd moving on a busy city sidewalk. "'Go placidly amid the noise and haste, and remember what peace there may be in silence,'" it says. A poem, then. A long one too, though on each page there are only a few lines printed. All the illustrations are black-and-white photographs, a lot of them grainy: some of people, some of nature. I read the whole thing, stumbling a little, trying to focus on reading it well out loud and understanding at the same time. It's a pretty poem, soothing in a nice, embrace-all-things-including-yourself message. When I get to the end, I'm surprised as Dad recites along with me: "'With all its sham, drudgery, and broken dreams/it is still a beautiful world. Be cheerful. Strive to be happy.'"

We're home but I stay put in my seat. "You have it memorized?"

Dad shrugs. "Parts of it."

I look at the cover again, running some of the verses over in my head. *Do not distress yourself with dark imaginings.* "I didn't know you were into that kind of thing."

"Eh." Dad exaggeratedly cracks his knuckles before unbuckling his seat belt. "You know, works with the ladies." When he sees me roll my eyes, he shrugs. "Used to, anyway."

Back upstairs in my room while Dad's cooking dinner, I reread the poem (my favorite line the one about how the universe is unfolding as it should) and examine the inscription in the front of the book. Someone with very swoopy handwriting has written, *To M, so that there may be peace in her troubled-water heart. —L.* I picture my youth group leader and her steely coolness, try to imagine her having troubled waters where her heart should be. I wonder who L. is, why she wanted Marilyn to have this, how it helps. There's a piece of small yellow notebook paper folded in half in the front, too, and though I worry it might be a more personal note Marilyn forgot about, I unfold it, anyway.

It's a note to me, in Marilyn's scratchy writing: *Found this, too. Thought it might help you more specifically.* It's a quote from the Bible, Mark 12:31. When I read it I take out my own Bible to look at the entire chapter: a story about Jesus talking to His disciples and a bunch of other people. Somebody asks Him if He knows what the most important commandment is. Though I've heard it plenty before, tonight I read His answer over and over, making it stay with me a long time even after Mom calls me for dinner. The first part's about loving God, of course, but it's the second part that echoes: *"'Love your neighbor as yourself.' There is no commandment greater than these."*

chapter 25

Monday and back at school. Figuring it's our new meeting place, I go to the library to look for Cara and Naeomi, and am surprised they aren't there. I sit at a table and wait for them, not sure if they're late or I'm early. I read ahead in history a little, and still they haven't shown. By homeroom bell neither of them has appeared, but since school's officially started I can't text Naeomi to see what's up. I head to homeroom, alone.

PE first period this week. Enough said.

Naeomi isn't at my locker before English, and no note from either her or Cara. *Did everybody drop off the face of the earth?* This feels way too much like the Monday after my fight with Morgan. So much so I almost wonder if I somehow time traveled in my sleep, but that Monday I had a totally different outfit on, so I guess not.

On the way to bio I steel myself to ignore Morgan completely. Clearly Mayhem and the dance and probably finishing touches to her renewal service were all way more important than fixing our friendship. Clearly whatever she felt on Friday was fleeting, and I suppose I shouldn't be surprised. *The love of Jesus is forever, Tab.* I guess, compared to that, not much else is. It's niggling me a bit what she said about not meaning to hurt Cara, and I wonder what extent of anything about Cara she really knows, but, if she really cared or wanted to know, she would have called me. If it's not important to her, then her lack of concern isn't important to me, either.

Except she's totally standing outside class, waiting for me.

"Hey," she says when she sees me, closing the distance between us.

"Hey."

"I'm sorry I couldn't call you this weekend."

I don't have an answer for this, and I'm not going to help her any.

"I really . . . think we have a lot to talk about. But I want to, like, do it in person."

What, so I can watch the contempt spread over your face again? So I can get my hopes up to have them dashed? I think of Cara's understanding, of Gemma saying "Cool." I have other friends. I don't need her.

"I have to work this afternoon, and there's yearbook tomorrow." My voice is flat.

She nods, eyes down. This is when I notice she still doesn't have her ring. It's bizarre, her naked hand, like someone else's—I haven't seen her close up like this in a while. I wonder if she worries the new one won't be done by Easter. A twinge of sympathy beats in my heart.

"Wednesday after school?" she tries.

I sigh, wondering what Cara would think if she found out that, since I can't really hang out with her anymore, I decided to just take back up with Morgan. Even Judas would know better. When I saw Morgan Friday, when she reached out for me, all these old feelings came rushing back. Now facing her, thinking about what she's done, how cold and hard *she's* been, I'm not sure what I feel. I never thought I could ever do anything without Morgan, let alone be happy to, but after the last couple of weeks I know different. So much has happened that she doesn't even know about, and a lot of it has been really great. Even if we do talk—even if she somehow apologizes in a way to make up for everything—what then? How do I even start to explain about Jake? Or what a good friend Cara's turned out to be? I feel like I've changed shape, and she has too: that the matching puzzle pieces we used to be have gotten wet and warped. And I'm not sure we'll be able to fit them back together.

"I guess I just want you to hear me out," she says, seeing my hesitation.

"I guess I can do that."

The look of relief on her face is almost heartbreaking. "Thanks."

Without saying anything else we both move to the classroom door and go in. I'm afraid for a minute that Morgan will try to reach out and hug me or something, act like everything's totally back to normal just by virtue of my agreeing to meet her, but it seems she really does understand. We go about our business in biology as we've been doing for the past several days, neither of us acknowledging the other much. After class she only gives me a small wave before she heads out. I'm confused about why I feel let down by this. I follow her a short way down the hall, staying several people behind, feeling the tug of the invisible tendrils that are trying to keep the two of us connected.

Even though she's been incognito all day, Cara is actually in chorus, and afterward we walk together to math. During history I'd tried to draw a little picture to give her, just something small and funny to sort of try to cheer her up, but everything I could think of came back in some way to either the formal we both missed, or else the two of us talking together about our boyfriends. It actually bummed me out, wondering what we'll have in common now besides school, so I decided to stop.

Still, I give her a big hug and smile after singing is over, and tell her I missed her this weekend.

"Did you get to do anything fun?" she asks, plain as possible.

I'm not sure whether to tone things up or down: "Jake took me to a party?"

She nods. "Cool."

I'm just about to tell her more about Gemma and how she didn't seem to think my ring was weird, but that would be talking about our rings, which is yet another thing I don't have in common with Cara anymore. This isn't going very well.

"Did you ride this weekend?" I try.

"It's practically all I did. Besides homework."

It's like she's—I don't know—a lump of clay or something,

how lackluster she's being. Not sad really, just kind of—nothing. I scan my brain for a good topic change, something we can chat about that doesn't touch on any sore spots. It's much harder than I want it to be. Even filling her in on youth group just emphasizes that she can't go.

"Naeomi says you went to Mayhem," she says after the crossroads.

I ignore my guilty twinge. "Are things really better with you guys?"

She nods but her eyes are still blank. "She's always been a really good person to talk to."

I can't help wondering how much Naeomi's gotten to talk, herself.

We're outside geometry now, only a minute or two before the bell. Cara's chewing on her bottom lip. "I told her this morning I think Michael and I are," she swallows, eyes on the floor, "breaking up or something."

My hand goes automatically to grab hers, and when I do the tears she's apparently been holding in swell up along her lower lids.

"I just don't know how we can make it work you know?" She tries to sound firm around the shaking in her throat.

I don't say anything. I don't honestly know how they can really make it work, either. Jake and I are doing pretty good with e-mails and phone calls and seeing each other a few times a week, but we're still getting to know each other and aren't that serious. If I was relying on him every day, and then we couldn't talk at all? Gah.

She sniffs in a loud strong breath and wipes her eyes with her fingertips, shaking it off in her horsey way. The bell rings over our heads and we flinch, but I tell her I'll stay with her until she's ready to go in.

"I think . . ." She sighs, clearing her throat. "If I broke up with him for good my parents might give me some of my privileges back. At least let me see you guys a little."

This is a mildly abrupt switch, but I guess a good one. "I hate it that you're going through this bad time and I can't talk to you except here."

She nods vigorously. "I know. I mean, I miss Michael and everything but not having you guys is worse almost."

Mr. Outif sticks his head out of the classroom then and asks if we'll be joining them any time soon. When he sees Cara's been crying, it takes him by surprise. I ask if we can have a few minutes and he tells us, "Of course of course," in his sympathetically embarrassed way.

"Have you heard anything from him?" I say when Mr. Outif shuts the door again. He can't not've e-mailed her, or written on her Wall, right?

But she shakes her head. "He messaged Naeomi on Facebook and said to tell me he's thinking about me, but that's pretty much it. I think he's scared maybe Skip is cyber-tracking him, in case. Like he'd know how." She makes the weird sad laughing noise. "I wrote him—Michael. A letter, you know? I thought he might . . . try to write me back or something, but I guess my dad would rip it up if he found it. Maybe it's on the way, though. You never know."

I think how weird that would be, resorting to the Pony Express just to talk to your boyfriend. Let alone having to maybe break up with him that way.

"I wish I could *do* something. I mean, I don't know any way to help. I don't know what to say."

"You've stuck by me," she says, smoothing back her hair and preparing her face for class. "That helps a lot. Not a ton of folks lining up for the job, you know?"

It strikes me then that I'm the only one who has stuck by her through all of this. You know, consistently. "Wow, I must be some kind of amazing friend then, I guess," I say, making it funny: pulling on invisible suspenders like a Good Old Boy.

And she actually laughs—not the bitter kind, even. "Well, I guess you kind of must be. You should have a crown or something."

That we've found even a tiny thing to joke about is huge. I catch a glimpse of my real friend: the girl who's rapidly becoming my—best? My stupid joke may be an itty-bitty island in a sea of troubles, but standing on it here, hugging her in the hall, I think maybe I can even see some other oases peeking out of the waves.

It's like she reads my mind. "Hey, don't go feeling sorry for me too much. I still want to know all about you and Jake. I need to hear some happiness, you know?"

"Okay," I promise, trying not to let my mind rush forward to a time when Cara can come to one of Paul's parties, even maybe starts to date one of the Sams.

"Okay."

Pure

We go in then, ducking past Mr. Outif as unobtrusively as possible. The rest of class I half listen, pretending to take notes, though really I'm drawing a picture of myself with a big jewel-encrusted crown, and little quote bubbles chattering about different things to Cara: meeting Jake's friends, the environment stuff we talked about at youth group, even the *Desiderata* Marilyn gave me. The more I write, the more I realize I have to tell her, though since my crown's so big in the picture, the paper fills up pretty fast. When I give it to her after class she opens it right away and laughs a second time. The resulting good feeling propels me through the rest of the day, especially the knowledge that, when the time comes, I'll be able maybe to fill another whole sheet with whatever happens with Morgan on Wednesday, though maybe after that it will be Cara who'll have to wear the Stick by Me crown.

When Mom and I get home after my afternoon of helping Lacey finalize things for the mock wedding at the Center, I check my e-mail, see that Naeomi's online too.

And I realize there's something I want to ask her.

u busy? I type.

It takes her a second before she IMs back: LITTLE BIT. BUNCH OF TESTS THIS WEEK.

ok me too.

WHAT'S UP?

have u tlkd 2 morgan?

HARDLY. WHY?

she wants 2 tlk 2 me.

Nothing from Naeomi for a full beat, so I plunge on: did u tell her abt C getting in trouble? & michael?

I don't know, really, how much Naeomi and Morgan talk at dance practice, especially not anymore. I can easily picture her saying absolutely nothing to Morgan. I can also imagine her losing patience, letting something fierce slip. Especially if she thinks what I think.

SHE'S PRETTY MUCH ESTABLISHED SHE DOESN'T WANT TO KNOW ANYTHING ABOUT CARA ANYMORE, HASN'T SHE? finally appears.

Good point.

AND BESIDES I DON'T THINK IT'S REALLY HER BUSINESS.

do u think she told? I brave. I haven't admitted to anybody else—not even my parents—that I think Morgan called Cara's family; it's hard enough to admit to myself.

Right away: HARD TO SEE HOW IT COULD BE ANYONE ELSE.

I look at the screen, wondering how I feel about this. I mean, I knew. But seeing that Naeomi thinks it too makes it more definitely real. And so—what? Morgan called the Rawlsons and ruined Cara's life. Cara's in a ton of trouble and her whole family basically hates her. Now she's even losing her boyfriend. On the other hand, I know Naeomi thinks Cara and Michael breaking up is probably the best thing that could happen for Cara. And in some ways, I guess I agree with her.

do u think m used c? I decide to ask.

Another bit of time before she responds: NO. HE LOVES HER. HE'S JUST NO MATCH FOR THEM.

she thinks they're breaking up.

SHE SAID THE SAME THING TO ME.

did u tell her what he sd?

I MAY NOT HAVE TO.

I sit with that a minute, everything swirling around: Morgan, Michael, Cara, good things turning bad and bad things turning good.

I BETTER GO. HAVE TO WORK ON A PAPER AND STUDY.

ok. me2. hey! great job fri.

THANKS.

cu 2morrow?

SEE YOU. XO.

xo.

When I sign off, I really do try to also sign out of the crazy maelstrom in my head. Spring break starts on Friday, and between now and then I have three tests and a Dickens response due in English, plus regular homework, including vocabulary sentences for French. It's not pleasant, but since schoolwork's the only certainty I've got right now, at least until I talk to Morgan, I almost kind of cling to it.

chapter 26

Wednesday morning when I get to school there are crowds of people in the foyer near the front office. When I look, I find the huge poster of proofs from the Mayhem Formal: tiny thumbnails of photos taken as people entered the dance that you can order and have enlarged for various gross amounts of money. They could just as easily do this on a website, but this way everyone sees everyone else looking at the pictures, and it's harder to avoid looking—or better yet, buying.

I stand at the edge, then squeeze my way closer. The pictures are pretty generic, really: everyone standing in couples or groups near this silly arch covered in blue, white, and silver streamers and a lot of fake plastic ivy. The boys are in ties and jackets and the girls are mostly in strapless black dresses, the main differences among them being the hemline and whether there's a sash or not. My eyes go to the popular people first: Seamus in a kilt, and his date with a giant fake magnolia pinned to her shoulder. Natalie and

McKay posing together. Tiny Tyler in a bow tie, his Platinum date towering over him.

Okay, yes, honestly I'm looking for Morgan and Cody. I can't help it. I want to see the dress she didn't consult me about and the makeup I didn't help her put on. I wonder if she even looked for me there, if she thought she might run in to me and Jake. I'm frustrated not finding her and am incredibly surprised when my eyes fall on Priah and Sprockett instead.

They look perfect. Sprock has this sleek black suit on with an electric blue tie, and he's smiling so much you can really see his handsomeness. Pree too has got a huge smile on her face, and is wearing not black but an incredible soft tangerine color that looks great against her dark skin. A huge burst of happiness explodes in me. *Hooray, Sprockett, for not taking my horrible advice! Hooray, Priah, for saying yes!* I wish I could just rush up to Priah and hug her.

And then, when I turn around to head to my locker, she's standing right there, looking dead at me. There isn't anything to do but go over, though her expression doesn't make me too eager.

"Yeah. In spite of you we went," she says, mouth tense.

A green curtain of shame sweeps from my forehead to my feet.

"Why did you tell him not to ask me?" she spits.

I feel myself on the verge of saying something cutting, but, as usual, I falter for just a second and it fails me. She is, after all, finally talking to me. She's mad, but she's talking. I've missed her so much I weaken.

"I'm glad he asked you, anyway," I say. "I really wanted him to."

The pleasure goes across her face. I watch it happen, watch her try to hide it, try to make herself fierce and mad again, but we both see it doesn't exactly work.

"My parents liked him," she admits, eyebrows going together.

"So . . ." I have to tread carefully. "Do *you?*"

Priah's never been good at camouflaging her emotions, and she still isn't.

I smile. "Pree, I—"

She leans back against the lockers and looks up at the ceiling. "When he told me he was surprised I said yes because of what you said, I was so mad at you. I wanted to kill you. I hoped you'd be there just so I could, I don't know, slap you in the face or something. I didn't know why you would do something like that. You're so—*nice.*"

My insides crawl up closer to each other. Yes, I usually am "so nice." Especially where my friends are involved. *But you haven't exactly been nice, either.*

"But then," she goes on, "it was so weird—I was there and we had so much fun on our own even though I was so mad, and I kept looking for you and looking for you, thinking 'Just wait until she gets here; I'll show her.' And Woody kept being so annoying, asking if I was okay—and I realized, mainly, I was just *looking* for you."

Her eyes are still on the ceiling, arms crossed and hands shoved far up under her armpits. She's so uncomfortable saying what she's saying I wish I had a chair to offer her, so she could sit down. And truthfully it's such an unexpected outpouring of honesty I wish *I* had a chair too. I had no idea that Priah would miss me, that *she* might've gone through a thing or two, too.

"Wasn't Morgan with you at the dance?"

She starts. "Has she talked to you yet?"

I shake my head, can't help glancing at the wall clock, notice we only have a minute or two before the bell. "No. Why?"

I can see her weighing how much to tell. "You should just talk to her."

A familiar, protective panic uncurls in me. "Is she okay?"

About six things to say cross Priah's eyes. "I haven't really talked to her since Mayhem, and everything was so crazy that night—"

"You were good by the way. I was there."

A fast smile. "I saw you." Then, serious again. "But—she's going through a hard time, I think. I mean, it's not like her to not call me, especially after—" She realizes what she just said sounds awfully Very Best Friend-ish. We both exchange a look. "Just talk to her, okay? I think she . . . really needs you."

I remember Morgan's ringless hand. "What about Easter?"

The school bell clangs glaringly close. We flinch together.

"They couldn't do it. For one thing her ring wasn't finished and then there just wasn't room in the service. She was pretty upset."

I can imagine. I know that was her dream: to get up there in front of everyone. It wouldn't occur to her that her minister might say no outright. "Look—" I start, but we both have to go. And yet we have so much to talk about, now that we actually are. "I'm really sorry."

Her face is so sincere. "I am too. But"—she looks down the hall a second, at everyone busy with their lockers and getting to homeroom—"I kind of deserved it."

I want to hug her then, but we are still a little awkward so I don't. Instead I ask her to call me or something, and she nods with a little smile before we wave and go in our separate directions.

I walk to homeroom, thinking about how long this day is going to be. I was dreading this afternoon before, mainly because I didn't know how to feel about it. Now I still am a little, but it's because, I realize, I'm actually worried about my friend.

When I get to Java Monkey after school, Morgan isn't there yet. I sip my iced tea and watch the door, worried—stupidly—that the next person who walks in might be Cara—that today, of all days, she's finally allowed to go somewhere besides straight home after school, and would, of all places, choose here.

It's only three people later that Morgan walks in, a little flustered and anxious herself, though she smiles when she sees me. I watch her go to the counter, order the raspberry tea I thought of getting for her but didn't in case I got stood up. I know she's tense because she doesn't smile at the girl at the register, doesn't scan the room on her way back to our table, looking for other people we might know. Instead she's focused, almost to a jittery degree. There's obviously a lot going on there. I imagine the conversation between Morgan and Priah about this meeting, if Priah told Morgan that she and I were talking now too.

"So," I say when she sits down.

"So, I was thinking about what to say to you all the way over here," she starts. "And the more I thought about what to say, the more things *to* say came up."

She's quiet just long enough to make me give in. "Like what?"

Her leg starts jumping under the table. "Like—" She flicks her eyes at me. "Like, I hated that article in the paper. That's not what I wanted, and it was totally unfair. Like, it was *so* good to see your parents and you at Mayhem. Like, I've lost five pounds because I can't eat or sleep because I'm so worried all the time. Like, I broke up with Cody this weekend. Like, I didn't tell on Cara." She looks at me again. "Like that."

I decide to process one of the easier parts first: "Are you sad or glad?"

She makes Are You Crazy eyes at me. "About which?"

"Breaking up with Cody. Sad or glad breaking up?"

"Um—" She assesses. "Sad then glad? I mean, sad when I realized I truly needed to, then glad to finally have it over?"

I nod.

"He did *not* take it well," she confides, leaning in and rolling her eyes. "Not like he couldn't see it coming. Nothing worse than a boy who whines when you dump him. That's why I missed the dance. Sucked."

I nod again, trying to picture Cody doing much more than shuffling and shrugging and following Morgan around. I wonder if their breakup constitutes a big enough reason not to call me.

"Have you been out with Jake?" she wants to know.

All I can do is nod. It's weird she doesn't know this.

"That's good."

We are both suddenly very interested in our drinks, instead of the giant elephant we're both still ignoring. I feel myself balled up, waiting: watching not just what she says but what she's not saying and perhaps is about to say. Though right now she seems regretful, and though just her wanting to make up would've been more than good enough in the past, one whole side of my body is still tense—ready to leap up from the table and run at the slightest sign of trouble.

"Look, you have every right to be mad at me," she says.

This is a surprise.

"I shouldn't've said what I said to you that day. I mean—I shouldn't have said it that *way*."

You mean the way you said you wouldn't want to be friends with me, either? Or, later, the way you basically said I was stupid for taking Cara's side? My head buzzes with this, but I just keep listening, waiting. For once I want her to be the one to make everything okay.

I'm flustering her. "Look, like I said, you can totally be mad." I give her the slightest nod. "But what you can't be mad at me about is telling. Because I didn't. I didn't call Cara's parents. I wouldn't do that. I know you think I did—and I guess I don't blame you—but I just needed you to know that it wasn't me."

My anger kicks in and I realize I don't believe her. "How do you know anybody said anything, then?"

She blushes, and her lips go together in an embarrassed frown. "I didn't—"

I just watch her, wanting, meanly, to see her struggle a little. Hating myself for it at the same time.

She takes in a deep breath. "I was upset. I mean, it's not exactly a picnic, your best friend not even making eye contact with you in class or anything—going through all this crap at school and not having her there, watching her take sides with someone you—" She stops short of "hate"; I can see it. "Someone you disagree with."

Yeah, tell me about it.

"And after everything got so messed up that week, I just didn't know what to do. I mean, I really thought I was doing something *good*. I thought it would help people. But everything got so whack and people were threatening stuff. And you still wouldn't talk to me. . . . "

Her eyes are looking everywhere except at me. "So, yeah, okay, on Sunday after youth group I talked to Wedge. I just needed some advice. I thought he would—I don't know, have some kind of wisdom."

I see Marilyn handing me a book, see myself lingering behind, wondering what exactly it is I want to ask her.

"So I told him. I mean, the prayer group thing had gone so badly and every time I saw you, you were always with Cara. And I was worried. About you. About what you might—" Again, she stops herself before going too far. And I have to give her credit, actually, for keeping herself in relative check. For thinking about what someone else might feel before she opens her mouth. "So anyway, I told him everything and he told me not to worry and that he'd do everything he could to help—he told me some passages to look up in the Bible—and for a while afterward I really felt better. But then about an hour after we got home Wedge called me back and told me he'd taken care of it, and I just—I just felt sick to my stomach."

I feel sick to my stomach myself, picturing Mrs. Rawlson answering the phone, Morgan's youth group leader on the other end telling her he's just heard something he feels she needs to know.

"They messed up his car," I tell her. "She's grounded forever and isn't allowed to talk to him."

"I know." Her eyes, shameful, on the table. "I mean, I didn't know exactly but I knew. I knew it would be something bad. I mean, it's the *Rawlsons*. But plus, she looks—gray."

"She pretty much is," I admit, and for a minute, it feels almost good: the two of us concerned about the exact shade of our friend's skin. And then I'm not sure. "Why do you suddenly care?"

She blushes, and I think she's angry at first. "I missed you, okay? I mean, Priah and I've been hanging out a lot more, but it isn't . . ." She falters. "It isn't the same. I'd see you and I'd realize I had no idea what was going on with you, and I hated it."

It's weird, this feeling. It's like I'm on delay or something. Her words are sinking in but I'm not reacting to them. I should be lunging across the table right now, hugging her, telling her everything she's missed, everything I've been wanting to share. So why aren't I? I mean, she's here, she admitted she was wrong, she's sorry—at least she seems to be. And I've missed her, too, right?

"What about Cara?"

I see her shoulders—just barely—slump a little before she gets her defensive shields up. "What *about* Cara?"

"I mean, what about Cara, is what about Cara." I'm looking at her now, dead-on.

"I told you I didn't tell on her."

"But have you apologized to her?"

She doesn't say anything.

"You know she's really a good person. A good friend."

She doesn't even hesitate: "What she did was wrong. Even she knows that."

This time I feel myself flush. "How would you know what she knows?" *How in fact do you know* any*thing for sure?* I've got marathon-running heart rate again.

She sinks her head into both her hands. "This isn't how I thought this would go."

I watch her staring down at the tabletop, fingers kneading at the top of her skull. I'm astonished at my resistance to her. So much of me wants to reach over, grab her hand, start over again, and talk like normal. It is a relief, knowing she didn't actually dial those numbers herself, and I do understand needing to talk to someone about all this. She couldn't know what Wedge would do.

And yet, it's still nagging me, how easy it all was for her, rejecting Cara. Rejecting me. Choosing sides. How she's still choosing them. How there's an ocean of things between us that we haven't talked about, and I'm not sure how we ever can. How I'm stuck between a place where I want to forgive her, and I still can't.

"Well," I finally say, "I'm glad you told me your side of it." And I mean it.

She's still staring at the table, shakes her head.

"And I'm sorry about Easter. Priah told me."

She looks up. "Priah talked to you?" I can't tell if she's mad.

"I saw her in the hall. Mainly she wanted to tell me about her and Sprockett."

"She had a good time, by the way. She likes him. But I think she feels bad, liking someone when me and Cody just broke up."

"Well, that's understandable."

"Yeah, I guess. But she's kind of a . . ." She glances at me, checking. "A hanger-on. You know? It's like, 'Gah, Priah. Give me half a second.'"

I shrug, trying to hide my pleasure. "Well, maybe a boyfriend will be good."

"Or maybe she'll want to call me every ten minutes to say what he said or what she's thinking about saying or what she's worried he might say about what she said."

We laugh at this, together. It's almost easy.

"So is your ring just not done or . . . ?"

She rolls her eyes and sighs. "Well, first there was—" But from the depths of her purse her phone beeps, and of course she pulls it out. She squints at the appearing text, then puts it back. "Mom's on her way. Final practicing for next week."

Next week. Her birthday. Her driving test.

"You nervous?"

She shrugs in a way that I know means she is. I ask her when she's going so I can pray for her at the exact right minute.

Outside, the sun is bright on the sidewalk and buildings, making us squint after the dark coziness of the café. "Thanks for meeting me," she says, watching the passing traffic for her mother's hulking white SUV.

I realize we haven't come to any conclusions, haven't—really—talked about much. Not the things I've wanted to talk about, anyway.

We both see her mom at the same time. "So can I call you?" she wants to know.

"I think we have more to talk about," I say, feeling anxious suddenly that she's about to leap in the car and go away, that I haven't gotten to say my piece, whatever it might've been.

"Well, duh," she says, digging into her purse again for her phone, beeping with another text. Her mom pulls up to the curb, leans across the passenger seat toward the unrolling window to call hello to me.

"Hi, Mrs. Kent."

"We miss you, honey," she chirps. "Hope to see you soon."

I realize Morgan has said nothing to either of her parents about any of this. I look at her, but she's squinting at her phone, punching keys.

"Okay then," I say, smiling at Mrs. Kent. I turn to Morgan, not sure whether we're supposed to hug.

She echoes me, "Okay then," distracted, dropping her phone back into her purse. "I'll talk to you later?" And then she comes at me, wrapping her arms loosely around the very tops of my shoulders and leaning her cheek close to mine in a quick air-kiss.

I find myself nodding okay and waving dumbly again as Mrs. Kent scooches to the passenger side so Morgan can drive. She's acting light but I can see she's tense and nervous. She waits until every other car in sight is safely past before pulling into her lane and driving away, neither waving nor honking, but both hands gripping the wheel.

On the walk home, everything runs through my head like a word problem: *Cara and Tabitha and Naeomi and Priah and Morgan were friends. Morgan and Naeomi got mad at Cara, but for different reasons. Tabitha did not. Morgan left both Tabitha and Cara, taking Priah with her. Naeomi left Cara. Tabitha's friendship with Cara improved. So did her friendship with Naeomi. Soon Naeomi and Cara became friends again. Priah has missed Tabitha; Tabitha has missed Priah. Now, if Morgan and Tabitha are talking, and Naeomi and Cara are talking, to what degree are Cara and Tabitha still friends?*

I can't make anything equal out.

I call Jake.

"Tabitha," he says.

"Jake," I say back, our new ritual. "Are you busy?"

"If you count watching my brother chase a bunch of other kids around a playground as busy, then yes."

I tell him I just talked to Morgan.

"Okay no, I'm not that busy. Are you okay?"

"I think so. I don't know what to think."

"Can't help you much there, I'm afraid."

I take a deep breath. "I can't tell if she's really sorry or if she just . . . wants things back to normal."

"Does it make a difference?"

I think about this. "I'm not sure I can go back to normal if she isn't really sorry."

"Well, there you go."

I laugh. "You're so helpful."

"And expensive," he teases. "That just cost you three milk-shakes."

"Am I being stupid?" I test.

"Again, can't help you much there. For what it's worth, I haven't seen you be very stupid yet."

"She said she didn't do it."

"Do what?"

I remember he doesn't know about my now partly confirmed suspicions. "Part of what I've been mad at her about."

"Austin! Put down the stick, buddy. Total foul. Sorry," he says back to me.

"No, it's okay. I should let you go."

"Austin! I'm serious, dude. Geez. Tabitha, I'm sorry—"

This is totally not the right time. And maybe even not the right person, though it is nice to have him close. "It's okay. Thanks for trying."

"Yeah, I better go. It's *Lord of the Flies* out here. Call me later?"

"If I can. Heaps of homework before break."

"You saving Saturday for me? Honest-to-God party at Paul's. And maybe you can meet my mom next week too? Come over for dinner?"

A jump goes in my throat. "Sure."

"Okay, we'll discuss."

"Sounds good."

"Okay, good luck with all that. And you're not stupid."

"Okay."

And we hang up.

Mom still isn't home and Dad won't be for a while yet, so when I let myself into the house I throw my bag down and pace. First, I go up to my room, but the bed's still unmade and there are clothes on the floor and I should probably really vacuum, so I go back downstairs. In the kitchen everything's clean and neat and sparkling and I don't feel like sullying it with a snack, so I wander into the den and stare at the computer a minute. But the computer means e-mail and Facebook and possible chatting and normal social run-ins, and since I don't feel normal, I don't even turn it on.

Morgan wants me back. And I want her back, a little, though I want her back-back and not back on these weird terms where we're both somehow different. But I can't time travel. I can't undo all the things that have happened. I can't make things not—changed.

I go to my bag, take out a notebook.

Dear Morgan, I write. I hold my pen over the very-blank piece of paper, thinking. It's been a long time since I wrote Morgan a note, and it's difficult to start.

I'm glad we talked today. I'm sure it was hard, and I want you to know it meant a lot to me. I stare at the paper some more. It was strange, all this stuff happening to both of us, and, for the first time, not talking to each other about it. I'm really sorry how things went at school, that your Renewal got postponed, you missed the formal, and you and Cody broke up.

I reread what I've written so far. I guess I'm not really that sorry that she dumped Cody—not even sorry, if I'm honest, that she didn't get to go to the dance, either. Mainly I'm sorry I couldn't be there for you, I add. I take a deep breath. But you weren't there for me for a lot of things, either, and though I know you're sorry—do I?—neither of us can change that.

I stare into space again. How can I tell her that things aren't so simple for me? She's still so certain about everything, and now I'm—not.

I'm glad you have your principles, I try. But I'm not sure we believe the same things anymore. I'm not sure you'll like, if we really talk, what I have to say. I realize I sound like I'm breaking up with her: realize I don't know whether I am or not. I guess I just need you to understand that things can't just go back to the way they were. I'm not going to stop being friends with Cara. I can't. There are just some things you're going to have to accept, and I guess I needed to let you know that before we really make up. I'll understand if you decide you can't, but I hope you'll try to be understanding too.

I look at the paper, hating what I've written but not knowing how to change it, what else to say. It felt so important to write, but now it just seems stupid and kind of whiny, even. I hear the garage door opening and shove the notebook back in my bag, snatch out my French book, and pretend to be studying. Later, I decide, I'll tear out the note and bury it in the bottom of my trash can. Maybe even burn it.

The next morning Cara, Naeomi, and I meet in the library before school. It's what I do now, and this morning getting dressed I made a conscious decision to stick to it. Just because Morgan might be reentering the picture doesn't mean I'm going to erase everyone else. At least that part's clear.

All morning, though, I keep expecting Morgan to come bounding up and start chatting about whatever. I'm not really ready for that to happen, but I'm also a little let down when it doesn't. Does she sense my hesitancy and want to give me some space to think about what she said yesterday? Is she waiting for me to make the next move? Or has she decided, after talking, that I'm really not worth it? That I have changed too much? That she can't talk to me really unless I dump Cara?

When I get to biology she isn't waiting outside for me to answer any of this, but she does look up from her desk and smile. I decide to go over.

"Sorry I had to leave like that yesterday," she says. I see that she isn't actually studying her lab notes, but is instead using them to camouflage the fact that she's reading the driver's handbook. She gives me a meek smile. "There's a lot to keep straight."

"You'll do fine. I mean, you really want your license, right?"

She smiles, picturing it.

"So you'll do what it takes to get it. You've always been good at that."

A weird look passes her face. "I guess so."

There's an awkward pause. I feel the letter I wrote to her yesterday practically burning through the side of my bag.

"You have a lot of tests this week?" she asks.

"Yeah, like everyone."

"Yeah." She looks at her lab notes. "I should've focused more on this, really."

"Probably more of it sunk in than you think." I realize I'm standing there, reassuring her, just like always. Maybe things haven't changed so much.

Mrs. Laboutin comes out of her office at the back of the classroom then, meaning class is about to start. I move toward my desk.

"Tab, wait." She reaches into her bag, takes out a small piece of paper, and hands it to me. *So I wasn't the only one scribbling notes.*

"Okay if I read it later?"

She nods. I hold up the note. "Thanks."

"Well, read it first," she says, though half her voice is covered up by the bell.

All during the test I can feel Morgan's note in my jeans pocket, and it's hard not to take it out and read it, but Laboutin would think I was cheating. I concentrate so hard on my answers that I manage to finish a little bit early. Only then, when my test is safe in front of my teacher at her desk, do I unfold the note from Morgan.

Tab: Yesterday was awful. I was so afraid you were going to hate my guts forever, and I didn't manage to say anything right. I just want you to know that I'm really sorry. I feel like I'm the one who's broken her promise—my promise to you. I know I don't really deserve it, but I hope you will someday forgive me. Love, M.

I finish reading for the second time right as the bell rings and everyone jumps up around me. I look to find Morgan, at least make eye contact with her, but she's already headed out into the hall, afraid of my response, I guess, which I can understand. I'm afraid of my response too.

chapter 27

Because today's the mock wedding at the Center, I get to leave French early. When I arrive at the pickup circle Mom's there, my not-Mayhem Dance dress in the backseat.

"You mind if I stick around this afternoon?" Mom asks. "I mean, are visitors allowed? I'd love to see you in that dress."

I'm not certain what the rules are about outside people coming to the wedding, but Lacey would love it if Mom stayed, so I tell her to come on in and we'll see.

When we enter the main foyer, Mrs. Rogers is behind the reception desk, since Coyle Ann's busy getting ready to be the mother of the bride. She frowns at Mom as though she doesn't really want to let her in, but hands her the visitor's roster and a Hello My Name Is badge, anyway. It's so easy I think the wedding day cheer must've sunk in even way up here, though as we head down the hall Rogers calls, "Make sure everything is clear by four thirty *exactly*," so then again, maybe not.

When we get to the Conservatory, everything's pretty much

already set up. Sterling's helping with the last of the chairs, and Mrs. Gifford is already in her place at the piano, wearing her corsage. Coyle Ann is helping the dining hall people lay out the food on the tables across the back of the room, where open space has been left for dancing, and the band is doing its sound check. It's like a beehive, with everyone moving and buzzing around their own little tasks, hurried and focused, but—since everybody loves a wedding—with an undercurrent of excitement. I think I must feel *my* endorphin levels rising, and try to remember to tell Lacey again how cool she is, doing this.

I'm looking for her as I hear a loud "Psssssst!" from the hallway. There, Lacey has her head poked around one of the nearby office doors. She waves me over frantically, veil flopping in one hand.

"I can't get this damned thing on straight," she hisses when Mom and I shut the door behind us. "No mirror in here. Hi, Mrs. McAbe. Sorry. Bridal nervousness."

"No, it's fine." Mom giggles, going over to help Lacey so I can change. When my own dress is fastened, we zip Lacey up and smooth her out and tuck the veil comb into the back of her ponytail. She expertly puts on her lipstick without even looking. As soon as she's done, we hear the piano start up outside, which means the patients are starting to come in.

The door opens suddenly, making all three of us yelp, and then giggle. Coyle Ann's thrusting the bouquets out toward Lacey, pretending not to peek. "You left these on the piano," she grumbles.

"Thanks, Mommy Dearest," Lacey winks.

"You look nice, Coyle Ann," I tell her, and she harrumphs, shutting the door on us.

"God," Lacey says, letting out a shuddering breath and handing me my small bouquet. "It's so stupid, but every time we do this I still get nervous."

"I'm sure it's a lot to coordinate," Mom says. "Anything I can do to help?"

Lacey scrunches her face, thinking. "Make sure Sterling and the minister are there, and maybe signal that I'm ready?"

The last two times this has been part of my job, but being the bridesmaid I can't very well do it. Good thing, actually, that Mom's here; when she leaves, Lacey lets out another breath, and I hand her the nearby glass of water. Briefly I picture someone doing the same thing for me, years from now, for real. Who will be standing with me then? Morgan? Cara? Someone I haven't met yet?

"You look dynamite," Lacey says, smiling.

"So do you." Her Salvation Army dress really is pretty: pouffy and flowy in the skirt with a simple strapless bodice that shows off her figure and her tan.

"Was it weird," it occurs to me to ask, "shopping for a dress when you weren't really getting married?"

"Nah. It was fun. I mean, the women were ridiculous, fussing and fluffing—it was silly in an interesting way. I played along. I figure all of this is good practice, anyway. Though maybe by the time I'm ready for a real wedding I'll be sick of all this and just run off to Vegas." She plucks at her veil.

I wonder if, after saying her vows falsely so many times, maybe they won't have as much meaning when she really does them, but just then Mom knocks. I peek out and she tells me everyone's ready. I turn to Lacey. "You all set?"

She shakes out her hands before I give her the bouquet. "For the record, it does feel very . . . serious," she laughs, "being in this dress."

"You look beautiful."

She smiles a little.

"Okay," I tell her, "I'm going out. Remember: twenty and then it's your turn."

She nods, and I go out into the hall to the Conservatory entrance, where inside all the old ladies and men are sitting in their seats, dressed up and patient. Sterling winks when he sees me, and Mr. Haybell gives me a nod, signaling I should start my little march down the aisle. The pianist begins the "Pachelbel Canon," and Mom turns around in her seat in the last row to wink at me, too.

Suddenly I'm as nervous and shuddery as Lacey. I walk slowly and carefully, one foot in front of the other, keeping my back as straight as possible, trying to be the prettiest, sweetest, and most proper bridesmaid I can. Though—I know, I know—this isn't a real wedding, if we don't treat it like one, the whole thing is kind of pointless. This is the first time I've been in the middle of the whole thing, and as I move slowly down the center aisle, everyone's smiles are aimed at me, and I can feel the happy factor raised already in the room. Even Sterling is alive with grin, and Mr. Haybell too, which then makes me smile even more hugely. When I finally reach the front and turn slowly to the other side of the minister, there's Lacey: poised and beautiful—and super smiling. Somehow, we're all transformed by this wedding thing. I hear Sterling take in a sharp breath, and then it does all feel very serious, whatever this is.

The piano begins the wedding march. Coyle Ann and Mom stand up at the same time, signaling that's what everyone else should do. Some of the patients stand with the help of nearby nurses, some don't make it, but as soon as any of them catch sight of Lacey, they all beam even more. Even old battle-ax Coyle Ann, when I sneak a glance at her, has got this giant goofy grin on her face, watching Lacey take her place at the front of the room between me and Sterling.

"Dearly beloved," Mr. Haybell starts when everyone sits, "we are gathered here today to celebrate the union of this man"—he gestures with his big pink hand to Sterling—"and this woman." You can feel the blank space where he's supposed to say "in holy matrimony" but Mr. Haybell refuses to bring God into a fake ceremony. "Who gives this woman today?" he asks instead, looking out as though he doesn't know.

Coyle Ann stands up then, jerking on the hem of her beaded jacket to unbunch it from her armpits. "I do," she says, almost sounding nervous herself. She sits back down quickly, looking around as though daring someone to challenge her.

"Will you please join hands," Mr. Haybell tells Lacey and Sterling, and Lacey turns to hand me her bouquet. It's time for the vows: standard-issue love, honor, cherish vows—lines a million brides and a million grooms go over every day, the same lines practically everybody knows by heart. Listening, I realize they aren't even lines that fully capture the monumentalness of really getting married, of giving your whole self—body, heart, and mind—to this one and only person forever. In fact, they almost seem like fake promises to begin with (or at least really generic ones), even if you do put the God parts back in where they belong.

It's when I look out of the side of my eye and catch sight of some of the people behind us, though, that it strikes me that Sterling and Lacey's promises do mean something, though maybe not in a literal way. Here they are, up here together, going through the motions of the most serious thing two people can do, and while it doesn't mean anything to them, it does mean something to the people watching. All of this: the dress, the performance, the food, Lacey and Sterling put together for the sake of some sick old people that aren't even their grandparents. They're up here making promises (promises that don't count, but still), not for themselves, but for the community of patients they work with. And maybe *that's* an important kind of vow, as well. Maybe enough to cancel out the other fake parts.

I'm so stuck on this thought that I almost blank out on the changing of the rings, which is the part I try to pay the most attention to. One day I'll be trading the one I have now for a totally different one, one that will come from my husband. I need all the clues I can get—even fake ones—about what this might be like. When I was the videographer I could see Lacey's face clearly, see the little turndown of her mouth as Sterling squeezed it on, and then her big smile up at him. Now standing behind Lacey this way I can only see Sterling's smile when his ring goes on, but it's a good one.

Then Mr. Haybell is saying, "I now pronounce you joined." (Again, fake.) Lacey and Sterling give each other a quick peck on the mouth and then turn to face the audience. Everyone claps as they stroll arm in arm down the aisle. Mr. Haybell has to reach for me, remind me to follow.

Afterward I stand with Lacey and Sterling at the back of the room in order to greet all the guests as they head toward the food and the band, which is starting up. I'm still kind of thinking about literal promises versus more abstract ones, but snap to when Mom approaches, helping a lady who was sitting next to her.

"You were beautiful," Mom says to me, smiling, before hugging Lacey. The lady with her grips Lacey's hand really hard and stares into her face.

"Thank you for coming," Lacey says sweetly, before lady finally moves away, leaning heavily on Mom.

There aren't, like, hundreds of patients in the Alzheimer's wing, but every one of them wants to get a chance to be near Lacey, to touch her or kiss her cheek. One old guy who's also suffered a stroke, and so can only really move one side of his face, struggles to tell Lacey what a good daughter she's been, how he wishes he could have been here today. Another couple of ladies smile and talk nonsensically—but clearly fondly—about their own weddings, while Mr. Fannin—one of my favorite old guys in the whole Center, because he used to be a chemistry teacher and so sometimes slips and uses the names of elements instead of adjectives—tells Lacey that she was "Borite like my Gwendolyn here," though his wife's name was Patricia and she died before he even came to the Center. Mainly, everyone is obviously really happy to be near the bride and groom, and Lacey's experiment is once again proving what it's supposed to.

When the line finally ends we head to the food, to mingle and watch a few of the nurses "dancing" with some patients. I suddenly wish Naeomi was with me. She, more than anyone, would understand what I'm feeling—feeling that maybe it isn't the thing you say out loud that matters most, or even whether it lasts. Instead it's what the doing of it brings you and everyone else.

Friday, the last day before spring break, I'm on a mission to find Cara. I think I know what I want to do now, but I need to talk to her first. Fortunately she's in the library, and fortunately Naeomi's not there, though I wouldn't mind talking to her, too. After the wedding last night I did a lot of thinking, thinking I need to turn into words before we're all off in different directions for the week.

"I have good news," Cara says when I sit down with her. The brightness on her face makes my stomach twirl a little: Michael. They're back together; he's finally e-mailed; they'll continue their love affair in secret. I try to get ready to be happy for her about it. Or at least pretend to be.

"I had a long talk with my mom last night," she starts. "The boys were out and it was just me and her and it was really good.

Pure

I told her how sorry I was for disappointing them: that I realize that was the worst of it, and I wish I could take it back."

"You do?" I can't help but be surprised.

She looks at me, thinks a second. "Well, to be honest, I don't know all the way. I'm not . . . sorry. About how I felt. And doing what I did." A worried look crosses her face. "I'm not sorry for being in love. Or for acting on it. But I am sorry for letting everyone down. I didn't realize how I was affecting everyone else." She flicks her eyes at me. "Including you."

"I've told you; you didn't let me down."

She shrugs. "Well, I certainly made a mess of a lot of things. And it's sucked. For everyone. Michael, too I guess, though you wouldn't know." There's an edge to her voice.

"Have you heard from him at *all*?" I can't imagine, still, that he's just—evaporated. That'd he'd really just leave Cara to handle everything alone, without at least saying good-bye.

"I don't get it," she says. "I mean, I'd never have guessed, you know? I've spent all week being shocked and sad, not wanting it to be true, making up excuses for him, but he's just—gone. And I'm tired of waiting for him."

It strikes me as a little funny, that sentence, but I keep my mouth shut.

"Anyway, Mom says she thinks I deserve a little break, and so next weekend when Naeomi's back from Chicago I want you and her to come out and we'll all go riding. Spend the night. Movies. Maybe you can come over while Nomi's gone, even."

"When are they gonna give your phone back?"

309

"I don't know. I've told them it's over with me and Michael but I think they think I'm just saying that so I can go behind their backs. Guess I don't blame them."

"Can I call your house?"

"You can give it a shot." She smiles.

"What about your ring?" I brave.

She looks at her naked hand. I think of Morgan. "I miss it," she admits. "You know? It's like a part of you or something. But I don't know what Walt did with it. Maybe he threw it out."

"He wouldn't."

"No, you're right. He wouldn't." She leans back in her chair. "Gah, he was so crushed. It was awful. I mean, Skip was *pissed* and I think Mack was just doing his Southern chivalry duty, but you should've seen Walt's face." She shudders. "I don't know." Her eyes twinkle a little. "I've heard about girls praying hard enough to reinstate their virginity. Think I can do it?" She grins.

"You better start on your Hail Marys right now." I laugh, then use the pause to plunge ahead: "Do you think you'd—do it again?"

"I don't know. I didn't think I was going to break it before, you know? But if I met somebody I really loved? Like, maybe in college? I don't know."

I remember Naeomi talking about promises she makes to herself. I remember yesterday, and how good even a fake promise could make everyone feel.

"I talked to Morgan," I tell her.

She leans forward. "You did? I mean, that's good, right?"

310

"Yeah, I think it's good." I study her face, try to see if she's hiding any letdown. "It wasn't her, you know. Who told. Well, I mean sort of, but—"

"I know." Cara nods. "It was Wedge. Mom told me last night. You know, I never liked that guy."

"I know. He is kind of . . ."

"Creepy?" Cara inserts.

"Well, or just really, really takes himself seriously."

"Too seriously," Cara mutters. "It was none of his business. Even Mom admitted I should've had a chance to come to them myself."

"Well, it made me feel better," I confess. "I mean, at least it wasn't her. She didn't . . . hate you that much."

"Not even after I stole her best friend?" She's joking, but she's right. Kind of.

"She's sorry we fought."

"Well . . . that's good, right?"

I sigh and lean back. "I don't know. I mean, yes, it's good. I'm glad she's sorry. Because it sucked. All of it." I picture Morgan's face, turned away from me in class; the exasperation in her voice before I hung up on her; the robotic smile she gave me, handing me a prayer group flyer. "But I just don't know if it fixes anything. And I feel terrible about it."

Cara nods. "She can't undo what she's done."

If anybody knows how true that is, it's Cara.

"I don't want to ruin our friendship," I finally tell her.

"What? Yours and mine? How would that ruin our friendship?"

"Well, if I started being friends with Morgan again, and she—"

"Look," Cara says, seizing my arm. "You've known her way longer than you've known me. You've been through so much together. I actually can't believe you haven't made up with her before now. Naeomi and I were only at odds with each other for a week or two, and just that was terrible. I mean, it was amazing of you to back me up like that—I don't think I've really told you how much that means, especially since I know how you feel about our promise—but if you and Morgan never spoke to each other again over all of this, it'd be horrible. I mean, I've messed up enough things."

"She's still mad at you, though."

"Well, she probably should be." This takes me by surprise, and Cara sees it. "I did something she thinks isn't just, you know, bad, but is totally immoral and against God," she explains. "Totally unforgivable."

"But nothing is—"

She shakes her head. "That's according to you and me. But to my brothers in their way, to Morgan in hers, to a lot of other people, it's not. They've got their rules—whatever they are. They *need* them. And even though I've seen it differently, I can't necessarily ask them to change their own worldview. The way that makes things work for them."

I look at her and know she's right. At least about Morgan needing her view to stay the way it is. But if I've survived *not* talking to Morgan for this long, maybe really talking to her won't kill me, either. I could use a giggle-filled manicure, too.

Trying to picture a normal talk with Morgan, though, makes

me realize it isn't just Cara that lies between us—and maybe it was never just her. "But what if we—I—can't get over it? Everything. What if we're just too different?"

"You're not gonna know until you try," she tells me. And with that the bell rings, starting school.

Since it's the day before spring break and the majority of tests and papers have already happened, most of my classes are no-brainers. In PE we don't even have to change out, and in English, Ms. Stackins brings in these cool short films to show us that have nothing to do with class—random weird things, one with stop-animation puppets, and another a cartoon about a singing duck and herring.

Even Mrs. Laboutin gives us a mild break in biology, showing us microscope slides of weird mutated cells and explaining the gene combinations scientists think happened to make them. It's still connected to what we've been studying, but in a cool, real-world application way, and even she is having fun with it.

Morgan I guess has figured, since I haven't written her back or called, that I must not want to talk to her, because when the bell rings after class she just quietly heads out the door without even looking back to wish me a good break. I remind myself she took a risk, saying what she said to me, and it must feel a little bad, not getting any response. I call out, ask her to wait. Even if I can't make myself jump across that gulf between us, maybe a tiny step will do.

"I just wanted to know," I tell her, "if you're going away or not this week. I realize we haven't—haven't talked about that."

She's let down, but she hides it pretty well. "Believe it or not we decided, since I can't do my renewal, just to skip Easter altogether and go to St. Simon's early."

"Shocking!" I say in mock horror.

She smiles a little. "I know. And it was Daddy's idea, to make it even more crazy. I think he thinks if we go to church like normal it'll make me feel bad or something. Like, if everything isn't about me I somehow won't want to participate."

It's not lost on either of us, her sarcasm. It surprises me a little, but in a good way. Maybe I'm not the only one who's gone through some important changes.

"I'm not against beach time, though," she sighs. "And since my driving test is right in the middle of the week like that, it chops things up weird. Going this weekend means we can be there a day longer."

"You leaving tonight?"

"After school. They're picking me up."

"Priah going with you?" I'm as light as possible.

She rolls her eyes. "Still not allowed, even with chaperones. Maybe next year."

"You gonna drive?" I try a smile of mischief.

"I guess I could," she says. "But I kind of want to chill, you know? Just . . . make my mind a blank."

I feel awkward, all of a sudden, getting this close to the Seriousness of Things, when we only have eighty more seconds to get to our classes.

"Anyway." She shakes her hair. "We'll be back on Wednesday for my test."

"Okay then."

"You can—call me. I don't get very good reception, but . . ."

I just nod. "Don't worry, we'll talk."

She wants me to say more, I can see. She wants me to hug her, to maybe cry a little, to—I don't know—ask her if they'll be any parties down there or something, but I don't manage to.

"All right. Well, have fun, I guess," she says, moving away.

"You too. Don't forget—"

"Yeah—my sunscreen." She smiles, rolling her eyes, already remembering, like me, spring break of eighth grade when we went to her family's house in St. Simon's and both got so sunburned on the first day we had to stay inside for the next two.

"Okay then," we say at the same time, reluctant to go, but needing to.

"Thanks, Tab," she says, lots of stuff happening across her face. But she's turned on her heel and is around the corner before I have an inkling of what I might be saying "You're welcome" for.

After school is over and everyone pours out of the building, free and elated and noisily chattering, Amelia calls to invite me, totally last-minute, to go roller-skating with her, Krista, and Opal tonight. It's actually a ton of fun, and it occurs to me while we spin and laugh under the colored lights with the crazy retro music, that I really should hang out with my chorus girlfriends more. Maybe Cara and I can move our morning meetings back to the chorus room after break, on days when Naeomi has SGA meetings or homework. Maybe, with all these new friends, I'll stage some different spend-the-nights.

Saturday, Mom and Dad and I go play tennis together in the morning (Mom always wins since me and Dad put together still aren't as good as one whole person), and then go eat a really big brunch at Feast. I spend the afternoon actually cleaning my whole room, in order to sort of get a fresh start to the long, empty week, and then try to make a list of things I want to accomplish during my time off. I write down things like Spend all day doing nothing but reading—NOT FOR SCHOOL! Try to cook dinner for Mom and Dad. Meet Jake's Mom and Austin. Go riding with Cara. I stop myself when I hit Do something for Morgan's birthday? and put the list away. It bothers me that I still don't want to think about her, but it bothers me even more trying to think about *that*.

Clearly it's time for new toenail polish. But I also take a second to sign on to Facebook and write on Priah's Wall, wishing her a good break. Maybe she won't want to do anything without Morgan. Or maybe we'll surprise ourselves and each other—go to the movies and maybe get makeovers. It's good to know, at least, I'm open to either.

At seven, Jake comes to pick me up and we head over to Paul's house, where, for first day of spring break, there is really *truly* a party. Thank goodness Jake warned me and I got myself a little dressed up, because even Pam, when she meets us at the door, is wearing this crazy sequined blouse and a pink feather boa.

Inside, the kitchen is crowded with kids, and the counter and table are even more crowded with soft drinks and food. People are still playing video games in the den, but Paul and his mom have also cleared the dining room, and there's a guy in there DJ-ing with his laptop for real dancing. The whole ceiling is strung with twinkle lights, and if you squint right and don't look at Pam's china cabinet, it could almost be a club.

"Wow," I say, when Jake pulls me onto the floor. "Pam really likes a party."

He just smiles and shrugs. "I told you, dude."

"Dude?"

"What, dude?" He rocks elbows and hips and knees in a kooky get-down.

"Okay then, dude," I snort and join in.

After a while of dancing and laughing and having a good time and getting sweaty, Paul screams over the music that it's Rocket Time and everyone cheers and heads for the back door. Gemma and some of her friends have been dancing around too, and as we move toward the kitchen and the patio outside, she grabs my hand to pull me along.

Outside, the anticipation is practically palpable, and when Paul comes forward with a bulging shopping bag, I can see why. This isn't just regular bottle rockets. Instead he's got these cylinder tube things he puts on a cinder block, ordering everyone to back off. Over my shoulder I see Pam standing on the patio, watching us, a small fire extinguisher by her feet.

Paul drops a small ball with a long fuse into the tube and then takes out a lighter and again tells everyone to step back another few feet. He squats down in an awkward hunch, ready to run, and holds the flame to the fuse. Immediately it lights, and Paul dashes to where the rest of us are standing, just before the tube erupts with a soft *poff* and a trail of sparks leaps into the sky above the lake. It whistles and then explodes in a shower of green and pink, and everybody cheers.

"Oh my God, he is so crazy," Gemma says next to me, delighted. Sam is standing beside her, his arm wrapped around her shoulders, squeezing her close. "My dad would kill me if he knew I was doing this. Pam is so cool."

I wonder, actually, if Dad would kill me or if he'd just want a chance to light one of those fireworks, which I'm not even sure are legal. It makes me smile, thinking of it. That and how friendly Gemma is being, how I really feel included and a part of this. How even out of broken things, you can make something new and maybe even improved.

Jake moves behind me then, puts his arms around my waist and chin on my shoulder. I lean into him. Paul lights another firework, and the sky glows with light and sound. More cheering as someone brings out a box of sparklers from Paul's giant bag and starts passing them around.

"You know," Jake says, taking a lighter and holding it to my sparkler. I'm watching the end of my sparkler and not his face when I hear him say, "I think I might kind of love you."

My sparkler blazes to life, showering us with its soft sparks. It startles me but not as much as what he just said.

"Is that okay?" he asks, trying to look at my face.

Pure

I hold the bright orange tip of my sparkler to his yet unlit one. I stare at the sparks, sizzling furiously just like me.

"I think it's okay," I finally say, smiling up at him. "And I mean, I think I love—"

"Icing, cupcake," he interrupts, as the tip of his sparkler finally burns to brilliance with mine.

chapter 28

Easter Sunday morning. There isn't time for waffles, since
I slept late after Mom and Dad extended my curfew to midnight
just this once. When I wake up I almost roll over again, let all
the wonderful images from the party wash over me, but then I
see what time it is and realize I really want—need—to make it to
church today.

Instead of being clean and quiet, on Easter Sunday church
is full and bright and buzzing. There are lilies exploding from
all the windowsills, and the pews are packed with the regular
congregation, plus all the people who only come to church for
this service and the one on Christmas Eve—the people Mom and
Dad *really* don't want to be, though I'm so used to being alone at
church it'd be weirder if they were here. I peek over the balcony
rail (downstairs is already too crowded) to watch little girls dressed
up in frilly pinafores and white patent-leather shoes, little boys
in clip-on bow ties and stiff new belts. Moms and Dads and
grandparents and teenagers and visiting college students are all in

their best too. Lots of women who normally don't wear hats have them on, and my eyes swim with clashing floral fabrics.

When the organ crashes out its beginning chords, the choir processes in, some of them ringing handbells as they sing. Behind them Pastor Tom and Pastor Catherine are in their fancy Easter robes, both of them singing along joyously and smiling at everyone they pass on their way to the pulpit. The choir goes all the way around the front of the congregation and then to their seats, and as they finish, the organist really lets the final notes rip, telling you this is a good day—one of bursting excitement.

"Good morning and welcome," Pastor Tom says, smiling broadly, lifting his hands toward all of us. "He is risen."

"He is risen indeed," we respond, and I get ready to make myself focus on the Good News.

The first hymn is booming and loud and wonderful, and the "peace be with you" is fun because there are so many people to greet, but when prayers come I start to get nervous. Today I want do my best to express everything in my mind to God, and try to listen to what He says in my heart, but I've had so much jumbled in my head for so long, and still everything feels unclear. Can broken promises be forgiven? Do fake promises still matter? Who are you making your promises to, really? And if you change, can your promise change with you? I know the questions, I just don't know if there are answers. As everyone around me bows their heads, my mind jumps from school to Jake to homeless veterans to Cara to my biology test to depleting fossil fuels. Even when we ask for mercy and forgiveness, all I can feel is my incredible doubt. When we're done and the handbell choir is playing, I realize I haven't even specifically prayed to be forgiven for not being able to forgive Morgan exactly. During the first Bible lesson, all I can manage is to ask God to maybe forgive us both.

We have the readings, and both the little kids' choir and the girls' choir sing, and then it's time for the Gospel Lesson. The service is almost half over, and I still don't know where my head is. I concentrate on Pastor Catherine reading the story from John where Mary goes early to Jesus's tomb to tend to His body, and she sees that the stone is moved away. She tells the disciples, and when they leave she sees a man near the tomb she doesn't know. She asks if he's taken Jesus's body and hidden it somewhere. She doesn't realize it is Jesus at first, but when He calls to her, she does. He tells her not to hold on to Him yet but instead to go and tell everyone else what has happened.

It's a good story, and after hearing the different tellings of Jesus's Resurrection over the years, it's one of my favorites, but I don't feel any kind of epiphany coming on, any sense of ease. I mean, Jesus is risen and we're all forgiven of our sins because of it, but I don't feel any better about anything, because I don't know what my sins *are*. As Tom starts the sermon, talking about Mary's grief and the fear of all the disciples—how they totally felt abandoned and beaten down—mainly all I feel is that I can relate.

"Everyone else has left, you see," Pastor Tom is saying, leaning comfortably on the pulpit. "Mary came to do her duty, and then, when she saw that Jesus was gone, went off again dutifully to tell the men. Even in her fear, she's done her job. Like all of us, she shows up.

She does what's asked. But after everyone takes off, she still lingers."

Tom pauses and looks at us a moment, then down at his notes. "You see, she can't go back to normal just yet. She's sad, she's confused, she's scared. She needs to spend some time processing the extra shock. I mean," Tom laughs a little. "*Gimme a break, God!*" He looks at us with a knowing smile—we've all felt this, even him.

"But then, consider: On top of His death, now His body has been *stolen*. Maybe it's being desecrated in some way; maybe now He'll *never* be able to come back, even if He was *going* to like He said. It's all too much. So Mary has to mourn awhile longer. She can't act like everything's okay. Not only is she still upset that He's *dead*, but now this. This thing that can maybe never be fixed."

I feel a creepy tingling in the back of my neck.

"The other disciples have gone back home to conduct business as usual, and she's left alone in her grief. And it's in *that* time, in her being there—in her sadness, her solitude, her doubt—that Jesus appears."

You can almost hear everyone letting that sink in. The cold feeling keeps prickling in me.

"But poor Mary." He shakes his head. "She's so caught up in all her fears, all her concerns about what's already happened and what might be happening, what she thinks about everything that's happened, that she can't see that it's Him. There He is"—Tom shakes his hands at us, demonstrating—"standing right there in front of her—her friend, her leader, her Lord, and she doesn't know it. She can't see that His promise has already come true, that He is here, that death does *not* win"—Tom's voice rises with the power of it—"because she's distracted by her own thoughts."

This is where tears start to sting my eyes, and my nostrils tremble.

"No, she can't see the miracle of God's love—the mighty power of His forgiveness—even though it's standing right in front of her. Only when He calls her by her familiar—the thing she's heard Him say for days and days and months and months—that she finally realizes her friend is standing right there, with her. He's changed, she can tell—the whole *world* has changed—but there He is. Just like He promised. And her fears?" Pastor Tom looks at us. "They don't matter anymore."

Now the tears come down my face in earnest. My shoulders start to shake. I hold my hand over my mouth and bite my finger to keep myself from crying more than I already am. There's more to the sermon, more about how Jesus forgives Mary's confusion, the disciples' fears, and how that extends to all of us now that He is risen, but mainly I'm too overwhelmed to absorb much.

Afterward, there's more singing, and then all the prayers and rituals of Communion, the rousing alleluias of the final hymn, and then church is over. I visit with a few people outside, but mainly I can't wait to get home and get started. Maybe God hasn't answered everything—maybe I haven't *asked*—but maybe that's not needed yet. For now at least I have some idea where to start.

chapter 29

On Wednesday morning, Dad drops me off at the Pointe before he goes in to work. I'm early but it was the only way I could get out here without spoiling the surprise, and even though I'm not sure what's going to happen, I had to do this.

There aren't very many shops in the complex, and most of them aren't open yet, but there is a little coffeehouse where I sit and read while I have to wait. I only check my hair and lip gloss, finger the two small boxes in my purse about six times before I see Mrs. Kent's white Explorer pull up across the lot a half hour later, with Mr. Kent and Morgan parking in the next spot, all of them getting out and heading into the DMV at the far end. I debate going and sitting with Morgan's parents while she takes her written test, and then waiting with them while she does the road test part, but having to make small talk while I'm this nervous doesn't seem like a very good idea. Again I think it was a mistake not to tell Morgan that I'd be here, and instead only told her Monday—she really does get horrible reception down at the beach—that I'd call when she finished.

It's another long hour of trying to read and not succeeding very well (I'm checking out the window now almost every thirty seconds) before I see Morgan cross the lot with a tidy-looking woman in a gray suit. They get into the Explorer and I watch as Morgan backs slowly out of the parking space, constantly checking all her mirrors and pointedly turning around to look behind her. She pulls out smoothly and they drive around the rear of the building, where I guess the rest of the test is taken. I only know they left the parking lot—some rear exit, I guess—when Morgan drives up from the front entrance about ten minutes later: sooner than I expected. I wonder if she failed immediately. Watching them go back into the building, it's hard to tell whether Morgan'll be excited or deflated when she walks back out that door: whether I'll be the first person she wants to see, or the last.

I decide to just wait until they all come out again, which is another excruciating twenty-four minutes. I realize this was a very stupid choice. I wish I had told Dad to come back and get me. I wish I'd just written everything in a card and left her present on the hood or something. If she's in there getting her license, she'll want to go drive off and show Priah. If she's not getting it, maybe she'll want to be left alone. I take out my cell phone, wondering how mad Dad will be if I interrupt him at work since Mom's in class now, but then I see the Kents start to cross the lot. Mr. Kent's arm is around Morgan, and she's beaming.

I take a deep breath, gather my things, and head out.

"Morgan," I call as she's unlocking the driver's side door.

Mrs. Kent sees me. "Why, what a surprise. Look, honey," she says.

"Morgan," I say again. I want her to hear me, want her to see.

Finally she looks. She's confused at first but then it registers.

"What are you doing here?" She checks to see if her parents knew about this.

"Happy birthday," is all I say. "I guess you passed?"

She grins and holds up the small white piece of plastic. "We were going to go celebrate." There's only a brief pause. "You want to come?"

Whoops. Of course. Family lunch. "Well, I don't want to intrude."

"Don't be silly," Mrs. Kent cuts me off. "We're thrilled you're here. It's even better this way. You girls take my car and we'll meet you there," she adds with a giggle, heading around to the other car, not allowing for any protest.

I look at Morgan to make sure this is really okay. I've thought a lot about today, and this isn't quite how I pictured it. Of course, my present to her isn't how I pictured it on Sunday, either—it morphed a few times in the making, and twice I had to start completely over—so maybe this is just par for the course.

"My first passenger," Morgan squeals, moving around to open the door for me. I get in, reminding myself to just start with one step.

"Oh my Gah, I'm still, like, shaking," she says when we're both settled. "That lady was, like, so *serious*. She didn't say anything the whole time. I did fine but she was so quiet I thought I was totally messing up. When I saw you I thought it was just some kind of nervous hallucination at first. I still haven't processed everything."

"You did it."

"I know!" she shrieks. "Can you believe it?"

"I told you you would."

I realize I sound just like I always do, that in spite of my intentions this seems a lot like being on the path of Everything's Fine, Nothing Happened, but then she looks at me and the giddiness drops. "Thanks for coming. I didn't know I wanted you with me until I saw you, but it's perfect."

"Happy birthday." I shrug.

"No, really." She turns in her seat. "It means a lot, your understanding."

"Well, I can't say that I all the way understand everything yet."

She looks out the windshield, more serious than I expected. "Yeah, I'm not sure I do either."

There's so much, I realize, *so much* I want to ask and to tell her. Even when I was maddest, I think I was more mad about her absence. And I've been absent too. "Maybe we can work on that."

Her head turns back to me. "You think so?"

Here's my moment to take out the two boxes from my purse. "I do." I hand her one and keep the other in my lap.

"What's this?"

I cock an eyebrow at her. "On three, tear it open, okay?"

"Okay."

"One . . . two . . . three!"

We each pull off our paper in pretty much one big tear. Since I know what's in my box I mainly watch her lift the lid off hers, and then take out the small ring. She holds it close to her face, examining the sparkly beads and how I wove them together with the flexible wire, crafted the tiny flower with tweezers and a lot of cussing.

"Did you make this?" She gasps.

"Remember that beading kit from my aunt Heather? Finally found a good use for it." I take the lid off my own box, show her the second, almost-identical ring.

Her face is a mix of things.

"I've been thinking so much," I start. "This has all been . . . really confusing. And I still don't know all the way what I feel about everything yet. I mean, it feels like, sometimes, everyone's right."

Out of the corner of my eye I see her nod just slightly.

"And I think I have to decide, kind of, on my own." I brave a glance at her. "But I do know, at least, that if I can forgive Cara, then I have to forgive you, too. I need to. Because one of the worst things about all of this has been not being able to talk to you." I swallow a little. "I'm afraid sometimes you won't want to listen . . ."

"But—"

I don't let her interrupt. "But that means I don't have much faith in you. Us." I think of the disciples then, frightened after Jesus's death, doubting. Mary unable to see. I let out a long breath, gearing up for the last thing. "But I do. Have faith. At least"—I shoot my eyes at her—"I still want to."

She looks down at her ring. "Me too."

"But I also want . . ." Again I have to swallow. "I want my promise to you to be separate from my promise to anything else.

I don't want them to be . . . dependent on each other. And I don't want your own to be tied up in mine. So I thought—"

She lunges across the seat then, grabbing me around the neck. "Oh Gah, Tab," she says into my hair. "I didn't think you would ever . . ." But she stops, pulls back to look at me. Her hand is still gripping my shoulder. She does Cara's horsey head-shake thing. "But it's just like you to figure out the perfect solution," she says, not looking at me and then looking again. "*This* is what I missed. I mean, I tried to come up with stuff by myself—I did—but none of it worked and it made me realize I can't—"

I stop her. "Well, I don't have all the answers. Not nearly."

"You're smarter than you think, Tab. Even Priah said so."

I laugh. "Well, then it *must* be true."

She blushes. "You know what I mean."

I smile, picturing Priah and Sprockett in their photo together. "Well, that's saying a lot, seeing how brilliant I was on her behalf."

She snorts. "Gah, I *wish* he had listened to you. She is so over the moon." She rolls her eyes. "It's kind of disgusting."

I remember Friday night, how Jake said "I love you" again yesterday on the phone, how wonderful that felt and how now, maybe, I'll get to share the boy-yay with Priah in the same way Cara got to share it with me. Maybe single-for-now Morgan will even be okay with it, or at least I'll be okay with her not being okay.

"You think they'll last?" I ask.

"Probably not." She laughs. "But truthfully I'm happy for her. For now." Oh Crap Face goes over her then. "I should call her though. She's dying. Do you care?" But already she's rummaging for her phone.

"We should probably get going," I say. The Kents have already left, and will probably wait by the hostess stand until we get to the restaurant. "But maybe she can meet us later?"

Morgan grins, finds her phone at the bottom of her purse. She's about to dial, but stops herself. Instead she gropes in her lap, pulls out her flimsy ring. I watch as she slides it from finger to finger, trying to find the best fit. Finally it nestles snugly on the pointer finger of her left hand, one finger between it and where her new purity ring will be.

"I promise not to leave you again," she says.

I think of all the things I still haven't told her: about Jake, about the *Desiderata*, about Paul's parties and the new friends I've made, about the mock wedding and what Cara's taught me, about Naeomi's conviction, my thoughts about promises. . . . It's all so much—more than we've ever had to handle. Maybe too much, no matter what we say or feel right now. Maybe, like our promise years ago, it entails more than we comprehend even this minute. Maybe it will change. Maybe, if it does, we'll be able to change with it, together. And if not, maybe it will do us and the world a greater good, just to have made the attempt.

"How about we just promise to try?" I tell her.

"Amen to that," she says, smiling broadly.

"Okay," I say, with conviction. "Amen."

Acknowledgments

All thanks and praise to my friend and editor, Anica Rissi, for putting "A Ring that Says No, Not Yes," into my hands and saying, "Do you think you could do anything with this?" and then for all the sparklingly miraculous work that happened afterward. Cannot—cannot—worship you enough.

Laud and honor also to Jennifer Klonsky and Bethany Buck at Simon Pulse for taking a leap of faith, and for everyone else at Simon & Schuster who touched this book and made it into a shining reality.

Hosannas also to Meg Howrey and Amy McClellan, for their insights, enthusiasm, and encouragement from Draft One; to Casey and Natalie, for contemporary high school consultation; and to Brant Copeland of First Presbyterian Church in Tallahassee, Florida, for his ministerial input, not just during the writing of this book but in my own spiritual life. To this end I also owe infinite thanks to Christy Williams and all the other First Pres grown-ups who lived their own faiths around me and showed me how to.

There is not enough reverence for the patience, support, encouragement, and love that I receive—now and forever—from my family.

Finally, offerings of love to Scott, for believing in me, always.

This moment changes everything.

after the kiss

Terra Elan McVoy

author of Pure

Turn the page to take a peek.

Camille

not getting ready for a date

it's not like it's a date. how could it be a date since you don't date anyone, because dating's a trap, because dating is totally dated? because you are the girl who stays unconnected to everyone. still, you do know he will be at the lake house tonight. and he knows you will be there. and you both know that right now you are probably getting ready to be there, knowing the other one will be there. it's why you're sitting here staring at your closet with a disaster of discarded outfits on your floor. it's why you can't decide between jeans or the deconstructed tuxedo pants. it's why you wish you'd bought those killer turquoise cowboy boots you saw with mom last weekend, and why you can't decide if your hair goes down or up. he'll be there. you'll be there. and eventually you'll be there together. and you're not sure what's going to happen—what's already happened is confusing enough—but you do know you're sure something will happen. maybe like last time you'll just talk. but that was still something. something for sure. he thought it was something too because what about those e-mails? so this isn't just going to another weekly party. it's more like kind of a date. even though you don't date. which is why you're not sure why you're sitting here getting ready as though it is a date. but why you're not able to act like it isn't one, either.

the kiss

he just comes at you. you barely drop much of a *hey, how are you?* there on the back deck where people can see—and he just comes *at* you, surprising as a tornado on a sunny day, blowing the roof off, pulling up the fence. you see him and you smile and then it's just one step, two steps and he's over you and under you and all over you and it's not some *you're cute i might like you* kiss, nor a confused and disgusting sloppy-slather fueled by all that vodka kool-aid he's obviously had. no, this is a mouth with momentum, a train on one track paying no heed to any warning clangs, a chemistry set just waiting for someone to put the wrong powder in the right tube and make something explode. this kiss says he needs you more than all those puppies put together, that he'll aim over and over at the tender haiku buried deep in your own trenches until he hits the right syllable. this kiss will wipe your mind of all things, will make you forget your name your face what town you're living in and who's driving you home. it is a kiss that, when it ends—after he's summoned laughing into the dark by shouting boys in the driveway—will leave you gasping and glossy-eyed for hours later, will follow you home as you stare in the bathroom mirror at the chewed-looking spots his stubble left on your chin. it is a kiss so loud and long that your whole mind will scream, *that can't happen again,* while your body will still twitch a little, wondering if it could just once more.

Becca

Telephone Evolution

In the old days (Mom says)
it would just ring and ring and ring,
callers counting
twenty, twenty-one, (he could be
just now running in from outside)
before giving up.
Next came answering machines
(we still have an ancient one for the telemarketers)
that allowed for screening—
deciding whether or not
to pretend to be out.
Now there is the cell phone:
more immediate, less discreet—
I can tell, for example, after two rings and a click
that for the first time
he has seen my number, hit IGNORE.

The Coffee (Heart) Break

After the superspeedway
of Sunday morning doughnut drive,
coffee chaos,
and tablewipe tumbling
there is a small lull
—a pause.
I can sip
my own coffee—break
my own doughnut into small pieces to savor.
This is the time
—Freya knows—
someone can come by
and I can do more
than wave at her like a drowned girl.
She can come
—fifteen minutes before the after-church lunchers—
and I can sit
on the patio with her a minute,
ask about last night.

It is enough time even
for her to show me her phone
—the photos she took last night at the Lake House—
and ruin my life
forever.

With Apologies to WCW

so much depends upon
the red (handed) cameraphone photo
glazed with pain
(of him) standing beside
(with his mouth all over)
the (creamy) white chick

Numb

At first a column of heat
—a lava charge—
bursts up from the tail end of my spine and
rockets
up to the top of my skull
—fills my eyes—
so that for a moment I can't see and all I feel is
heat.

But it is the last thing I will feel—this fever wind—
because after that I am ice:
a white tundra of unmoving blank:
a glacier only very slightly drifting
—unaware of its own motion—
across a dark and frozen sea.

Fury

Freya's face is a fist,
her frustration a force
unfurled and frenzied—lashing
against the redhead, my boyfriend,
the entire (cheating) world.

Coming from her each hate-filled word falls—
one poisonously sour grape after the next,
leaving a miserable, permanent stain
on everything touched.

Island of Relief

After Freya leaves, the sorrow is a tidal wave,
pounding me so hard it is difficult to see
—strident tide smashing
everything in sight.

I am a drowned girl:
lungs grabbing dark water,
filling with—[seeking]—the source that will
silence and bury.

A pale hand plunges—grabs—
and insists: rise.
I am a gasping, sputtering face,
looking for a life raft.

Nadia is calm, cool, solid—
an ivory island.
In her comforting concern I will rest and think,
gulp for air,
try to breathe again.

Helpful Advice

Janayah's left alone at the counter
and I will get in trouble,
but I don't care I
can't breathe after all.
Back in the kitchen Nadia
holds me by the scruff of the neck,
helping me stand,
cleaning me up.
I know it hurts, Nadia says calmly,
but if he cheats, it's over.
Maybe not over for you
but over for him
and in that case it is just
over for you both.
Over like the last pizza crust.
Over like hitting E with forty miles
to the next fill-up.
Over like a blackout.
Over like an execution.
Her face is still a new doll to me—something
to admire but not yet fully know.
But her voice is serious as the grave:

concrete, set and poured.
Break it off, she tells me,
sounding like some Old Testament Bible verse
about a right hand and its offense.
You have no choice, she says.
This girl usually so full of sunshine,
now black clouds sweep across her brow.
Against her finality my heart thuds, once.
But around it my soul echoes empty,
her words careening back and forth and back,
ringing like truths.

Kisses. Sunshine.
Sunburn.

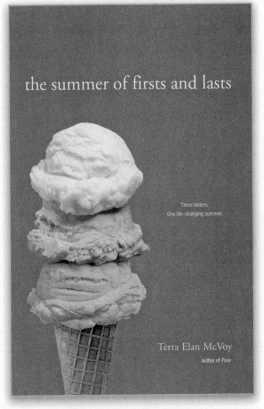

the summer of firsts and lasts

Three sisters.
One life-changing summer.

Terra Elan McVoy
author of *Pure*

Three sisters.
One unforgettable summer.

S neaking out to meet Brynn was so easy and uneventful and normal the first time, I almost forgot it was against the rules. When I see her tonight at karaoke, we don't talk about yesterday's thing at lunch at all, or her "camp apology" cloaked in disdain. All that happens is that she plunks down next to me, and then we laugh a ton together. When I hug her around the neck to tell her how awesome her Janis Joplin was, she only husks in my ear, "Tonight again."

And this time I'm way more excited than I am scared. Because of karaoke, though, it takes everyone else a lot longer to settle down to sleep, which makes me antsy. I'm a little less confident, too, since I can't tell if Natalie's really asleep or faking being asleep before she sneaks out. I am cat-burglar tiptoe quiet. But before I know it, I'm outside under the stars, figuring we're going up to the fire pit again to hang with whatever counselors are there tonight. Meaning James, I hope. Maybe we'll finally talk.

Brynn has other plans, though. She barely even says hey when I get to the boathouse, and just starts walking down to the dark edge of the lake, far away from all the cabins and their lights. Without a word, she shimmies off her pajama bottoms. She's wearing a boy-shorts swimsuit underneath.

"What are we doing?"

"Going for a swim, dummy. What does it look like?" She is half smiling.

"But I don't—I mean—"

"So swim in your pajamas." She whips her T-shirt off over her head, showing smooth white belly and too many ribs.

I go down and stick my foot in the water. It's chilly, but not totally freezing. It won't be comfortable at first, but I know I'll get used to it. But the air's too cool now to dry my pajamas before I get back to the cabin if I swim in them. And I am not very enthused about wearing wet underwear, which will then soak my pajamas, too. Taking things off and hanging them up will be a way too complicated chore when I'm trying to sneak back into my bunk. If I do this, I'm doing it au naturel.

"Or you can go back, it's cool," Brynn says, seeing me hesitate. Her voice is genuinely indifferent, not teasing or challenging. And I could go back. I kind of want to. But this is my last summer as a camper, and I don't want to be the girl who only heard about the crazy, rule-breaking things people did at camp, or saw them in the movies. I want to be the girl who did them. I want to be able to tell James about this whenever we do get to talk—to watch his face light up in surprise, imagining me out here. And naked. So off goes my top, and my sleep shorts and underpants are quick to follow. Brynn takes our clothes and shoves them in the seat of one of the kayaks chained to its rack.

"C'mon," she giggle-whispers. Something about how she sounds makes it seem like she's never done this before either.

The water is. Freezing. If it weren't midnight and I weren't breaking camp rules, I'd be squealing. Instead—somehow—I just grit my teeth and go under. It is so cold.

Hasn't stopped Brynn, though. When I come up, she's already knifing herself toward the floating dock in a freestyle that looks Olympic. I am not a swimmer. I mean, I can swim, and I like to, but we never got lessons or anything like that. My stroke is more like a turtle's.

By the time I make it out to the floating dock, I'm definitely warmer, and being in the water with no clothes on feels surprisingly good. You'd think, because a bathing suit sticks to you when you're wet and really isn't that much clothing to begin with, there wouldn't be much of a difference, but there definitely—well, there just is. I almost don't want to get out, partly because in the water at least, no one can see me. Gripping the ladder, I still get the feeling—even though it's impossible—someone might be looking out their cabin window, able to catch a glimpse.

But even Brynn can barely see me, and she's six feet away, though I'm sure my butt is white as chalk in whatever small moonlight there is. I haul myself up the ladder and sit down quick, bringing my knees up to my chest, wrapping my arms around myself and making sure my feet are blocking any view of my—you know. Since the three of us stopped taking showers together when Calla was about ten, I've really only been in my birthday suit when I'm by myself. Parts exposed, with different people, sure, but not, you know, the whole deal. I feel a little mad Brynn has her suit on. And a little proud I don't.

"You're a good swimmer," I say. My voice sounds loud, though it isn't.

I think she shrugs.

"How come you're in Equestrian and not Water Sports?"

"Their routine is messed up here," is all she answers.

"So you are on a team at home?"

"Yeah." She says it without enthusiasm, but without snarkiness, either.

"I can never get that," I say after a minute. "The arms and the head thing."

"My favorite's the butterfly. It's hard, but that's why I like it. Not many people are good at it."

And so that explains the serious shoulders she's got. Though as a swimmer I'd think she'd be more muscle-y and not so Skeletor. I decide not to ask her if she's won anything. I can't tell, from the way she's talking, if she wants me to be asking all these questions anyway or not. Though this is the first time we've really hung out alone, she's half acting like we're already best friends who are completely comfortable with each other, half acting as though she doesn't care if I'm here.

Still, I have to talk to fill the quiet. "My mom took my little sister to those baby underwater classes—you know, where you throw babies in a pool and they just naturally hold their breath and paddle around?" I tell her.

She snorts.

"But it didn't make her some great swimmer. I mean, she swims, but none of us are real swimmers."

Mom said Daisy was the best baby in that whole class, though. She'd practically leap out of Mom's arms to get into that water. Sometimes if she got fussy we'd just fill up the tub and plop her in there, even when she was really small and couldn't even crawl or anything. She loved it. Why Mom never took me and Calla to those classes, I don't know. When I asked her about it once, she just cocked her head way over and frowned into space for a minute before she said, "You know, I have no idea. But it just never occurred to me for the two of you."

Brynn still doesn't say anything. Instead I hear Saran Wrap rustling. I don't know what she's doing until there's a spark and a surprising flame, and then the fire goes up to her face and she inhales, holds it a minute, and then lets out a mossy-smoky breath.

"How can you be a swimmer and smoke?" I can't help blurting. She only chuckles. The orange dot that is the lit end of what she's smoking comes toward me.

"You want some?"

Which means it's pot. Which I should've figured anyway by the way it smelled. And it's stupid and embarrassing, but all I'm thinking is that if I smoke that with her, I won't be able to swim back. I picture myself naked, in the water, just floating there in the dark and unable to move my arms and legs, totally numb. I picture Calla having to come down to the lake to take away my pale, wet, bloated dead body.

"Where'd you get it?" I ask, big dummy. The orange dot goes back to her and she takes another inhale.

"Brought it." Her voice is tight, like she's holding in her breath.

The smoke that is somehow oilier and not as gross-smelling as regular cigarettes comes out at me again, and I feel like an idiot, sitting here with no clothes on, just some dumb girl Brynn brings along to keep an eye out while she smokes weed and drinks beers and hangs out with counselors and does whatever she wants. I don't even know why she's letting me tag around with her. She could probably care less whether I was here or not. She would do all these things with or without me. She isn't at all worried about making the swim back.

"Okay," I say.

"What?" The smoke comes out from her again. She coughs a little bit.

"Yeah, I want some, duh."

"Here," is all she says.

My fingers pinch around hers where she's holding the end of the joint out to me. It is warm, and a little bit damp. Shorter than I think it should be. The ember burns only an inch or so from my thumb. It's hard to get it close to my mouth without thinking I'm going to burn my nose off. I have to tilt my head a little. The nonburning end is mashed pretty flat, and when I suck in I'm not sure I'm going to get much, but then the ember glows brighter and a searing scratchiness goes into my throat and my mouth fills up with this grossness that is the exact same taste as the smell of flower water that's been in a vase for too long.

Like the dumbasses smoking pot for the first time in the movies, I cough and cough and cough.

"Do it again," she says in her Johnny Cash voice. "It'll help."

So I take another hit, still scratchy and gross, still making me cough, but not as bad. My eyes are stinging with water. I hand it back to her.

She smokes the rest. I don't ask for any more and she doesn't offer. I just sit there, arms wrapped around myself and my butt starting to hurt from sitting on these hard planks. I watch her shape in the dark, and the orange dot growing and dimming and moving from her mouth to somewhere down around her lap, back and forth a few times before she's putting it out and there's the sound of Saran Wrap again. She tucks the lighter and the butt somewhere and stretches out on the planks of the dock, staring up.

I'm waiting for something to happen. For my head to swirl or to start giggling uncontrollably or my tongue to swell up or the skies to explode in comets or—something. But nothing does. Only my scratchy throat and kind of a warmish feeling in the front of my face. I take a deep breath and look up at the stars anyway, because stoned or not, they do look remarkable. And here I am, naked in the great outdoors and everything.

"My stepdad—" Brynn says out of nowhere. "He's who got me into swimming. At first I hated it. My mom wanted me to is why I did it, really. She wanted him and me to have something to do together, wanted me to be active. He would get up really early to go to work before everyone else, so he could leave at three to take me to swim lessons. I was, I think, ten. I wasn't fat or anything, but when I started swimming I got really . . . skinny. And by sixth grade I was wearing a zero. Sure, in my school, most of the sixth-grade girls wore zeros. But by seventh, eighth, all of them started getting boobs and hips and puberty fat and all that. And me, with all my swimming, I was a total board—flat. And you know how girls are always made fun of for having no chest?"

I hear her head turn on the wood planks as she looks over at me. I grunt a kind of yes, to keep her going mostly, to see what she's going to say.

"Well, I didn't care. I wanted to swim harder, more often, more. I wanted to keep all the girl fat off me I could. And even though now I go to this school that has a pool, like, three blocks away, one I can walk to and don't need a ride anymore, my stepdad's still going into work early, still coming to my practices, all my meets."

She's quiet for a minute. "At first I hated him so much. And my mom. And he knew that, and he probably hated me for a while too, this total brat little bitch, but he just kept driving me to those swim lessons all those years and keeps on watching and clapping and taking us out for pizza sometimes afterward and buying my coach a beer—just smiling and happy and pounding me on the shoulder like I'm his real kid or something."

She's quiet, and I don't say anything. I've stopped being cold. I've stopped feeling my sore butt. I've even kind of forgotten that we're actually at camp, instead of just in some private dark place that is totally our own. Which is what makes me remember, suddenly, that we are at camp. And I'm out here on the dock, naked, and I just smoked pot for the first time, and Brynn, this girl I barely know—this tough, shocking girl—is out here with me being, in her own way, completely naked too. And I think, how can this be against the rules? How can something like this be against camp policy? Because this—this—is exactly what camp should be all about.

Love. Heartbreak.
Friendship. Trust.

Fall head over heels for
Terra Elan McVoy.